A Court at Constantinople

Anthony Earth

Published by Eorthe Books, LLC, 2023.

This is a work of fiction. Similarities to real people, places, or events are entirely coincidental.

A COURT AT CONSTANTINOPLE

First edition. March 29, 2023.

ISBN: 979-8215602690

Written by Anthony Earth.

For Tony and Joy, who secured my passage.

Part I

Preliminary Examination

Preliminary Examination.

305. Where the accused comes before the Court on summons or warrant, or otherwise, the Court before committing him to prison for trial, or admitting him to bail, shall, in his presence, take depositions on oath (Form 39.) of those who know the facts and circumstances of the case, and shall put the same in writing.
— *Rules of Her Britannic Majesty's Supreme Consular Court and other Consular Courts in the Dominions of the Sublime Ottoman Porte, 1860.*

Chapter 1
A Proposition

"Bingham," a gravelly voice emerged from behind the red velvet curtain.

James Bingham twisted in surprise toward the curtain at his back, rendering his wig askew. He hastily adjusted it to restore lawyerly decorum.

"Bingham," the voice rasped with guttural urgency.

"What?" James leaned closer to the curtain and smelled alcohol.

"Bingham, you're up against Shepherd's Pie," the rum-rancid breath exhaled.

For some reason, judges called Samuel Rye, his foil in the case, Shepherd's Pie. James did not know whether he had a nickname.

Gravel-voice continued, "When Shepherd's Pie begins again, say this."

A wrinkly hand splotched with liver spots thrust a scrap of foolscap between the curtain panels. Someone belched behind the velvet, provoking school-boy snickering.

James took and read the scribbled note. It addressed the case that he and Rye were arguing, but it contained legal terms, Latin words, and assertions of law foreign to him. This experience was not unusual; he was still relatively new to the Bar. However, he would usually define unfamiliar words, decipher unknown concepts, and dissect unusual claims by candlelight in chambers before uttering them in court. And the first session had already gone badly. The judge had hammered him and Rye with questions, exposing that neither barrister was up to snuff. James knew that his lawyering was suffering. Because of Emma.

"May I ask who you are?" James was becoming unsettled.

"Boy," came the indignant response. "Read it and watch that bugger get ripped."

The voice trailed off, taking the reek of rum with it.

James was not fond of Shepherd's Pie either. But reading a note he did not understand before an already peeved judge on the orders of a tipsy voice behind a curtain hardly seemed worthy of his responsibilities as a lawyer. James tried to treat courts as cathedrals and law as scripture. He bent his knee to the juridical hierarchy, liturgy, clergy, and canon that brought society order and his life stability. But too often judges and lawyers—mostly of privileged birth—behaved as if courts were playthings.

As James fretted about the note, Cranford Pennington, the senior barrister in his chambers, walked up. Looking imperious as always, Pennington straightened to his full, intimidating height as if preparing to pontificate. Instead, he saw the paper in James's hand, plucked it, skimmed it, curled a wicked prefect's smile, and, in that Pennington baritone, said, "Read it, as instructed."

This command made a confusing situation more disconcerting. It was gospel among barristers in London not to cross Cranford Pennington, who combined an impeccable lineage with one of the sharpest legal minds in the realm. He was in no position to defy Pennington, even over an incomprehensible note written by inebriated jurists. James was not finding enough clients and cases on his own. He survived on "table scraps" that other barristers in chambers were too busy to handle or considered too boring to bother with. Whispers and rumours about him served as warnings about his prospects in chambers commanded by Cranford Pennington.

As Samuel Rye resumed his argument, James begged the judge's permission to intervene. His Honour's eyes twinkled, and the judge granted him leave to speak. James read the note, pausing where the rhythm of the rhetoric invited some reason in the words.

When James finished, the judge said, "Mr. Rye, this seems fatal to your plea. What is your response?"

Samuel Rye swivelled a panicked gaze between the judge and James. He had no more idea than James what the note meant. Rye's bewilderment confirmed to James that he was a pawn in a prank to burn some Shepherd's Pie.

The session did not go well for Rye, who dug himself deeper into trouble the more he pretended to know what he was saying. Despite the humiliation, the judge did not dismiss the plea. He eventually halted the proceedings and scheduled more arguments for Tuesday next, with the admonition that Rye be better prepared. The judge nodded his ancient, wigged head at James, then flashed a wink. Rye hissed, "Boot-licking bastard," as he hurried past James in leaving.

Upon exiting the courtroom, James heard the Pennington baritone again, "Bingham, with me." Pennington indicated the direction with his walking stick.

Burdened by carrying a stack of beribboned briefs, James trailed behind Pennington's lanky strides. He entered the chambers of Judge Oliver Norton shortly after Pennington. The judge was conversing with a man James did not recognise. James had not appeared before Judge Norton, who had a reputation for being ferocious in the courtroom and generous at the public house.

"Bingham, sit," Pennington pointed at a worn, upholstered chair.

Judge Norton manoeuvred to face James, leaned his abundant backside on his desk, lowered his ample double chin onto his chest, and grimaced.

"James Bingham."

"Yes, Your Honour," replied James.

"Your parents?" enquired the judge.

"Deceased." James thought the question very odd.

"Your wife, she is gone," Norton asserted without feeling.

"No," James tried not to betray emotion. "She is ... she was my fiancée, not my wife."

"Even so," Norton continued, "your woman is dead."

Four words of scouring clarity. James looked at the floor.

It had rained during Emma's sparsely attended funeral and when he had trudged back to the churchyard a week later. He had courted her, but on returning to the grave, he struggled to understand what had passed between them. He had acquaintances for whom courtship and marriage were transformational because love germinated, status elevated, or wealth flowed. Staring at the wet headstone again, James sensed his relationship with Emma had been more transactional.

Shortly before their engagement, he had been grooming his horse, Bones, after riding to Emma's village one glorious fall morning. He talked softly to the horse as he brushed its blackness toward an obsidian sheen. When finished, he fed it a small, tart apple and touched his forehead to its forelock.

He did not know she had been watching until she spoke, "You treat your property well."

She walked away without looking back, her auburn hair swaying across her shoulders. What she meant, or what she was feeling at other peculiar moments in their courtship, he had never asked.

He missed her soft laugh. It had, perhaps, been a promise of possible happiness.

"Bingham," Judge Norton's voice forced James to lift his eyes. "We have a proposition."

"A proposition and a duty," added Pennington.

"A duty arising from empire," said the man James did not know.

"And an empire in need of law and justice," Norton layered on.

Pennington sensed that the barrage disoriented James. Failures to persuade other lawyers to accept the proposition and the duty had not produced a more effective way to present the matter.

"James," Pennington unusually deployed Bingham's Christian name. "The Foreign Office has approached Judge Norton and heads of chambers to find a young lawyer to become a law clerk in Her Majesty's Service. I don't believe you know William Willett, of the Foreign Office."

Willett nodded at James and explained, "Edmund Hornby, chief judge of the British Supreme Consular Court at Constantinople, needs a junior law clerk. Under the Foreign Jurisdiction Act, this court has authority within Ottoman dominions. Judge Hornby requires more help in his efforts to reform how Her Majesty's Government handles legal issues in those lands."

James now realised that Judge Norton's questions had established that he had no family to keep him in London. But a British court in the Ottoman empire? His irregular perusal of *The Times* produced some awareness of Britain's foreign endeavours, but he knew little, if anything, about law beyond the sceptred isle. More intellectually restless young lawyers took up international law. He struggled sufficiently with English law applied in England.

"I'm a barrister not a clerk." James tried a positive way to say he was not qualified.

Pennington sensed that James had never heard of the judge, the court, the act, or maybe even Constantinople. The boy was not the cleverest junior barrister in chambers, but like a draught horse, he pulled and plodded with tolerable results. For Pennington, such commonplace competence was fungible, when the price was right.

"James," Pennington interjected. "The post of law clerk in Her Majesty's Service is different than being a clerk in chambers—and certainly more adventurous."

This explanation, even leavened with enticement, did not answer James's questions. Despite the shame he felt about his ignorance, he spoke up, "Why do we have a court at Constantinople?"

Willett responded, "We have a treaty with the Sublime Porte."

"With the what?" James remained lost.

"With the Ottoman government," Pennington answered, "which diplomats often refer to as the 'Sublime Porte' after the fancy gate that gives access to Ottoman government offices."

James still did not understand. "The Foreign Jurisdiction Act is a treaty with the Ottoman empire that created a court at Constantinople?"

"No. Parliament passed the act in the 1840s to guide Her Majesty's Government in the exercise of the extraterritorial jurisdiction that our treaty with the Ottoman government grants," Judge Norton used his tutorial voice. "Her Majesty established the court a year and some months ago."

Agitated, Willett stood up. Finding a clerk for Hornby had already taken too long. He wanted these ignorant questions to end, and the matter concluded. "As a barrister, you have what this post requires—an understanding of the law and the ability to apply it."

Pennington noted the irritation in Willett's voice and posture. Pennington needed the Foreign Office's help with the commercial ventures a growing number of his clients had—or desired to have—in the Ottoman empire. Obtaining that help was more important than Bingham's place in chambers. He deployed his deepest voice to send a clear message, "Bingham, take this post. It would be best for you."

James went cold with the threat. But he grasped that calling Pennington's bluff courted professional ruin, and that capitulating meant professional exile.

To indicate that more significant business awaited, Pennington retrieved his pocket watch, pretended to gauge the time, and deposited it back into his waistcoat. Then he ordered more than asked, "Could you have an answer by the morning?"

James saw no way out. Pennington held the power. *Read it, as instructed*. Pennington had exploited his misfortunes. *Your woman is dead.* Pennington had the leverage. *Take this post.* He did not need until morning to choose when he had no choice.

"Tomorrow, I would like to be bound for Constantinople." James attempted to appear decisive in defeat.

"That's done," Pennington said more to himself than anyone else. "The Foreign Office will communicate with you through chambers. William, may we speak about other matters?"

Willett made it clear that James would not be departing tomorrow, but he promised that the Foreign Office would brief him and arrange passage thereafter.

The departure of Pennington and Willett left James with Judge Norton, who stared blankly at James before breaking the uncomfortable silence. "Well, that turned unpleasant. It would have been better for Queen and country had you accepted the proposition that empires need justice. As it is, you will perhaps depart with a bad taste in your mouth."

"Perhaps?" James asked more with sadness than sarcasm.

The judge held up an admonishing hand. "In the East, selfish pathos will not serve you well. Look at me, boy; don't stare at the floor again. You will see injustices done by Christians and Mussulmen. You will see men with power by blood or capital behave as if the law is a trifle. How you respond will be a measure not just of yourself, as a man, but of our civilisation."

Making his way home that evening, James shivered with Bones in the bitter, late December cold. He could not fathom what had just happened to him. Emma's death took a wife from him, but as people assured him, he would find another woman to wed. Her passing altered nothing else in his life. Pennington had threatened his place in chambers and his career in England—things he had fought poverty and prejudice to have. He had no idea what burdens parliamentary acts, treaties, courts, and judges would pile on him in a faraway land. He did not know why a British court had to provide the Ottoman empire with justice. His export seemed expedient for the Foreign Office and Cranford Pennington, whatever the status of law in British foreign affairs. The appeal to "our civilisation" made no more sense than the note he had read against Shepherd's Pie. How could he be disposable as a lawyer in England but duty-bound to serve justice in empire?

Chapter 2

Ottoman Voices

"Mehmed," said the *mufti*, "we don't raise our voices against each other here."

This student impressed and worried Kazim Hasan. Ideas that experts in and judges of Islamic law—*muftis* and *kadis*—spent years learning came naturally to the young man. The boy grasped languages quickly and argued at every opportunity with Europeans in English and French. He annoyed Ottoman officials in coffee-house conversations because they stumbled with his arguments and resented his attitude. He resisted advice to be patient and humble. Osman Mehmed was thunder without yet the lightning.

"Teacher, when will we raise our voice?" asked Mehmed.

Hasan waited for Mehmed to continue, as he invariably did. Instead, the young man left the question hanging. It was a good question, made more so by the silence that followed.

"Do we have a voice to raise?" Hasan asked Mehmed, who did not anticipate the query, but whose dark eyes flashed the wildness that concerned Hasan.

Mehmed's hesitation created an opportunity. The *mufti* looked at a rotund student near the back of the room. "Mustafa, what voices do we raise against which wrongs?"

Mustafa tilted his fleshy head to look thoughtful. "I think Mehmed meant—"

"I can speak for myself," interrupted Mehmed, causing the *mufti's* eyebrow to arch, a gesture the students understood as disapproval.

"Mustafa," said Hasan, "tell me what you think."

"Mehmed is right. When do we speak out against the Europeans? What the Prophet, Peace Be Upon Him, gave to the people is being desecrated."

"Under whose power do we ponder Mehmed's and Mustafa's questions?" Hasan's hands indicated that any student could answer, but the young men seemed confused.

"Mustafa?" The *mufti* attempted to keep Mehmed quiet a moment longer.

"The Sultan," Mustafa replied as perspiration beaded on his forehead. But when the *mufti* did not respond, he tried with even less confidence, "The Prophet, Peace Be Upon Him."

"Mehmed, do you agree?" enquired the *mufti*.

Mehmed glared at Hasan. "No. We are under the power of the English and the French. They stopped the Russians from humiliating us."

Hasan did not agree with Mehmed's summary of the Crimean war. It devalued the bravery and sacrifices of Ottomans during the conflict. But he sensed a teaching rather than a preaching moment.

He began to pace before his students. "And yet, we want to raise our voices against the English and the French, who defended you against Russia?"

It still tormented Mehmed. The Russians had crossed the river, but he did not stand and fight. He was not a man when that crisis came, but other boys his age—and younger—had met violence with violence. He was ashamed that, in the decisive moment, he did not spill or shed blood for his people. With his father, he had fled from the danger.

"The English and the French are not our protectors," interrupted Ali, another student. "They make us suffer the humiliation of obligation."

A muscular, physically imposing young man, Ali was Mehmed's rival in the class. He had a hot temper like Mehmed but not the same intelligence. Ali talked tough, but as far as Hasan knew, he did not act on his belligerent rhetoric. Hasan had recruited both for the new school. He knew Ali from his mosque, the son of a military officer who had served valiantly under the Ottoman general, Omar Pasha, during the war. Hasan first encountered the sinewy Mehmed at a coffee house arguing with customers rather than cleaning tables, floors, and dishes as he was paid to do. Ali tried to bully Mehmed, calling him "coffee-house boy." But Mehmed was clever—and he knew it—which infuriated Ali.

"Why did we need Britain and France?" The *mufti* stopped before Ali, who sullenly scratched his thickening beard. "Why are we obligated? Why are we humiliated?"

The questions produced only silence.

Hasan began pacing again. "Let me tell you a story. In conducting imperial governance, two officials travel to different provinces. Each one stops at a village for the night. A family is chosen to feed and house each official. After food and drink, each one is escorted to a bedroom. Each hears a knock on the door, and when he opens it, a daughter of the host stands on threshold. The first official points to the bed and forces himself upon the girl. He leaves in the morning—not saying a word to his host about the girl—and looks forward to the next village.

The second official in the other village looks with puzzlement at the girl. He thinks she might have brought water, but her hands are empty. Unsure what she wants, he retrieves some coins, puts them in her hand, smiles, and closes the door. He leaves the next morning—not saying a word to his host about the girl—and looks forward to the next village."

Hasan stopped pacing and perceived discomfort in his students. "Against which official should we raise our voice?"

Mehmed responded, "Your stories concern individual choices, not decisions that empires make. Good and evil men are everywhere. Your tales could happen in any country, at any time."

"But," replied the *mufti*, "what country and which time do these stories illuminate?"

His students knew the answer. Mehmed certainly did. But no one spoke until Mehmed broke the quiet, "One man's virtue does not make an empire just."

"Indeed," agreed the *mufti*. "But when we raise our voice, it should ring with clarity of purpose, not hostility spawned by our weakness and failings in governing our people. There is nothing in European behaviour that explains what has happened to girl after girl, in village after village, year after year at the hands of Ottoman officials. Our treaties with European powers are not responsible for the degradation of daughters or sisters becoming a custom, answered only when fathers or brothers run vengeful knives across guilty throats."

"Or mothers," Mehmed muttered.

Mustafa spoke with trepidation, "I can believe the first story, but perhaps the second requires fiction to be true."

Hasan laughed at Mustafa's observation. "No, both are true. I was present at the first village, and I heard the second story from the official involved."

"You were at the first village? And you did nothing?" Mehmed's emotions flared.

"You see this scar?" Hasan knew that anyone who looked at him saw it. The students kept a close eye on the scar, which turned blood-red when the *mufti* was displeased with them. But none had asked the origins of this oft-crimson cut down their teacher's face.

"The Ottoman official slashed my face with his riding crop after I confronted him. But he died before we reached the next village. His horse spooked; he fell off, broke his neck."

"*Mashallah*," his students quietly said, acknowledging that Allah had willed it.

"You've heard of the second official, whom people call the Supreme English Judge. I have talked with him at dinners he has hosted for Ottoman leaders."

Mehmed's eyes flashed wild again. "You eat and talk with this man? Who brings his law here? Where it displaces the law of the holy Koran—our *sharia*? Where it cannot bring us justice?"

"You could learn from this man," the *mufti* responded.

"Only as an enemy." Mehmed's blood was up.

Hasan's scar darkened. "Are you prepared to meet the enemy? Our military is not. Our government is not. Our religious leaders are not. No wonder Europeans think the Ottoman empire is sick, feeble, decrepit.

"We have established this school because we need advocates for our laws and our justice. The government responds to this transforming world by importing European laws. Why? Because many believe that *sharia* is inadequate. Because we cannot compete by looking backwards. Because we only know the past. Because we haven't developed our laws and lawyers to balance the scales of justice among nations in this time of great change. Because we have no answers for today or tomorrow. That's why we copy French law. That's why the English have a court at Constantinople. Our complacency, our confusion, our failing confidence, our lack of purpose—all threaten to make humiliation a permanent obligation."

"How can we compete," interjected Burak, a quiet but perceptive student, "by trying to learn everything? When we study *sharia*, we aren't learning the legislation adopted by the Sultan. When we study the Sultan's law, we aren't learning European law. When we study European law, we aren't learning *sharia*. If we only know a little about a lot, we will not be prepared."

The *mufti* shared Burak's concern. The new school lacked an identity. It was not an Islamic place of learning, like Al-Azhar in Cairo, where he had trained when the shadow of European power was not as dark and long. The school was to be an Ottoman institution, an Ottoman voice in a rapidly changing world. But what "Ottoman" meant was fiercely contested. For some, only *sharia* and Islam could define Ottoman justice. For others, Ottoman law must embody ideas about justice from beyond the caliphate. As he once heard a *kadi* lament, "I do not like this modern world. We have more laws but less justice."

"Teacher," interrupted Süleyman, a waifish, bespectacled student. "Why is this English judge traveling around giving money to girls?"

Mehmed shot Süleyman a look of disdain. Of the students, Süleyman was the least informed about what was happening all around them. He insisted on wearing a traditional turban that was too big for his head, which made him look trapped in a distant time when the people of Islam taught the world fantastic things.

Hasan asked, "Who can answer Süleyman's question? Why is the English judge here?"

No one answered. The *mufti* lowered his head in disappointment. How often had they looked at the treaties with the Europeans? How many times had they discussed why these treaties had been transformed from acts of magnanimity by powerful sultans into marks of ignominy for a disoriented people?

"You want me," Mehmed's surly tone lifted Hasan's head, "to learn from this man?"

"I want—" Hasan paused to contain his frustration. "You—all of you—could learn from this man. He is a man of law and is here to end the injustices his government perpetrates."

"Learn from a man ignorant of *sharia*? Learn from a man who considers us uncivilised?" Mehmed boiled.

"Mehmed," the *mufti* felt the scar on his face grow hot again. "We are, in this school, studying how our jurists, judges, and officials apply law and seek justice amidst bewildering change. Do you believe that we are the only people who confront this challenge?"

"The change this English judge brings is not of our making," Mehmed answered angrily. "And it cannot be a source of justice for us."

"And how have we fared against the waves of change crashing over us? Do we believe that we can respond only to the change we create?" The *mufti* challenged his students.

"Change may come from within or beyond our shores," Mehmed replied in a more measured tone. "But foreign ideas should not determine why and how we change. The latest law—the Imperial Criminal Code—reads like it was written in Paris. This English judge applies his law here. We mimic and appease the Europeans, but it's never enough. They want more laws written in Paris, more English judges here, more European power, more Ottoman surrender. In all this, we lose our dignity and our destiny. How is this just?"

"You're all fools," Ali stood and puffed out his chest, looking around the classroom with contempt. "Becoming better lawyers than the infidels won't matter. We need to shelve the books and shoulder our guns. Talk to me about dignity, destiny, and justice when we march on Vienna again."

Ali added one more insult, "And you're the biggest fool of all, coffee-house boy."

Provoked, Mehmed rose aggressively to his feet.

Hasan wanted to reprimand Ali and Mehmed for their behaviour. He was trying to train confused and angry young men to make a future through means other than fury and violence. Mehmed and Ali, the *mufti* feared, were confusing rage with righteousness.

But Süleyman spoke first, uncharacteristically refusing to be ignored, "Who is this Supreme English Judge?"

"Hornby," Mehmed answered, his eyes still locked on Ali. "A *kaffir* named Edmund Hornby."

Chapter 3

Build an Empire, Burn a Wig

The Foreign Office never briefed James. He received his formal appointment—title, salary, and so forth—and instructions for arranging his journey, but nothing else. He organised his travel, including transport for Bones. James devoted the time before his departure to educating himself about his new post. Growing up in the shadow of the workhouse had deprived him of opportunities to learn about the world and its ways that his betters had enjoyed. Sensitive about his ignorance, he had honed the skills to hunt down the knowledge he needed.

He was to join the Supreme Consular Court at Constantinople, presumably part of the British consular service in the Ottoman empire. He rummaged London booksellers until he found *The British Consul's Manual: Being a Practical Guide for Consuls, as well as for the Merchant, Shipowner, and Master Mariner.* It contained much useful material, including about Turkey and the Levant. Published in 1856, the *Manual* did not mention the Supreme Consular Court. He located Her Majesty's Order in Council from 1857 that established the court and authorised the appointment of a judge, vice legal consul, law secretary, and subordinate officers. As a junior law clerk, he was now a subordinate officer. James ran his hand pensively through his hair. All this seemed rather important. But he lacked what the *Manual* said a consular officer must have—"A virtuous and manly confidence that he possesses the necessary qualifications for the performance of the duties of his office."

London to Dover by coach proved uneventful, but the following day, rough Channel waters to Calais made the crossing miserable. Torrential rain and other never-explained problems delayed the rail journey from Calais to Lille to Paris. The train from Paris to Marseilles crawled through a small station near Avignon when sunlight finally broke through early January clouds, illuminating a young woman on the platform. He mistook her, ever so briefly, for Emma. The woman smiled at the man staring at her, one hand pressed against the carriage window.

After the *Sphinx* departed Marseilles, James focused on studying the materials he had collected for the journey. In his berth or in places onboard where he could be alone, he read and re-read documents and reviewed and revised his notes to make sense of what awaited him at Constantinople. This monastic behaviour left him outside various communities of passengers forming on the ship, and he was on his own even when not communing with the *British Consul's Manual* or *Murray's Handbook for Travellers in Turkey*, another bookseller find. For some reason, one couple, George and Jemmy Oakeston, noticed and, perhaps taking pity, invited him to play cards in the evening.

The couple seemed overly concerned that James had no wife. During cards, George would eye a young woman passing by or sitting elsewhere in the room, elbow James, and say, "There, Pup." Thanks to Jemmy, James would then find himself meeting the ladies whom George had "pupped." James thought one young lady fetching, but, despite opportunities, George never pupped her. She was, James surreptitiously learned, a missionary's daughter named Caroline. His nerve failed when he had chances to make her acquaintance on his own.

As the voyage progressed, James continued reading books and papers during the day, occasionally meeting young women courtesy of Jemmy, and playing cards in the evening with the Oakestons. At first, he did not notice, but a pattern formed with each successive *tête-à-tête* that Jemmy arranged. Each pupped lady was a merchant's daughter, every single one. It seemed odd. Given that he had not mixed much with other passengers, he might simply be unaware how many merchants with families in tow were onboard. Or perhaps there was another explanation.

As the *Sphinx* steamed through the Dardanelles for the last leg of the journey, cards began as usual, but after the first hand, the evening's focus shifted.

"James, you look as if something's on your mind," Jemmy observed.

"I have a question for you," James replied.

"You may ask your question if you would be so kind as to first answer a question I have for you," Jemmy said.

The request was unexpected, but James tentatively nodded his assent.

"How is Caroline?" Jemmy asked.

"Pardon?" was all James could muster.

"Caroline—the young lady you fancy—how is she?" Jemmy asked again.

James had never mentioned Caroline; but in failing to meet her on his own, he had no answer to Jemmy's question.

"Shame. She's rather pretty, especially in that green frock," George commented.

Jemmy titled her head to signal that James should ask his question.

"Why only the daughters of merchants?"

"It served our purposes. A young barrister in Her Majesty's Service without a wife was just enough of a curiosity on this ship to be somewhat useful to us," Jemmy replied.

The response was not what James expected.

"Pup," George's voice turned hard. "You've hidden away with your books. You didn't meet Caroline. You haven't made friends, learned from people you will serve on behalf of Her Majesty, or marvelled at living in a moment when the arc of history is bending. You'll leave this vessel as lonely and ignorant as when you embarked."

"And my ignorance is any of your business?" James felt insulted but regretted the retort.

"Our business is information," George shot back. "So your ignorance is, literally, none of our business."

Our business is information? James's confusion about the Oakestons was now in flood.

"Pup," George's voice softened. "Many on this vessel are part of the burgeoning guild of professional men. Power is spreading from the mouldering aristocracy into the motivated hands of the engineer, scientist, industrialist, merchant, journalist, and attorney."

"And their wives and children," Jemmy added.

George continued, "What the people on this ship do, and how they think, will shape our empire. Information from them can be as useful as the state secrets that spies steal."

The shift from personal critique to imperial exegesis deepened James's discomfort.

"James," Jemmy touched his hand, "if Britain merely builds an empire, it will suffer the fate of all empires. The question is, what will our empire build?"

"Our empire is in India and elsewhere, not in Turkey." James tried to lawyer the matter instead of answering the question.

"Our empire has India, which is our destination," George said. "But what did we build there?"

"You're going to India?" The question underscored that James was as ignorant about George and Jemmy as when he had played his first game of cards with them.

"Eventually," answered George, "but what did we build there?"

"A rebellion." James remembered a mutiny in India that took place not that long ago.

"Pup, we are building—you will be building—at Constantinople too. But you will never understand what you are creating and becoming unless you open your eyes, open your mind, and open your soul to life," George implored in a fatherly tone.

"Perhaps I can still make Caroline's acquaintance and arrange to meet her again in Constantinople," James managed to say.

An awkward pause preceded Jemmy's reply, "Caroline and her family are going to Africa."

"All for a religion in need of an empire." George's testy comment drew a reproachful glance from Jemmy, produced an unsettling silence, and brought the evening to an abrupt close.

In the afternoon of the penultimate day of the voyage, James leaned on the ship's rail, trying to discern where the sea ended and the sky began. A quiet voice interrupted this effort, "Mr. Bingham?" James turned to see a young woman in a green dress.

That evening, James could not find the Oakestons to thank them. Enquiries of other passengers suggested that George and Jemmy were dining with the ship's captain on the journey's final night. He meandered around the vessel until sunset, before returning to his berth.

He woke late the next morning, having slept through the ship's arrival. Most passengers had disembarked when he hauled his possessions topside. As he circled the deck looking one last time for George and Jemmy, a steward handed him an envelope. Inside was a note in a woman's hand: "For a man in need of heart—When doubts come to conquer, remember Caroline."

—

"Emelia," Edmund Hornby called out. He tried again to knot his tie just so, but irritation spiked as the silk did not acquiesce.

"Emelia Bithynia Hornby!"

"Sir?" Giovanni, the butler, appeared after the louder, more agitated appeal for Mrs. Hornby.

"Where is she?" Edmund made another attempt at sartorial perfection.

"On her morning constitutional, up the garden. Would you like me to help?"

"No," snapped Edmund, providing Giovanni sufficient permission and incentive to leave.

"Gone for a walk?" Edmund grumbled, miffed that his wife was not there to help him prepare for an important meeting.

Just as he coaxed the tie into tolerable form, Giovanni reappeared to say that Mr. Henry Wroth had arrived and was in the study. Edmund brushed his black suit, bristles removing grey hairs prematurely deposited on his shoulders. His wife had stopped picking them off at breakfast before he left for the court. He considered himself in the long mirror. Once, years ago in bed, Emelia had moved her hand over his bare chest, recalling how, when they first met, she was attracted because he looked part pugilist, part philosopher. He was not sure what she thought now.

"Here." Henry Wroth, vice legal consul at the court, handed Edmund a folder as he entered the study.

Edmund opened it and fingered the document inside. "How many?"

"Twenty. Enough for today," Henry replied, moving to warm himself by the fire.

Edmund glanced at the names of British subjects and persons of other nationalities, such as the residents of Malta and the seven Ionian islands off the western Greek coast, protected by Her Majesty's Government under its treaty with the Ottoman empire. These persons were in Turkish gaols in violation of the capitulation provisions in the treaty. As head of the judicial department of the British consulate at Constantinople, Edmund wanted these violations to stop. The British ambassador, Lord Stratford, had arranged an audience for him with the Ottoman Foreign Minister, His Excellency Mehmed Fuad, or Fuad Pasha, to discuss the matter.

"Has the junior clerk arrived?" Edmund returned the document to its folder and inserted the folder into his satchel.

"Yes, the ship arrived this morning. He has instructions to report to the Ambassador before teatime today," Henry replied. "And Stratford wants you there as well, so don't dawdle with

Fuad. You'll be hard pressed to get from the Sublime Porte to Therapia on time."

Edmund nodded. "Giovanni can get you some tea or coffee before you go."

He pulled on his coat, hat, and gloves, collected his satchel, and exited into the courtyard of his residence. His horse, Sultan, and police escort were waiting. In Constantinople, one Turkish policeman—a *cavass*—or at most two, provided him with security. Today, Halil, the *cavass* who most frequently accompanied him, and four others were ready, dressed in splendid uniforms, their polished swords glinting under the winter sun. Halil and his colleagues had been military officers who were selected to provide security for foreign diplomats and Ottoman officials because of the intelligence and courage they had demonstrated during the Crimean war. But Edmund's escort had never been kitted out as it was this morning.

"Such a handsome sight, and all just for me." Edmund winked at Halil.

Halil laughed. "When you meet Fuad Pasha at the Sublime Porte, nothing is too good for the Supreme English Judge."

Edmund mounted Sultan, and from the Bebek area in which Edmund lived, Halil set a quick pace, cutting across the Pera district toward the Golden Horn. Halil slowed things down to put the little phalanx on display as it crossed the New Bridge into the old city, and to add pomp to their arrival at the Sublime Porte. Edmund anticipated having to wait before his audience with Fuad Pasha, but he was ushered directly into the Foreign Minister's office. Fuad sat behind a document-strewn desk but did not stand to welcome the Englishman. He motioned to a chair in front of his desk for Edmund to use.

"Lord Stratford tells me that you have complaints about the capitulations in our treaty," Fuad began. "I want to complain about the capitulations, too."

"Yes," Edmund reached into his satchel. "I need to bring to Your Excellency's attention violations of the capitulations committed by Turkish officials against British subjects and other persons protected by Her Majesty's Government under our treaty."

"Another list of people tried by our courts without a British representative present." Fuad's staff had briefed him.

"Yes, Your Excellency," Edmund responded. "Our treaty is clear—a Turkish court cannot try a British subject or protected person for a crime without a British official present, who decides the case as an equal with the Turkish judicial authority. Turkish courts continue to decide cases against such subjects and persons without the British government's involvement."

"Tell me," Fuad leaned forward. "If a Turk is tried in London at the Old Bailey, does a Turkish diplomat have the right to be present and decide the case as an equal with the English judge?"

"No, Your Excellency." Edmund tried not to appear irritated by the question.

"So this treaty is not equal because you do not consider us civilised, not your equals in law," continued the Foreign Minister.

"Treaties do not always contain reciprocal obligations." Edmund used a pedantic legalism to deflect political criticism.

The two men sensed that the conversation had already entered the *cul-de-sac* almost every diplomatic discussion about the capitulations reached. Turks, especially reformers such as Fuad, hated the capitulations. The Ottomans believed the capitulations manifested in treaty law the European conviction that Ottomans were uncivilised in matters of justice. The British were adamant that justice required the Ottoman government to comply with treaty law.

"Do you mind?" Fuad retrieved a cigarette.

When the judge did not object, he offered one to Edmund, who declined despite his taste for tobacco.

After a prolonged inhalation of smoke, Fuad went in a new direction. "I understand that, if we adopt forms of European law, the capitulations could end. So, we must go beyond treaty compliance to be considered civilised. Is that correct?"

"It would be one strategy, Your Excellency," Edmund cautiously replied.

The Foreign Minister smiled at the answer's diplomacy. "We have just enacted a temporary code of criminal procedure, informed by French law, to supplement the new Imperial Criminal Code, also based on French law. So, we are adopting European law, despite opposition from religious leaders, nationalists, and radicals. Are we making progress in becoming civilised?"

Edmund had read the temporary code and harshly critiqued it in a despatch to the Foreign Office. More tact was required with Fuad Pasha.

"My concern is that your new criminal codes mimic French law, but they have no roots in your traditions of law and justice. Implementing them requires a new approach to legal education and changes in how the Ottoman justice system operates. Without appropriate training for jurists and harmonised guidance for judges, Turkish tribunals could apply these codes in inconsistent, arbitrary, and unjust ways—and that wouldn't be progress."

The Foreign Minister did not immediately respond. The Ottoman embassy in London had produced the code of criminal procedure to quiet British criticism without consulting Turkish judicial officials or *muftis*. This approach was not a solution to the trouble the capitulations caused for the Ottomans.

Fuad let his cigarette smoulder before asking, "You had a problem. How did you fix it?"

"I'm sorry, Your Excellency?" Edmund was perplexed by another change of direction.

"The Foreign Office wants you to improve how British consular officers perform judicial functions. So, how did you fix your problem?" Fuad asked, crushing out the cigarette.

Edmund was unsure whether Fuad was curious or was setting a trap. "Your Excellency, before I arrived, my government did not provide consular officers with rules, training, resources, or supervision on handling legal disputes among British subjects in Ottoman dominions. Without a blueprint, without uniform rules and procedures overseen by a supervising authority, consular officers did not administer justice consistently or transparently. This arbitrary, unjust system developed because great distances, slow communications, and immediate temptations to gain influence or wealth allowed the discretion of men to displace the rule of law."

"So, you wrote a code," the Foreign Minister interjected.

"We had to build—we had to engineer—an entirely new system capable of delivering justice and withstanding the relentless forces that seek to bend the law to the demands of power, the greed of profit, or the whims of passion. We began by establishing the consular court here as the supreme legal authority, and we are presently drafting a code of common rules and procedures for our consulates in Ottoman lands to follow. One system, one set of rules. With railroads, steam ships, and telegraphs, geography no longer excuses divergence in the application of the law," explained Edmund.

In Edmund's answer Fuad heard echoes of Ottoman reforms—centralising government power at Constantinople and reducing the discretion provincial officials had long exercised. Such localised autonomy had served the far-flung, diverse Ottoman empire well enough for centuries, but this tradition had become a liability as the world beyond ceaselessly encroached on the empire. In response, the Sublime Porte was attempting legal reformation. New legislation standardised law across the imperial realm. Faster transportation and communication facilitated the centralisation of authority and harmonisation of law throughout the empire.

Fuad sensed Edmund had more to say. "Go on, judge."

"But our code does not simply copy what English courts do in England. We need a code that adapts the most important principles of justice to the realities that British consular officers and subjects face in the Levant. It is like building a suspension bridge—using the immutable laws of nature to span a singular river."

"I need such a code. One that does more than copy French law. A code that applies the most fundamental principles of justice with Ottoman conditions in mind," the Foreign Minister said. "So, let's create it together."

Edmund hesitated because of the diplomatic implications of such a project. "With the Foreign Office's permission, I can work with you, and I can assign a law clerk to the effort. However, you're a very busy man, so the task also requires—"

"A Turkish law clerk," Fuad completed the thought. "You leave that to me."

—

James slipped Jemmy's note into his pocket, lifted his two small trunks, and entered the gangway. Halfway down he realised he did not know where in Constantinople he was disembarking. Crew from the ship were pounding down the gangway carrying large trunks, so he continued toward the dock, where a young man stood watching him.

"James Bingham?" the man asked in accented English.

James nodded.

"You took a bloody long time." The man thumped an envelope into James's chest.

James took it, and the man left without another word. Inside the envelope was confirmation from the *Hôtel de Byzance* of a reservation for Mr. James Bingham. The slip included the hotel's address on the *Grand Rue de Pera*.

Shifting out of the way of sailors and stevedores crisscrossing the dockyard, James set down his trunks and retrieved *Murray's Handbook for Travellers in Turkey* from his satchel. The handbook placed the hotel in the Pera district on the *Grand Rue de Pera*, just south of the British embassy. Farther down the *Grand Rue* was the British consulate, near something called the Galata Tower that overlooked where the Golden Horn met the Bosphorus. All quite interesting, but James still had no idea where he was.

Someone interrupted James's orienteering. "Hotel? Bono Johnny, hotel?"

James looked up, and the man reached down and took hold of the trunks. James began to panic, recalling warnings he had heard in London about oriental thieves on every street and around every corner of Constantinople. Instead, the man stood before James, trunks in hand, repeating, "Bono Johnny, hotel? Hotel?"

"The *Hôtel de Byzance*," James answered. "*Grand Rue de Pera.*"

The man signalled with his head for James to follow, and James put *Murray's* away and fell in behind his apparent porter. James guessed that trekking by foot meant the hotel was nearby. As the route became steeper, the walk became more challenging physically and disorienting sensorially. The familiar and the foreign swarmed all around. Horses and riders that would have been fashionable on Rotten Row sauntered past. Camel trains seemingly straight from the Arabian desert bellowed and plodded across his path. The accustomed pungency of animal dung mixed with sharp, alien odours. The swirl of English quotidian and Eastern exotica left James distracted and barely able to trudge in a straight line up the road's increasing incline.

Eventually, the *Hôtel de Byzance* appeared, and its deliberate occidental ambience calmed James as he presented the confirmation of his reservation to the hotel staff. In return, he was handed a light blue envelope printed in dark blue ink with the British royal coat of arms centred underneath "ON HER MAJESTY'S SERVICE" and above "Her Britannic Majesty's Supreme Consular Court Constantinople."

Inside was a brief letter in a crisp hand from Consul-General Carlton Cumberbatch, welcoming him and instructing him to report, upon arrival, to the ambassador, Lord Stratford Canning de Redcliffe, at his country residence at Therapia. The letter stated that Judge Edmund Hornby would also be present. James also found inside the envelope a scribbled note from "H. T. Wroth,

Vice Legal Consul," instructing him to wear his barrister's robe and wig for formal investiture by the ambassador.

James asked the hotel to arrange transportation. After depositing his belongings in his room and taking a light meal, he washed and shaved. The carriage took James northeasterly along the Bosphorus. He saw grand houses lounging on the banks of the strait. He observed men in traditional turbans and cloaks talking on street corners with Turks in European coats and hats. The carriage passed women playing with children in a park. When the road curved away from the Bosphorus, he saw soldiers marching on a parade ground. Rounding back toward the water he glimpsed, at a distance inland, a cemetery with damaged headstones.

The carriage picked up speed as the road exchanged city for countryside. The pace tousled his hair and brought cold air hard against his cheeks. When the driver slowed to navigate through a muddy stretch, James locked eyes with a young Turkish man on the roadside waiting for the carriage to pass. The man spat at the carriage, his ice-blue eyes filled with reproach and defiance.

Made uneasy by the encounter, James sank back into the leather bench of the carriage, closed his eyes, and faced up to soak in whatever warmth the winter sun offered. After some moments, he opened his eyes and saw a bird with large wings soaring high above. Black against the azure sky, its wingspan was too large for a hawk or falcon. An eagle, perhaps, or a vulture. A jolt from the carriage brought his gaze down and turned his mind toward meeting the British ambassador.

After arriving at the ambassador's residence, a taciturn footman shunted James into the building, through dark hallways, and up frigid staircases into what appeared to be Lord Stratford's study. He shed his coat, donned his barrister's robe and wig as instructed, and warmed himself before a fireplace.

Alone with the heat and sound of the fire, James remembered putting on his robe and wig for Emma, at her request, by the hearth of her cottage on a gloomy Sunday afternoon. She had brushed at a spot on the front of the robe before realising the fabric was frayed and discoloured rather than merely dusty. She had stepped back to get the full effect, placed her hands on her hips, and stared at him without expression. "Another James," she had said, before her parents ended the inspection by trundling into the cottage.

A door at the back of the study suddenly opened, and out came a man with unkempt white hair, clothed only in a tatty, grey dressing gown. This sight alone was unnerving, but the gown had not been closed, leaving the occupant's manhood exposed.

"Where the hell is Hornby?" growled the man.

For all its gruffness, the voice sounded distinguished to James. The man, even naked under a dressing gown, exuded an authority bestowed by privilege and burnished by sacrifice.

"What, in God's name," the man moved toward James, "are you supposed to be?"

"Sir?" was all James managed.

The man brought his long, thin face close to James's, as if inspecting a species unknown to Darwin. James saw stress and age in the thinning hair and leathering skin.

"Were you invited to a *bal costumé?*" The man stepped back with his own costume parted.

"Sir, I am James Bingham, Judge Hornby's new junior law clerk." James executed a slight bow and extended his hand, which he withdrew when the gesture was not reciprocated.

"May I, Her Majesty's ambassador plenipotentiary to the Ottoman empire, have that thing on your head?" asked Lord Stratford.

"Lord Ambassador, sir?" James fumbled out.

"Nervous, are we?" A twinkle flashed in Stratford's eyes. "Give me your wig."

James handed his wig to Lord Stratford, who shifted James from before the fireplace and tossed it into the flames.

"Lawyers," Stratford muttered, as James caught an acrid whiff of burning horsehair.

Stratford took a pace back and looked James up and down again. "Tell me, Mr. Junior Law Clerk, now that you have joined the enterprise, what do you make of the British empire?"

James struggled for something to say, before he remembered, "We are builders."

The furrows on the ambassador's brow communicated puzzlement at the response. Stratford sat down in a chair by the study's window, crossed his bare legs, ignored the worn-out slipper that fell from his foot, and looked out the frosty glass panes.

"Years ago," Stratford's voice went quiet, "I read a despatch from some far-away place newly touched by British power. I don't recall where. There have been many such places."

Stratford ran a bony finger through dust on the windowsill before curling it back. "According to the despatch, a British soldier had killed all the inhabitants of a hamlet he encountered while scouting ahead of the main force. Men, women, children, livestock, everything living was slaughtered. His officers, arriving later, beheld the carnage and asked what had happened. The soldier replied, 'For Queen and country.' An officer asked, 'What queen and what country?'"

Stratford paused, uncurled his index finger, extended the adjacent thumb, and angled the finger onto his temple. "The soldier smiled, put a pistol to his head, and blew his brains out."

Stratford lowered his hand. "Then the despatch described the unit's map-making efforts."

James stared at the ambassador, unable to grasp why he told the story or what it meant.

"What, pray tell, did the Foreign Office tell you about your mission—what you are building? Glory for the Queen, justice for the empire, civilisation for the Turks?" Stratford asked.

"Yes," James replied, "my recruitment featured those concepts."

Stratford began twirling the white hairs on his sternum. "What sort of lawyer are you?" The ambassador's tone suggested he was not curious about James's areas of legal expertise.

"The sort who agreed to come here."

Stratford grinned. "Like a diplomat, you answered my question without answering it. Lawyers, I have found, do not make good diplomats. Lawyers in Her Majesty's Service appear to have struggled in England's juridical jungle, all red in tooth and silk, and experience some chance event that brings them to diplomacy. What happenstance explains why you're here?"

"My fiancée died." James avoided the less sympathetic parts of his story.

Stratford showed no sympathy. "The Turks will hate what you do here. They resent the changes we ask or force them to make. Hornby is reforming the British consular judicial system in Ottoman domains, but he believes British reform provides a plan for Turks and other oriental peoples. He seeks convergence among nations on a shared body of law that operates under some universal concept of justice. But this push for convergence crashes against the divergent national interests that governments have when the balance of power is at stake. Do you understand?"

Before James could respond, footsteps from the hall entered the study.

"Welcome, Lucifer!" Stratford clapped his hands and, with some difficulty, stood.

Startled by Stratford's appearance, Judge Edmund Hornby stumbled out apologies for being late, sent a concerned glance at James, and asked whether everything was alright.

"Splendid," replied Stratford. "I've had a chat with Mr. Junior Law Clerk."

"Your Excellency," Edmund slowly brought his hands together, "your dressing gown."

Stratford looked down, shrugged, folded the gown over, and tied its belt. Edmund shook James's hand, noticed his barrister's robe, and looked in the fireplace. He feared that James had experienced one of the ambassador's infamous rages.

"Mr. Bingham, is that your wig in the fire?"

"Come, gentlemen," interrupted Stratford. "Let's have a drink."

The ambassador retrieved a carafe of madeira and glasses from behind some books and papers. He poured, they clinked crystal, and drank. The judge and ambassador conversed about things James did not understand—Fuad Pasha, a code, a Turkish law school. A finely dressed woman then entered the study to inform Lord Stratford that so-and-so had arrived. James surmised from the displeasure she expressed about the dressing gown that the woman was Lady Stratford. The ambassador pouted like a guilty schoolboy and departed through the back door of the study. Lady Stratford escorted Edmund and James to the front entrance of the residence and, *en route*, pried from them the ambassador's behaviour during the audience.

"Let me apologise," Lady Stratford said.

"Lady Stratford," began Edmund, "there's no need."

"No," she insisted. "His burdens do not excuse such antics. But, Edmund, I am worried. He's under great strain. The *et tu* knives are out for him. He's too old for all of this."

The tiredness in Lady Stratford's voice told Edmund that all the labours of British diplomacy at Constantinople did not fall on her husband's shoulders alone. She insisted on hosting a dinner at the embassy to welcome James, properly, to Her Majesty's Service. The judge was enough of a diplomat to know the offer should be accepted.

Despite Halil's protest, Edmund insisted the *cavass* ride in the carriage waiting to take James back to Constantinople. Halil tied their horses to the back and climbed in. Edmund stuck a cigarette in his mouth, shared one with Halil, and offered another to James, who declined. Edmund and Halil lit their cigarettes and settled back to enjoy their smokes.

As dusk fell, Halil softly started humming and singing folk songs. Edmund was silent, reflecting on the day, which featured predictable disagreement about the capitulations and more inexplicable eccentricity from Stratford. But it also produced a commitment to forge something new. A legal code of Turkish and English making. A code to teach the diverse nations of a shrinking world how to build justice together. And what better place for such a code to arise? The touchpoint between East and West. The terrain where Greeks and Persians, Christians and Moslems, Ottomans and Europeans met in war and peace. The fabled city whence the Code of Justinian shaped the law of Christendom. The seat of an Islamic empire confronting a transformed world. A place where justice should never be wholly ours or entirely theirs.

Edmund smiled wistfully at the pulse of idealism. Halil's gentle singing caught his attention when the *cavass* struggled with a verse in a song. Edmund asked whether the song told a story.

"Yes," Halil replied, "about a boy and a girl. The happiness love promises. The tragedy love creates. The final part always catches in my throat."

"Why?" asked Edmund, touched by such sensitivity in a man scarred by war.

A fragile smile crossed Halil's face, "It is about another boy, another girl. The happiness love promises ..."

Chapter 4

Dinner at the British Embassy

Lady Eliza Stratford's desire to make amends for her husband's behaviour during James Bingham's audience produced invitations for a Saturday evening dinner at the embassy for James, Judge and Mrs. Hornby, and other guests. But Eliza had other motives. Within British society at Constantinople, she felt obliged to nurture relationships among Her Majesty's subjects and suture wounds they inflicted on each another. Salving slights—real, imagined, and calculated—was tiresome, and increasingly so as the number of British subjects arriving in the city multiplied. But it was, in her mind, part of the woman's work of diplomacy. With this dinner, she wanted to repair the damage between the Wattling and Colborne families and, perhaps, foster a new liaison.

After conversation over drinks, the guests were shown into the dining room. At a stunning table, James was seated between Judge and Emelia Hornby and Garrett and Mary Wattling. Beyond the Wattlings sat Dr. Charles Hoyland, chief surgeon and superintendent of the British Seamen's Hospital at Constantinople, and his wife, Emily. On the other side was Lady Stratford, next to her husband who sat at the head of the table, and a young woman sitting with what appeared to be her father and mother, whom James had not met before dinner because they arrived late. Next to this family were Robert and Jane Norris.

Lord Stratford welcomed his guests and let the dining begin, with a promise of formal remarks later. Lady Stratford told James she had crafted the menu to feature Turkish cuisine that she had come to love. At the hotel, James had already grown fond of Turkish coffee and pilaffs. With Lady Stratford's guidance, he tucked into new dishes, including Circassian chicken. Lady Stratford encouraged him to leave room for something delectable to end the meal.

As dinner progressed, James's attention shifted toward Mrs. Hornby, who peppered him with questions about how he was adjusting to life in Constantinople. The inquisition abated long enough for him to eat when Mrs. Hornby talked about her years in the city. James was surprised when she offered to lend him a book that she had published about her time in Constantinople during the Crimean war.

After the main courses and before dessert, Lord Stratford asked Judge Hornby to introduce the evening's guest of honour. Edmund obliged with a heartfelt welcome. James smiled and nodded to acknowledge the remarks, knowing that protocol required him to thank Lord and Lady Stratford for their hospitality and express gratitude to Judge and Mrs. Hornby for their kindness.

Before he could speak, the young woman across the table addressed him. "Mr. Bingham, I see that you are without a wife this evening. Did she not make the journey to the East?"

The question, and its timing, was impolite. Lady Stratford had hoped Rosamund Colborne would notice James, but demurely. Perhaps, Her Ladyship wondered, Miss Colborne had not tempered herself after the consequences of her behaviour last year.

Edmund attempted to provide James another opportunity to do protocol justice. "Miss Colborne, James's fiancée died before he accepted this post."

"Well then," Rosamund continued without sympathy for James or concern for protocol. "We must find you a wife. Here, as in England, men without wives find wickedness the prime occupation for idle appendages."

The mouths of Rosamund's parents dropped open, Mrs. Hornby's eyes went wide as Wedgwood saucers, and Lord Stratford burst out laughing. Eliza glared at him, and he took a guilty gulp of wine.

Garrett Wattling did not let the remark pass. "Well, women without husbands find bitter loneliness a poor salve for withered spinsterhood."

Now Mary Wattling looked like she wanted to hide. The Wattlings son, Henry, had courted Rosamund. Eliza had helped bring the two together. A handsome, rakish lad, Henry had been eager. The courtship began during Henry's unsuccessful stint in the British army and continued after he joined his father's business. The impediment to the match had been Rosamund, who eventually refused Henry. Her rejection was thought by most to have been imprudent and by many to have been impudent. On frequent occasions, Rosamund had provided a cutting catalogue of Henry's faults. She had noted the British army's willingness to take almost anyone as cannon fodder, except cowards. The personal scorning and public humiliation had a deleterious effect on Henry, who took to drinking, gambling, fighting, and whoring.

Fearing the dessert portion of the evening was headed in an uncomfortable direction, Lady Stratford tried again to let James speak. "Mr. Bingham can take care of himself, Miss Colborne."

"As can I," interjected Rosamund.

"Rosamund, please, not again," pleaded her embarrassed mother.

Mrs. Hornby glanced at James to discern what he made of Miss Colborne. Lord Stratford had whispered to her about Eliza's scheme concerning James and Rosamund, but his face provided no clues. James sensed that Rosamund's provocative behaviour could not be about him, so he did not engage, but he found it hard not to look at her.

Rosamund's father, Hugh, surveyed his wife and daughter with contempt. "Katherine and Rosamund, stop being rude. Enough already."

"Indeed," replied Rosamund. "I've already had enough."

"Enough of what, Miss Colborne?" The rumbling timbre of the ambassador's voice gave him control of the table. Eliza rolled her eyes, surrendering to the evening's demise.

Stratford sensed his wife's displeasure. "No, my dear, this young woman provokes our guests, embarrasses her parents, and, most unforgivably, keeps us from the baklava. As host, I apologise."

"She should apologise," mumbled Mr. Wattling, his intent apparent to those familiar with Rosamund's treatment of Henry.

"No, with my apology, we are beyond apologies." Lord Stratford's declamation caught the table off guard, and the guests were unsure what was next.

"In diplomacy," Stratford's voice segued into a contemplative tone, "we engage in ritual dances—demonstrating skills, testing knowledge of the steps, and seeking the smallest advantage to lead. But the mark of a great diplomat, at least a British one, is the ability—amidst the music, movement, and misdirection—to grasp the heart of the matter, the sources of competing national interests. I believe, Judge Hornby, the same is true in law."

Remembering Lord Stratford's earlier bizarre performance with James had soured Edmund's mood as he made his way to the embassy dinner, which irritated Emelia, who craved such soirées as escapes from the solitude her husband's endless duties forced upon her. But with his question about law, Edmund wondered whether Stratford was starting another eccentric episode.

"In legal disputes," Edmund replied, "the two sides argue about the facts, what law applies to the facts, or what the law means. The best lawyers cut through statutes, case law, and the cunning of opposing counsel to locate the critical issue on which the case will turn."

"Very nice," Lord Stratford continued. "But in diplomacy, the hardest issues arise when the heart of the matter touches questions deeper than truth or law. We have our rituals, but my encounters with foreign diplomats distil into their resistance to how we vindicate our power."

The guests turned toward Edmund, who hesitated, not sure where Stratford was going. "The law creates legitimacy through a commitment to process. Parliament makes laws. Courts render decisions. Merchants negotiate contracts. Countries conclude treaties. These ways of making, applying, and relying on law make the legal system resilient. This resilience sustains the support the law receives from the governed. Our rituals help shield the law from resistance."

"But," Lord Stratford replied, "people argue about another thing important to law, the same thing that informs resistance to power. Do we not, as diplomats and lawyers, have a responsibility to acknowledge it?"

Edmund hesitated again, and Stratford needled the judge. "Perhaps Mr. Bingham can answer the question—a lawyer less encumbered by age and tobacco."

James had no ready reply, believing that he would escape further questioning. But curiously, Stratford did not look at him after sending the question in his direction. Instead, the ambassador set his eyes upon Rosamund.

She did not hesitate, tilting her head to acknowledge that Stratford wanted her to reply. "Justice. However skilled our diplomats are at ritual, other nations chafe at how we abuse our power. Subjects resent the law, for all its liturgy, when it becomes a means of oppression."

"What rubbish!" Mr. Wattling snorted.

The ambassador held up his hand as if to deflect Wattling's outburst, but he did not take his eyes off Rosamund.

"And you feel that you've been done some injustice that justifies your breaches of ritual and liturgy tonight?"

"Here and in England," Rosamund answered. "Everywhere I've been as a woman."

The riposte caused the other ladies around the table to glance at each other.

"What does being a woman have to do with justice?" Mr. Wattling asked.

"Apparently nothing," Rosamund replied.

Lord Stratford laughed again, spontaneity at the expense of Mr. Wattling, who only crinkled his forehead at the retort.

"Mr. Bingham," Rosamund continued before Stratford could regain control of the conversation. "Would you do me the honour of answering a riddle?"

"A riddle?" James repeated flatly, hiding his irritation at being put on the spot again.

"What is the difference between a civilised Englishwoman and an uncivilised Turkish man?" Rosamund asked, her eyes sweeping around the table to indicate that the riddle was for everyone.

"Miss Colborne, please," tried Emelia, as Edmund glanced angrily at Lord Stratford to get him to end the discourteous spectacle.

"I see that Mr. Bingham does not like riddles," Rosamund ignored Mrs. Hornby's plea. "So, Mr. Bingham, let me ask a simple question instead. Was your wife a diplomat?"

"What an absurd question," Mr. Wattling complained.

"She was my fiancée," James coldly replied, finally looking away from Rosamund.

"Was your fiancée a diplomat?" Rosamund ploughed ahead.

"Rosamund, stop this at once," a red-faced Mr. Colborne commanded.

"Was your fiancée a lawyer?" Rosamund would not be put off.

"Miss Colborne," Eliza interjected. "Please refrain from interrogating Mr. Bingham."

"Lady Stratford," Rosamund turned on the ambassador's wife. "Based on the ages and genders of the guests tonight, and your reputation, did you not intend to introduce me, a woman without a man, to that person"—she pointed accusingly at James—"a man without a woman?"

Eliza did not reply, but Rosamund needed no answer. "Then am I not permitted to learn about Mr. Bingham and the woman who ... Oh, I shouldn't be so presumptuous, so one more question, Mr. Bingham. Did your woman actually love you?"

Hugh Colborne's fist crashed onto the table, making the china jump and the crystal rattle. Everyone recoiled at the concussive act, except Rosamund, who merely looked at her father with haughty satisfaction.

Lord Stratford heaved himself upright and, in the resulting silence, ordered more than proposed, "Gentlemen, shall we retire?"

"To answer my riddle? To talk of justice? Are we not invited?" Rosamund dared more than asked. "Ladies, shall we?"

The women rose in unison, twirled from the table in synchrony, and left the dining room together. The men mutely watched this ballet before mumbling off for smokes and whiskey.

Left at the table, alone with the baklava, was James Bingham.

Chapter 5
Something Happened

James stopped writing to massage his ink-stained hand. His first full week at the Supreme Consular Court was occupied with legibly copying documents hastily drafted by Judge Hornby, vice legal consul Henry Wroth, and law secretary Donald Logie. Those who normally did copyist work for the court were, for some reason, unavailable.

James struggled with the task because his penmanship was poor. His mother had berated him with an inexplicable insult when he was learning his letters. "You write," she had yelled, "like you're deaf." It was not the yelling he feared, but the violence that often followed it. Fear that taught him to hide when she was alone at the kitchen table with a bottle and a battered face.

Emma had reacted to his handwriting differently. Once, on a picnic, she wanted him to read a letter he had posted because she could not make sense of it. He apologised for writing like he was deaf. Emma had fixed him squarely with her eyes, "You write like you're lazy."

At first, James believed copyist duty was ritual initiation, like Wroth's robe-and-wig jape for his audience with Lord Stratford. This notion faded as James saw the pace at which Hornby, Wroth, and Logie worked on cases, drafted correspondence, and managed seemingly endless meetings. Copying legal documents and despatches to the Foreign Office proved an excellent intro-

duction to the court and people, places, and issues still unfamiliar to him, despite the reading he had done on his voyage.

As his first week ended, James contemplated what he might
do for the weekend. Bones had finally arrived, so he could ride
around to develop a better sense of the city. Courtesy of Her
Majesty's Treasury, James could lodge at the *Hôtel de Byzance*
a few more weeks, obviating any pressing need to find accommodations. After Saturday breakfast, he visited clothiers for European gentlemen in the Pera district to ascertain whether any
sold barrister wigs. None did. After lunch, he rationalised his ret-
icence to explore Constantinople by remembering all the work
waiting at the court. He rode Bones to the court and spent the
rest of the weekend copying despatches, notes, and reports into
final versions.

To take some breaks, he explored the court building, looking
particularly for its library of legal materials. For James, there was
no law without books, reports, treatises, and periodicals. Words
on pages contained the law. Pages in books created the rule of
law. These words, pages, and books constituted justice for him,
not some sentimental sense of right or wrong or philosophical
prattle about an ideal society. In England, he always had books,
pages, and words to clarify confusion, keep chaos at bay, and provide comfort when solitude tempted despair. But he found no
legal materials in the court building's offices. He went into the
courtroom, but it housed no books, reports, treatises, or periodicals.

James lingered in the courtroom. It was arranged like most
English courtrooms, and it was chilly, as English courtrooms
were in winter. Its best feature was the light streaming through
windows, starting behind and extending high above the judge's

bench. He walked to the front, faced the bench, and raised his face to the sunlight. He imagined people packed in the courtroom watching him argue a criminal case for the Crown, in a wig worthy of a Queen's Counsel. The fantasy vanished as he realised that he was unlikely to argue cases in this courtroom. How his work as a law clerk would affect what happened here remained unclear.

When James arrived at the court on Monday morning, Donald Logie was preparing to depart. Donald took James by the arm and positioned him so that they were looking into the clerk's room, where James had been toiling at copyist duties. Sitting at the table was a young Turkish man dressed in European clothes and looking very uncomfortable.

"Who is he?" Donald asked, and James shook his head.

Donald whispered, "He was outside when I arrived. He's here to see the Supreme English Judge."

"What's his name?" James asked.

Donald hesitated, "Mohammed. Mahmoud. Moomah. M-something. I still have trouble with their names. Can you?"

"Can I what?" James responded.

"Find out why he's here. Entertain him until the judge arrives." The request was an order, but James just looked blankly at Donald.

"I have to inspect a Turkish gaol with Dr. Hoyland," Donald said as he moved toward the back door. "So I can't deal with this."

James continued looking at the Turkish man. Perhaps sensing he was being watched, the Turk turned his head and stared back. He was handsome, with dark, strong eyes. As James resolved to enter the clerk's room, pounding on the court building's main doors began. James pivoted and took a few paces toward the banging.

"Please open, we need the police, please help," a loud female voice called.

James knew he had to open the doors. There was no one else to do it. But the urgency of the appeal made him hesitate. More pounding on the door produced more pounding in his chest. Suddenly, the young Turkish man was standing next to him. More banging ensued. James locked eyes with the Turk, who nodded, and James opened the door.

"Oh, thank God," the woman puffed. "I need the police. Something happened."

"Please come in," said the Turk, with initiative that surprised James.

They shepherded the woman into the clerk's room and sat her at the table, but she remained agitated because neither man said anything.

"I'm Mrs. Emily Hicocks," she broke the silence. "My daughter. I need the police."

"Mrs. Hicocks, I am James Bingham, a clerk with the court."

"Who's that?" Emily pointed at the Turk.

"My name is Mehmed. I am also a clerk."

James gave the Turk a sideways look.

"I need the police," Emily returned to her mission. "Can you help me, please?"

The main doors of the court building opened, followed by footsteps approaching the clerk's room. A nattily dressed man stopped short as he glanced into the room on walking by. He entered and raised his eyebrows to indicate that he had no idea why two young men and a middle-aged woman—none of whom he had seen before—were seated at the clerk's table.

"May I help you?"

"Oh, sir," Emily responded first, "I need the police. Are you the constable? Our Susannah. My little girl. Something happened."

"Wait," said the man, "who are you, all of you?"

Bingham stood, "Sir, I'm James Bingham, the new clerk, and this is Mrs. Emily Hicocks, who wants help from the police."

"Ah," the man reacted, then spoke to the Turk, "who are you?"

Emily lost her patience, "Can somebody help me?"

"Mrs. Hicocks," the man took control, "I'm Frederick Guarracino, the dragoman."

"The what?" Emily's agitation deepened.

"I help the court with Turkish officials, act as an interpreter, etcetera, to ensure the Ottoman government treats British subjects fairly," Frederick explained.

Emily looked exasperated as tears appeared. "Are you a policeman? For the love of Christ, I need the police. Our Susannah."

"Mr. Bingham, go to the gaol building—out the back door, past the stables. Find Thomas Williams and bring him here." Frederick issued the instruction with authority.

As James left the room, Frederick turned to Mrs. Hicocks, "Mr. Williams is our police constable."

He then asked Mehmed in Turkish, "Who are you?"

Mehmed, also in Turkish, informed Frederick that he was the law clerk that the Foreign Minister, Fuad Pasha, made available to Judge Hornby for work on a legal code. The dragoman knew nothing about the arrangement, but the matter at hand took precedence.

"Do you know what this woman wants with the police?" he probed with Mehmed.

Mehmed replied that something happened to her daughter, Susannah. Mrs. Hicocks, who spoke no Turkish, repeated "Susannah" after Mehmed said the name. Mehmed added that he had only just arrived this morning and had no idea what was going on. James returned without Williams, who, according to someone in the gaol, was elsewhere.

"Gentlemen, take notes," Frederick said to the law clerks. "Mrs. Hicocks, tell me what happened. I don't need all the details now, but I want to know why you're here."

James fetched paper, pens, and ink. Mehmed looked uncomfortable as James gave him a pen and paper. Frederick noticed the discomfort and asked in Turkish, "What's wrong?"

"I speak and read English good enough, but not writing," Mehmed replied.

"Take notes in Turkish." Frederick's sarcastic tone was apparent even to James, who did not understand what had passed between the dragoman and the Turk.

The clerks inked their pens, and Mrs. Hicocks began. Frederick had to slow her down, but she settled into a more measured pace. Frederick did not notice when James and Mehmed stopped writing, which happened when Mrs. Hicocks described what transpired after her daughter went into the room where Mr. Sinclair was smoking his pipe.

Frederick left to escort Emily home. James and Mehmed knew they had to finish their notes, but they did not speak for some minutes.

"Do you have a daughter?" Mehmed eventually asked, remembering his sister's shame.

"No, do you?" James replied, recalling his mother at the kitchen table.

"No," Mehmed said. "We should finish. Mrs. Hicocks has a daughter."

Chapter 6
Serendipity

The invitation was irritating. The message to be delivered likely would be irritating. Nevertheless, Rosamund was preened, primped, and cognisant amends were in order after the dinner at the embassy. Waiting in the foyer, she inhaled and squirmed to escape irritation from her corset. The solidarity among the women at the dinner's end had not survived the rage at home, recriminations in society, and rumours spread as far as London courtesy of Jane Norris, a notorious gossip monger who had attended the dinner.

She sighed. Had she gone too far one too many times? She was concerned enough about the calculating anger in her father's reaction to appear today as summoned. She now needed something she lacked—the ability to be contrite over tea and cakes.

The butler escorted her into a room where Emelia Hornby was on her feet, holding a parasol. Mrs. Hornby was in her thirties, experienced as a wife and mother and seasoned beyond the home by the demands that her husband's place in Her Majesty's Service imposed on her. There were women in the British community at Constantinople with more status and influence. But, Rosamund surmised, the lot had fallen to the judge's wife, who possessed sufficient youth and worldliness to speak more convincingly to a troublesome younger woman.

"Miss Colborne, let's take tea in the garden given today's un-seasonably warm weather. Giovanni will have refreshments ready where we can look across the Bosphorus while we talk."

Mrs. Hornby's tone was business-like, an acknowledgement that this was not an ordinary social call. Mrs. Hornby exited on-to a small courtyard. Rosamund followed, deciding not to speak unless spoken to, hoping that such an approach would shorten the encounter.

The garden extended uphill on terraces traversed by a gravel pathway linked at terrace ends by small sets of stairs. Although the climb was not particularly steep, Rosamund laboured as Mrs. Hornby strode ahead, accustomed to the upward stroll. Upon reaching the last terrace, Mrs. Hornby walked to its front edge and enjoyed a clear view across the Bosphorus to the Asiatic side of the city. It was such a nice day, hinting of spring. The breeze had a slight chill, but on this fine day, it came gently and inter-mittently. She closed her eyes and let her face feel the sun.

Emelia expected Rosamund to join her for the panorama. She turned to find Rosamund behind her, looking at a very old statue of Diana that still sat on this vantage point over the Bosphorus. The marble had seen better days and too many birds, but even so, Diana remained breathtaking. With a confident face fixed on her target, the goddess was reaching for an arrow in her quiver—a motion that still seemed alive. The arrow was for the goddess's bow, but the weapon and the hand that held it were gone, taken from her in the mists of time.

"Miss Colborne?" Emelia called over her shoulder.

Rosamund turned and walked to stand beside Emelia. "My apologies, Mrs. Hornby, I have a soft spot for ancient things. The past often seems more fertile for dreams than the future."

Feeling more alive in the world of the dead? In other circumstances, Emelia would have probed this curious confession. She knew little about Rosamund, beyond her father's wealth and her reputation as a difficult young woman. She had interacted superficially with her at social events, often taking note of Rosamund's intriguing attire. One evening gown was composed of satin panels that glinted in candlelight as she moved, giving the fleeting impression that Rosamund was wearing armour. Another was jet black with strikingly medieval adornments. Small, embroidered silver circles interlinked across one side of the bodice and down one sleeve—as if she wore a half-vest of chainmail—and a long, black leather belt with silver metal accents girdled her hips, the tip of which ran down the skirt nearly to the floor. If nothing else, the daughter was fleecing the father's pocketbook at the dressmakers.

Rosamund's gown for the embassy dinner that produced this day's rendezvous hinted at what British nurses wore during the Crimean war. The effect was touching, recalling what the lady with the lamp, and all her ladies, had accomplished during the conflict. The gown was also discordant, a reminder of a war that had not aged well. Today, Rosamund had on an ivory-hued dress adorned with what faintly resembled a nun's collar and bib. Was this garment, Emelia wondered, chosen for a ritual of scolding and penance?

"Miss Colborne," Emelia began, "your performance at the embassy and past behaviour means you've just about squandered your advantages. My, you're a gorgeous thing, and your father's wealth means you come with money. What most women wouldn't give for what you have."

Rosamund did not reply. Surprised that the young woman's infamous tongue was still, Emelia continued, "You're at the proverbial crossroads, but you don't control the path you'll take."

Rosamund remained quiet for a few moments before speaking, "You forgot God."

"Excuse me?" The response surprised Emelia.

"My father harangues me on my duties under God to honour my father, obey my husband, and forgive their sins. My mother just gazes past me as if she lost something long ago that she never actually possessed. What's a girl to do?" Rosamund's voice was like a metronome.

"You talk as if you're the first woman to have such thoughts," Emelia scolded.

"I've been here since I was a girl," Rosamund spoke again without inflection. "If other women have such thoughts, I've never heard them."

Emelia did not wish to prolong something approaching petulance, so she remained silent.

Rosamund continued, "But here we are, with you—the representative of some self-appointed committee—to tell me to surrender. I might as well be living in a harem."

"Have you ever been in a harem?" Emelia sharply asked.

Rosamund closed her eyes in trepidation of Mrs. Hornby talking about her book, parts of which recounted visits to harems. *In and Around Stamboul* compiled letters that the judge's wife had written to friends and relatives in England during her first voyage to Constantinople and her time in Turkey during the war. When the book was published, Rosamund had read it, hungry for insights from a woman about that time of great events.

Rosamund appreciated Mrs. Hornby's anguish at the devastation the war had wreaked on soldiers and civilians. During the conflict, Rosamund's mother had volunteered to help Florence Nightingale and her nurses care for sick and wounded British soldiers. Only once had Rosamund visited her mother at the military hospital in Scutari. Maurin Hancock, wife of Geoffrey Hancock, her father's business partner, took her daughter, Margaret, and Rosamund to see Katherine Colborne at the hospital. Mrs. Hancock acted as a mother hen to Rosamund during Katherine's time caring for soldiers, which Rosamund loved because Maggie was her best friend.

They had crossed the Bosphorus by steamer and clambered into a carriage. Mrs. Hancock, in her best governess voice, told the girls that, once upon a time, the Roman emperor Constantine won a battle at Scutari and changed the city's name from Byzantium to Constantinople. The history lesson was met with silence. She and Maggie, holding hands in nervous excitement, were more interested in looking out of the carriage at a part of the city neither had seen before. Mrs. Hancock commented that, just as well, the day was not about dead men. No, she wanted them to see what females could do. Rosamund remembered how odd it sounded when Mrs. Hancock said "females."

The smell hit them first, well before they heard the screams, reached the ward, and saw the gore. In the closest row of beds, a soldier with a bloody head bandage thrust his hand up the skirt of a nurse, whose attempt to evade the invasion while holding bedpans sent her spilling onto the floor. The soldier laughed, "Just a bit of fun, lass."

Half-way down the ward, Rosamund spotted her mother, covered in blood—hands, apron, arms, and face glistening with crimson. She was restraining a soldier, who was screaming and writhing in pain. The soldier's hand snatched at her mother's hair and twisted her head so violently that mother saw daughter. Her mother's eyes registered shock upon seeing her dear girl there, amidst the horror. With gritted teeth, her mother slowly wrenched her head back to face the soldier and gently extricated his hand from her hair while talking or whispering to him. The soldier began to weep. Maggie vomited, Mrs. Hancock wheeled the girls out, and Katherine never talked to Rosamund about that morning or any of her days and nights at the hospital.

Rosamund had so wanted to talk. About what she saw, what her mother was doing, what all the heated arguments between her mother and father about it meant. She had only one exchange with her mother about the hospital. Shortly after her mother began to volunteer, she asked one night at bedtime, "Mummy, why have you gone to war?"

Surprised, her mother remained motionless before tenderly kissing the top of her head and saying only, "I suppose I have, Miss Rosamund. In so many ways, I suppose I have."

But much of Mrs. Hornby's book bothered Rosamund with its superficiality and detached descriptions of exotic things passing for engagement with real people, important places, and historic events. The letters describing visits to harems were particularly frustrating. Rosamund had heard that Turkish women in harems were only educated to excite and satisfy the carnal desires of men, a description she found horrific and implausible in equal measure. Mrs. Hornby wrote of her visits to harems as if she had been at a zoo, commenting on strange, unfortunate creatures without attempting to understand how these women felt about their lives, their world, their hopes. In the book, Mrs. Hornby agreed with another Englishwoman that Turkish women, "being degraded to an animal state," could only find contentment by "eating, drinking, and basking in the sun."

Once, when Rosamund was much younger, she spent a Sunday afternoon with her parents at the Sweet Waters of Asia. She wandered off toward something that caught her eye—a group of beautifully dressed and veiled Turkish women sitting in the sun near a fountain. The woman in the centre of the group motioned for the curious child to come closer. Rosamund had walked up to the woman and lifted her nearly sheer veil, pairing kind eyes wrinkled by a soft smile. The woman whispered something that she did not understand. "Thank you," she whispered before putting the veil back over the woman's face.

"No, I haven't," Rosamund finally said. But Emelia noticed the hesitation, which had not arisen because the young woman had trouble remembering whether she had visited a harem.

"Perhaps your imagination exceeds your experience, and what little experience you have means you don't know how to listen when women speak," Emelia observed, turning to gaze again over the Bosphorus.

Rosamund liked that Mrs. Hornby had some bite in her. But she remained silent, assuming the real lecture would soon commence. But, as moments passed, she sensed Mrs. Hornby was somewhere else and became unsure what the older woman was preparing to say.

"Edmund saved me from drowning," Emelia suddenly said.

"Saved you from drowning in the Bosphorus?" Rosamund ventured.

"What?" Emelia came back from her memory. "No, that's how we met."

Emelia turned her face back toward Asia Minor. "I was punting with my friend Charlotte near Weybridge one Saturday afternoon. I was being careless with the pole and gossiping too much. I lost my balance and splashed into the river. The water turned my crinoline dress into an anchor, so I couldn't keep afloat. Charlotte was a wee thing who couldn't pull me above the water. Then, as I was sinking, someone grabbed my dress, hauled me to the surface, dragged me to shore, and deposited me on the bank. It was Edmund, who just happened to be walking by as I fell in. Can you believe it—he was only in Weybridge after an impulsive decision to escape London for the weekend."

It was quite a story, but Rosamund went queasy. Emelia had shared something that had changed her life, and Rosamund was emotionally lost.

"We married a few months later," Emelia kept her eyes on the horizon. "Imagine that."

"Was he a judge then?" Rosamund felt she had to say something.

Emelia smiled quizzically at Rosamund. "No, he was just a struggling young barrister. When we met, his prospects didn't point to him being a judge in Her Majesty's Service involved with the great men and events of the British empire. But none of that mattered. We fell in love as fast as I fell in the river."

Emelia paused to signal a shift. "Your parents agreed to have me talk with you because I'm conventional, sensible, and have status in society, etcetera. But please know, when you asked James Bingham whether his fiancée loved him, my heart leapt because, dear girl, I knew why you asked. Your question—however cruel in the circumstances—touched me. Love ... It can be sustenance, even in the most trying times. That's why I wanted to talk with you."

The conversation's turn surprised Rosamund, even though she knew that Mrs. Hornby did not understand why she had loosed her questions at Mr. Bingham during the dinner. Before Rosamund could craft a response, Emelia signalled with her parasol for Rosamund to head toward a table and chairs farther along the terrace. As they sat, Giovanni appeared and poured tea. Rosamund took milk, buying time before having to speak. Mrs. Hornby spooned sugar into her tea and seemed ready to recall other memories, but Rosamund was again mistaken.

"You haven't found your Edmund," Emelia returned to a formal tone. "And, if it's love you must have, then you should return to England."

"Is this a command from my parents?" Rosamund asked.

"No. Well, perhaps advice from your mother, but not your father, who is beyond furious, or he's putting on a good show of it. He appears set on making you bend to his will, and he's not interested in whether you find love. He seems to believe that you've made it possible for him to dispose of you according to his purposes. Your father won't bankroll your future until he's broken you, or at least until he thinks he has."

Rosamund did not speak, and she did not move. Had she miscalculated? Was her father no longer afraid?

"I don't know," Emelia went on, "what, besides love, you want from life. You are intelligent, which is perhaps why you have disdain for the lives that I, your mother, and other women lead."

Rosamund began to protest, but Emelia cut her off. "Let me speak plainly. You might, as men do, dismiss my book as frippery.

But publishing a book that people in two empires would read was never something I dreamed I could do. And falling in love was not the direct cause of the opportunities that came my way as a wife. Edmund encountered his own unpredictable incidents that brought us here. You must be ready for life to produce what you never expect."

Emelia could tell Rosamund was not sure how this sermon spoke to her situation. "As odd as it sounds, you need to build space in your life for serendipity. Your father's wrath threatens to dictate what happens to you. You are hostage to a powerful man with the reputation for getting what he wants. You need room in your life for things just to happen."

Emelia halved a scone and spread jam on one piece, as a cue for Rosamund to speak. Rosamund remained silent, staring at the ground. Emelia had a bite of scone and a sip of tea, which was growing cold. She motioned for Giovanni to refresh their cups.

"You mean I should capitulate?" Rosamund finally engaged without looking at Emelia.

"No, child. You really are an innocent in the world of men. I mean manoeuvre, tack and trim, navigate, have the weather gage, do not leave the initiative to the raging storm."

Rosamund leaned her head to one side, sensing something but not quite grasping it.

Emelia touched Rosamund's knee, "Show more interest in the pursuit of justice."

Rosamund furrowed her brow. "You cannot mean I should become a lawyer."

"No, goodness, I have confused you," Emelia replied. "So, like a good lawyer, let me be more precise. You should show more interest in those who pursue justice."

Rosamund arched her eyebrows, "You mean Mr. Bingham?"

Emelia winked, took another bite, and, with scone slowing her words, said, "Perhaps you didn't notice, but he couldn't take his eyes off you, no matter how much you tormented him."

"You mean marry Mr. Bingham?" Rosamund scowled.

Emelia frowned, "Navigate, not plan nuptials. Manoeuvre, not prepare the marriage bed."

Rosamund leaned forward. Emelia nodded, believing that the young woman was now understanding the idea.

Rosamund sat back, "Poor Mr. Bingham. It wouldn't be fair."

"You can manoeuvre and not manipulate, but yes, threading that needle will be very difficult. However, men too often leave women with no good options. Resisting that fate is a type of justice. And, in the flesh-and-blood world, justice produces unfair consequences for the innocent as well as the guilty," Emelia offered.

Rosamund had misjudged Mrs. Hornby.

"Thank you," she half-whispered.

"Well, who knows, you might unexpectedly fall in love with a struggling young barrister."

Rosamund laughed and asked whether there was another scone. Emelia handed Rosamund the plate and asked, "Miss Colborne, tell me, what is the answer to your riddle about the civilised Englishwoman and the uncivilised Turkish man?"

Rosamund sliced her scone in two, applied jam to one half, and held it up. "Only one is accorded the opportunity to be equal."

Emelia did not immediately comprehend, but a moment's reflection provided clarity. She nodded at Rosamund, who slathered jam over the other half of her scone.

Emelia broke off a piece of her own, plopped it in her mouth, and with crumbs on her lips, said, "Now, clever girl, tell me what you think of my book."

Chapter 7

R v. Sinclair

It seemed like a good idea. Now integrated into the court's legal work rather than buried with copyist chores, James had been so busy that he spent no time looking for housing. Her Majesty's Treasury forced an end to his stay at the *Hôtel de Byzance*. Judge Hornby offered a spare room at his residence. However, living within the judge's reach expanded James's workload and extended his hours. He was constantly exhausted. Instead of arriving at the court before anyone else, as had become his habit, this morning he decided to complete overdue work in his room.

He retrieved an unruly pile of papers from his satchel and sorted out what took priority. Documents for the code of Turkish criminal procedure that he and Mehmed were supposed to be drafting were, again, placed to one side. Neither he nor Mehmed ever had time for the task. Other matters were always more pressing for James, and Judge Hornby often gave Mehmed more urgent work unrelated to the code. Mehmed also volunteered to copy final versions of draft documents to improve his written English and understanding of English law and diplomacy.

Although tireless, Mehmed was not always collegial. Like most Turks, Mehmed loathed the treaty capitulations. Judge Hornby insisted that Mehmed be a protected person under the capitulations while he worked with the court. Mehmed was, in effect, a British subject under treaty law. He was not pleased.

Hasan, the *mufti* who had recommended Mehmed, had to have Fuad Pasha intervene to keep Mehmed from leaving the court.

James decided to focus on documents related to *R v. Sinclair*, the criminal case coming to trial based on what allegedly befell Susannah Hicocks. The case involved only British subjects, and even for the Ottoman government, it fell under the jurisdiction of the British consular court. However, Mehmed argued that Turkish courts should handle the case. James cited treaty law as clear on British jurisdiction. Mehmed countered that the treaty was unjust. Mehmed also claimed that, because the Ottoman government employed Sinclair as an engineer, this employment status brought Sinclair under Turkish jurisdiction. Mehmed used his own status as a protected person under the capitulations, created by his role at the court, to support his argument.

Judge Hornby overheard James and Mehmed arguing this point one day and sat at the clerk's table. He had Mehmed go through his argument. Edmund then asked Mehmed whether he would be protected under the capitulations for engaging in the acts that Sinclair was accused of committing. Mehmed said he would not be protected because the acts were not related to his official functions as a law clerk. Edmund stood, put a hand briefly on Mehmed's shoulder, and left. Mehmed was unusually quiet for the rest of that day.

After toiling a few hours in his room, James went to the court in the late morning. A smirking Henry Wroth greeted him. Donald Logie noticed and came to stand by Henry.

"Well, well," Henry's smirk became a grin. "A wig and a woman all in the same morning."

Henry and Donald enjoyed James's confused look, and from behind his back, Henry tossed James a new barrister's wig. "From Lady Stratford."

James caught the wig. It was gorgeous, unlike the smattering of horsehair he had been able to afford when called to the Bar. With mock solemnity, he crowned his head with the wig.

"Donald, we were wrong," Henry feigned surprise. "He had us fooled with his befuddled demeanour, dishevelled wardrobe, untamed hair, and monkish disinterest in female company."

"I know," Donald played along, "and who would have thought that, of all the female company, she—the scourge of Constantinople's suitors—would call on our Mr. Bingham?"

"What are you on about?" James asked, not without some amusement.

Henry pulled an envelope from his pocket and presented it with *faux* formality. "Miss Rosamund Colborne requests your presence at her residence this Saturday at three for tea."

"You opened it?" James took the envelope, not amused that Henry knew its contents.

"No," Henry replied. "It's still sealed. Curiously, she told me, as if I needed to know."

"She delivered it here?" James was incredulous.

Henry tapped the envelope and said to no one in particular, "Back to the salt mine."

James read the invitation in the clerk's room. She probably wanted to apologise for her behaviour at that dinner. He put the invitation in his satchel and sorted through some documents. Concentration was difficult. He kept seeing her pointing at him from across that glittering table.

"Bingham!" loudly requested Judge Hornby from down the hall. The judge was holding a copy of *The Levant Herald* when James entered his office.

"Did you see this about the *Sinclair* case?" Edmund growled and thrust the newspaper at James. "We're going to trial on Monday, and this appears. Salacious. Wrong on the facts. Falsehoods about the court. It will feed the proclivity of Europeans here to spread false reports and rumours on every subject. It must be why we received a telegraphic message this morning from London about the case. Can you believe it—the Foreign Office knew about a story published in Constantinople last evening before I did? This telegraph, it spreads contagion with no chance of quarantine."

The outburst surprised James. Judge Hornby had praised the telegraph as a means for spreading the rule of law. James had seen a few telegraphic messages, scraps of paper recording brief information sent across land and under the sea through wire cables. It was a technology for brevity and speed—not the detail, time, and formality that diplomatic despatches reflected.

Edmund instructed James to prepare a report on the *Sinclair* case for the Foreign Office. He wanted to send it before the trial began to give the Foreign Office all the information the court had prior to proceedings before the jury. James burnt the candle at both ends preparing the report, which Edmund enclosed with a despatch to the Foreign Office on Friday. The trial was to begin on the Monday following, and James's work for it was not finished. He laboured most of Saturday before galloping Bones to the Colborne residence through crisp February air. He arrived, fresh in neither body nor wardrobe, at the appointed time.

A servant led James through a smoke-scented study in which Hugh Colborne sat, reading *The Levant Herald*. Hugh stood up as if taken off guard and looked James up and down quizzically. He mumbled "Bingham" in a confused tone as James exited the study.

Rosamund was seated on a divan when James entered the parlour. He apologised for his appearance and explained the reasons. She did not seem interested. After serving him tea, she apologised for her behaviour at the embassy dinner. She offered no explanation or excuses. Her apology was, in his experience of polite society, a spartan *mea culpa*.

Then, awkwardly, she changed the subject. "Tell me about *R v. Sinclair*."

He hesitated, telling her that, given his involvement, he should not talk about the case. He did not say that his reluctance also stemmed from the indecent nature of the alleged crime, which he did not wish to discuss with a young woman. Rosamund looked disappointed. She glanced at a clock on the mantel. With the conversation stalling and his nerve ready to fail, James was about to take his leave when he remembered George and Jemmy.

"What about the case interests you?" he risked.

The question improved her countenance. The case, she explained, had become notorious given its shocking nature. She described how the trial was turning into a bread-and-circus spectacle, with wagers placed on the accused's guilt or innocence. How, she asked, will justice be achieved in the case? What, she wondered, does justice look like in these kinds of cases?

He had no experience as a barrister with these kinds of cases. He did not know whether justice could be done. No one had witnessed what Susannah claimed and Sinclair denied. He desperately wanted the notorious and shocking kept away from the tea and biscuits, so he tried to move the conversation away from the case.

"Have you ever seen a trial?"

She shook her head.

"Perhaps you should attend the trial and see if it answers your questions."

Rosamund liked the idea and said she would sleep on it. She would not attend, however, if James refused to visit her for tea next Saturday. He agreed with perhaps too much eagerness. She escorted him to the front entrance through an adjacent sitting room where her mother sat alone, not working on unfinished embroidery. James nodded at Mrs. Colborne, who expressed wordless astonishment at seeing him. Rosamund did not stop to talk to her mother.

With arms tight across her body against the cold, Rosamund waited outside with James until Bones was brought around. She laughed when she saw his horse—a spontaneous act that, for James, warmly ended the afternoon.

—

Judge Hornby brought the Supreme Consular Court to order. The case attracted more people to the trial than the courtroom accommodated. Procedures for managing a crowd did not exist because the court had never faced this challenge in its short life. Thomas Williams, the constable, and Frederick Guarracino, the dragoman, improvised well enough that the proceedings started without much delay. With the jury seated, Judge Hornby motioned for Sebastian Knight, Queen's Counsel for the Crown, to begin. Knight was tall, stately, and possessed an exquisite aquiline nose.

"Your Honour, members of the jury, the Crown will prove that the accused, Thomas Sinclair, did indecently assault Susannah Hicocks in his house on January 22nd of this year. The crime is shocking, made more so by the context in which it happened—a gathering of families that the accused and his wife initiated. Amidst this wholesome endeavour the accused indecently assaults an eleven-year-old girl. The nature of this case produces the need for the jury to hear testimony from a child, the victim of this attack on her virtue. Through every step of this case, this child's story has remained consistent, despite how frightening all this must be for one so young and innocent. Such consistency bears the imprimatur of truth, and the truth provides ample grounds for conviction, which is the only just end for this tragedy."

When recognised by Judge Hornby, Maurice Butt, Queen's Counsel for the defence, stood for his opening statement. A short, stout man, Butt resembled a cannonball and had a voice that boomed like the guns of a man-of-war.

"Your Honour and gentlemen of the jury, the Crown has no evidence sufficient to convict Thomas Sinclair under English law. The Crown has no physical evidence, none, that Mr. Sinclair assaulted Susannah Hicocks. The Crown has no witnesses, none, who saw Thomas assault Susannah. The Crown has identified no motive, none, that explains why Thomas would assault her. The Crown has identified no pattern of behaviour, none, by Thomas that would support the story told by the Hicocks. I do not know why this girl told her mother what she did, or why her parents persisted with the allegation. What I do know is that, under English law and justice, no evidence of a crime means no conviction for that crime."

With opening statements completed, Judge Hornby asked the Crown to proceed with its case. Knight called Emily Hicocks to the witness box.

"Mrs. Hicocks," Knight extended to his full height. "Can you tell the jury how you came to be in Thomas Sinclair's home on January 22nd?"

"My husband, John, doesn't have a job, so we—me, John, and our Susannah—we're looking for food round where we live. Food that people might have thrown away. Mrs. Sinclair comes out of her house, and she figures what we're doing and invites us for dinner."

"Did you know the Sinclairs before this day?"

"No," Mrs. Hicocks replied.

"What happened after you accepted this invitation?"

"We have dinner, and I help Mrs. Sinclair clean up in the kitchen, and Mr. Sinclair, his three children, and Susannah go into another room. A Mr. Harris and his son knock on the door and ask if Mr. Sinclair's Gordon wants to go to watch a steam tug dock. So Gordon goes, leaving Mr. Sinclair's other children and Susannah in the room with Mr. Sinclair.

"After helping in the kitchen, I find Susannah in the hallway—crying and scared something bad. My husband comes along, and he's worried when he sees her. I ask her if she wants to go to the water closet, and she says yes. I find blood in her drawers, on her legs."

"What did you do next?" Knight asked.

"I'm trying to calm her down. She's shaking, can't hardly stand up. I'm thinking, she's too young, this doesn't make sense. She's only just turned eleven. I ask—"

"Mrs. Hicocks," Knight interrupted. "I have a question on this point. Since the incident, has Susannah started?"

"No, she hasn't. She's too young."

"Thank you, Mrs. Hicocks. Let's go back to the water closet. You find blood on your daughter—on her legs and on her clothes. She's upset, shaking, and can hardly stand. What happens next?"

"I ask her what happened. She says Mr. Sinclair did it. Caused the blood. Made her hurt. With his hand. I say to Susannah we'll go, and I tell John we needed to leave because Susannah feels sick. I don't tell my husband what happened, not with him in the house. So, we left. I took Susannah to Dr. Hoyland, who examined her and found harm done to her."

"Thank you, Mrs. Hicocks." Knight sat at the prosecution table.

Maurice Butt stood and adjusted the wig on his close-cropped head. "Mrs. Hicocks, did you see Mr. Sinclair touch your daughter during your time in his home?"

Mrs. Hicocks shook her head.

"Did your husband tell you that he saw Mr. Sinclair touch your daughter during your time in Mr. Sinclair's home?"

"No," she replied.

"Did you hear Susannah scream or make any noise that made you worry about her?"

"No, I only heard noises from the children playing in the other room."

"Mrs. Hicocks, would you say the noise indicated that the children were playing strenuously or roughly with each other?"

Knight stood and observed that Mrs. Hicocks was not in the room and could not testify as to how the children were playing. Butt acknowledged the point but said he would return to the matter.

"When you saw Dr. Hoyland, did you ask him whether Susannah might have started, or whether it was possible for such a thing to happen?" Butt enquired.

"No, I told Dr. Hoyland what Susannah said to me, but he said—"

"Yes," Butt interrupted. "We'll hear from Dr. Hoyland later. Now, you're so alarmed by what your daughter tells you that you leave Mr. Sinclair's home immediately after the visit to the water closet, correct?"

Mrs. Hicocks did not answer.

Butt persisted. "Mrs. Hicocks, you suggested that you left immediately after informing your husband that Susannah felt sick. Did you leave immediately? Before you answer, remember we have a written statement from Mrs. Sinclair, and I will be calling Mr. Sinclair to the stand later."

"No," she replied, casting her eyes into her lap.

"No?" Butt repeated with surprise. "What did you do after the visit to the water closet?"

Mrs. Hicocks looked at the jury and then into her lap again. "I told Susannah to go play, and I went to talk to Mrs. Sinclair and tell her that we would be leaving."

"Did you tell Susannah to stay away from Mr. Sinclair?"

"No."

"Did you confront Mrs. Sinclair with what your daughter accused her husband of doing?"

"No."

"What did you talk about with Mrs. Sinclair, as you sent your allegedly assaulted child to play in the alleged perpetrator's house?"

"About our lack of food because my husband doesn't have a job."

"Mrs. Hicocks," Butt continued. "Why did you wait two days before taking Susannah to Dr. Hoyland, and then seven more days before you went to the police?"

"We didn't know what to do. My husband was angry and wanted to go after Mr. Sinclair. I had to get him to promise not to. I had to find food for us." Mrs. Hicocks started to tear up.

"Did you give the bloody clothes to the police?"

"No."

"No?" Butt let the interrogatory linger in the air. "Why not?"

"I washed them. Susannah hasn't many other clothes. None of us do—we're poorly off. I didn't want her to see the blood again."

"During these days after the incident, did you and your husband discuss using what allegedly happened to get money and food, perhaps from the Sinclairs or from people shocked by what you said happened?" Butt's voice went hard.

Mrs. Hicocks looked at Judge Hornby, who said she must answer the question.

"No, we didn't," she replied.

"Have you and your family received food and money after the allegations against Mr. Sinclair became known?"

"Yes."

"Has your husband been employed since your allegations became known?"

"Yes, odd jobs, and more regular work at the docks."

Butt looked for a long moment at the jury. "No further questions, Your Honour."

Next to be called by the Crown was Susannah Hicocks. As she was being seated in a chair in front of the witness box, Judge Hornby and the barristers for the prosecution and defence whispered at the bench.

After the barristers returned to their tables, Knight approached Susannah and bent toward her. "Can you, Susannah, tell me what took place in Mr. Sinclair's home?"

Susannah did not hesitate, "Something happened."

"What happened? It's important for you to tell me," Knight encouraged the girl.

"Something happened to me," she said.

"Please tell me what happened to you," Knight used his kindest voice.

"Mr. Sinclair put his hand up my clothes. The front part. I was wearing drawers."

Knight did not speak when Susannah stopped. He wanted her to continue, at her own pace. He nodded that she could continue.

"I felt Mr. Sinclair's hand up my clothes. On my thigh. I felt his hand between my legs."

Neither Knight nor anyone else in the courtroom knew whether the girl would proceed. But she did. "I felt his hand somewhere else. Inside of me. It hurt me. He pulled his hand out. Blood was on it. Blood was on me."

Knight leaned down even more, "You're a brave girl, thank you."

Butt stood and cut through the tense silence with an unexpectedly gentle voice. "You are a brave girl, and I have only one question, Susannah. It has to do with what happened earlier that evening. We know that, after dinner, you and the Sinclair children went into another room to play. Your mother, who was in the kitchen, heard you playing. Can you tell me what kind of playing was happening? Was the playing gentle? Or was it rough, like romping?"

"We were romping."

"Thank you, Susannah. No more questions, Your Honour," concluded Butt.

Sensing the emotions stirred by Susannah's testimony, manifested in muffled attempts by numerous women to avoid weeping aloud, Judge Hornby adjourned the proceedings for an hour. James had glimpsed Rosamund in the courtroom before Mrs. Hicocks testified, but, as people filed out, he could not see her. He went to find her, but Donald Logie stopped him with an instruction from Judge Hornby to find cases on assault in the court's legal materials. James found the instruction irritating. The court still had next to nothing in terms of legal publications.

Mehmed found James in the clerk's room looking through the few scraps available and asked if he needed help. James said the task was impossible without a proper library. Mehmed reluctantly left. He wanted to talk about what he had just seen. It was his first exposure to an English judge, jury, and court. Even after weeks with English barristers and English law, the trial was a strange experience. He remembered a question James had asked during one of their arguments—how would a Turkish tribunal handle the case? He imagined James observing Turkish legal proceedings and feeling equally out of sorts.

But he had never answered James's question. In arguing with the barristers, he fixated on the illegitimacy of an English court adjudicating anything in Turkish territory. Watching the court forced him to think about the legitimacy of a proceeding under English law and in an English court. What he saw, stripped down, was what a *kadi* would do in a *sharia* case—investigate the facts, hear testimony, and apply the law. But he did not readily know what specific law a *kadi* would apply to this alleged act, how a *kadi* would manage facts and testimony in this case, or even whether such cases came before a *sharia* court. Nor could he describe how an Ottoman court, applying the Imperial Criminal Code enacted by the Sultan, would approach a case like *R v. Sinclair*. He insisted that Turkish courts and law resolve such disputes, no matter the nationality of the parties. However, he was insufficiently trained to understand the consequences of applying this principle to Mrs. Hicocks's daughter. He also had no answer for why Ottoman jurisdiction and law did not protect his sister or produce justice after what she had suffered.

James had no luck finding what Judge Hornby wanted, and he reported as much to the judge. Edmund believed that Butt would use case law in his closing argument to support his position that English law does not support conviction under the facts of the case. Edmund wanted to do research before instructing the jury on the case, but he did not have the materials needed. He did not want to ask Knight or Butt for help to avoid any perception of bias.

"Sir," James had an idea. "Send a telegraphic message to the Law Officers of the Crown in London with your questions. Ask them to send answers back."

"No, to Philip Francis, at my old chambers. He'll make it a priority." Edmund was excited. "My goodness, James, that never would have occurred to me. How very modern of you."

The judge, with James's input, formulated the questions to which he wanted answers from recent British cases on assault. He then instructed James, "Find Guarracino. Have him telegraph this, right away, for the attention of Philip Francis, 6 Fig Tree Court, Temple, London. Have Frederick tell the embassy staff there is no need to cipher the message."

James dashed off to find Guarracino, while Edmund began to make notes on the trial's opening session. The testimony of Mrs. Hicocks and her daughter had not diminished his fear that the case pitted a girl's unverifiable claim against a man's unverifiable denial.

When the court reconvened, Knight called Dr. Charles Hoyland, surgeon of the British Seamen's Hospital at Constantinople.

"Dr. Hoyland, when did Mrs. Hicocks bring her daughter to you for examination?"

"Late on the afternoon of January 24th."

"Why did they want their daughter examined?"

"They said their daughter had been harmed by an indecent act, and they wanted to make sure that, if she needed treatment, she would receive it."

"Did Mr. or Mrs. Hicocks tell you who they believed committed the indecent act?"

"No, and I didn't ask," replied the doctor.

"Did Mr. or Mrs. Hicocks indicate that they wanted their daughter examined for purposes of legal action against the perpetrator of the indecent act?"

"No, but I encouraged them to contact the police."

"Can you please tell the jury the results of your examination?"

"As requested by her parents, I examined the child. As you can imagine, the examination was frightening and unpleasant for an eleven-year-old girl. I determined she was slightly injured. She had some injury to the vulva, which had minor inflammation. There was no scarring. This injury looked as if it had recently occurred. I also determined the hymen was absent."

"In your opinion, Dr. Hoyland, is the inflammation and the absence of the hymen consistent with the act the accused is alleged to have committed?"

"The inflammation of the vulva and the absence of the hymen are consistent with the alleged use of a hand or fingers to force penetration."

"One last question, Dr. Hoyland. Would injury to the vulva and rupturing of the hymen through force produce the bleeding reported by Susannah and her mother?"

"The injury to the vulva was minor, so it's unlikely to have caused the bleeding described. However, rupturing of the hymen by force produces bleeding, as is well known."

"No further questions, Your Honour." Knight sat down.

Butt rose for the defence. "Dr. Hoyland, concerning the inflammation, can you confirm that it was minor, of no serious threat to the girl's health?"

"Yes, the inflammation was minor and posed no threat to her health."

"Did you see any indications that the inflammation had been anything but minor?"

"I saw no indications that the inflammation was caused by some greater injury."

"Could minor inflammation have resulted from Susannah trying to stop the bleeding?"

Hoyland paused, "Yes, that's possible."

"Could minor inflammation have been caused by Mrs. Hicocks trying to ascertain herself what her daughter was experiencing?"

Hoyland paused again, "Yes, that's possible."

"Thank you. Now, concerning the absence of the hymen, is it possible that a child can lose the hymen in ways that do not involve the acts Mr. Sinclair is accused of committing?"

"Yes."

"In your experience, does the loss of the hymen, in contexts not involving penetration, happen rarely or frequently?"

"Such a loss is not uncommon."

"Can you describe when the loss of the hymen without penetration commonly occurs?"

"Ruptures frequently happen, for example when a child is engaged in strenuous play and stretches her legs too much in playing."

"In romping perhaps, Dr. Hoyland?"

Knight stood up, but Judge Hornby put his hand up to signal him to sit. Hoyland understood that he had to answer the question.

"Yes, romping is a form of strenuous play."

"One last question, Dr. Hoyland. Is it possible for a young girl of eleven to start her courses, but then for them to become irregular until she is older?"

"Yes, that's possible. Not frequent, but possible. I have seen such cases."

"No more questions, Your Honour."

Butt did not sit down. It was time to present testimony for the defence. The circumstances of the case meant he had only one card to play. The law did not permit him to call Mrs. Sinclair to testify or the Sinclair children who remained in the house at the time of the alleged incident. Moreover, the police talked to Mrs. Sinclair and the children and recorded what they said, which produced nothing that other testimony did not cover. He called Thomas Sinclair to testify.

"Please state your name and occupation," Butt instructed.

"Thomas Sinclair, engineer."

"How long have you lived in Constantinople?"

"Seven years."

"In your years here, have you ever had problems with the British or Turkish authorities?"

"No."

"Did you know the Hicocks before January 22nd?"

"No."

"Were you angry when your wife invited the Hicocks to have a meal in your house?"

"I was annoyed, but not angry. My wife, she's got a good heart, and they did look like they needed a meal."

"Were any angry words exchanged at the meal, between you and any of the Hicocks?"

"No. I had to clip my Gordon's ear because he wasn't minding his manners, grabbing food before our guests were served."

"What did you do after the meal was over?"

"I went into the room where I smoke my pipe. It's the biggest room, so it's also where the children come after eating. I asked Mr. Hicocks if he wanted to join me, but he declined and went outside. I think he was embarrassed that another man fed his family."

"Mrs. Hicocks testified that your children and Susannah came into the room where you smoke your pipe. Is that correct?"

"Yes. Gordon left to see the tug. My other boys stayed and played with the girl."

"What, or how, were your boys and Susannah playing?"

"They're making noise, pushing and pulling each other. I told them to quiet down, but that only lasted a few minutes, and they're at it again."

"What did you do next?"

"I saw they were roughhousing, but this time it seemed my boys were being too rough with her. They're tangled on the floor, wrestling around, and I came and pulled them apart."

"Did you touch Susannah as you pulled them apart?"

"Yes, I grabbed Edward by the collar, and the girl by her arm, and pulled them apart. My Norman scampered away on his hands and knees."

"What did you do next?"

"Went back to smoking my pipe."

"What did Susannah do after you went back to your pipe?"

"The next time I looked, my boys were huddled in a corner planning mischief. I didn't see the girl."

"What did Mr. and Mrs. Hicocks say to you after this point in time?"

"I was cleaning my pipe when I heard steps toward the door. I went and saw that the Hicocks were leaving. They said they're grateful for the meal. Mrs. Hicocks said, 'God bless you.'"

Butt paused and repeated, "God bless you."

Butt continued his questions. "What did Susannah say as they were leaving?"

"Nothing, at least nothing I recall."

"When did you first learn that Susannah accused you of assaulting her?"

"When I came home from work on the 31st, when the constable was there to arrest me."

Butt looked at the jury and sat down. Knight, for the Crown, rose to his feet.

"Mr. Sinclair, are you an engineer in the employ of the Ottoman government?"

"Yes, I am an engineer working for the Ottoman government on construction projects."

"Do you have work clothes that you wear as an engineer?"

Sinclair was confused. "Do I have work clothes?"

"Yes," Knight continued. "Do you have clothes for work that you do not wear at home?"

"Yes," Sinclair replied, glancing at Butt.

"Now, January 22nd was a Saturday, not a workday, correct?"

"Yes, that's right."

"What was Susannah wearing on that day, when she was in your house?"

"A blue frock of some kind."

"What was your wife wearing?"

"A grey dress; wool, that's warmer for winter."

"What were you wearing on January 22nd?"

"What was I wearing?" Sinclair repeated the question.

"Yes, what were you wearing?"

"Clothes."

"Yes, but what clothes?"

"Shirt, waistcoat, trousers, boots."

"Mr. Sinclair, can you be more specific—colours and fabrics, etcetera? Remember, sir, we have statements from everyone who saw you that day." Knight kept his voice stern to hide the bluff he had to try.

Sinclair did not respond.

"Mr. Sinclair, shall I read from the preliminary examination taken of your wife about the events of January 22nd?" Knight pointed at papers on the prosecution table.

"She didn't say anything about my clothes," Sinclair said quickly before Butt managed to stand to protest the question.

Knight stood still, crossed his arms, ignored the now-standing Butt, and stared at Sinclair.

"You are correct, Mr. Sinclair, she did not. But you've never read the notes from her preliminary examination—yet you know what is not in them. Curious, don't you think?"

Butt growled noisily at the question from the defence table, but Knight waved his hand, "Question withdrawn."

Butt sat again, scowling at Knight.

"Now, Mr. Sinclair," Knight resumed. "You remembered what Susannah wore on that day, and what your wife was wearing. And, as I said, I have other statements, but I would like you to tell the jury what you were wearing."

Sinclair's face went blank. "My warmest white shirt, yellowed around the collar. Black waistcoat. Brown trousers. Brown boots."

"Can you confirm that you do not wear those particular items of clothing for work?"

"No, they're not work clothes, except for my boots."

"Mr. Sinclair, you are right-handed, correct?"

Sinclair nodded but cocked his head at this query.

"Did you shake hands with Mr. Hicocks when he came into your house?"

"Yes, that's polite and the custom."

"Did you shake his hand when he left your house, as would be polite and the custom?"

Sinclair opened his mouth to respond but closed it with no answer voiced.

"Mr. Sinclair, did you shake his hand when he was leaving your house? I can read from the preliminary examination taken from John Hicocks to help you remember."

"No, I don't think so. I don't think I did."

"Why not?"

At this point, Butt stood to challenge the relevance of this line of questions.

"Mr. Knight," Judge Hornby said, as Butt sat down.

"Your Honour," Knight pivoted toward the judge. "The circumstances of this case leave very few people to testify. I beg your indulgence with some questions I would like to ask the defendant. I think you'll see their relevance in due course."

Judge Hornby looked at the jury and then at Butt and nodded for Knight to proceed.

"Why didn't you shake Mr. Hicocks's hand? They were expressing gratitude, and Mrs. Hicocks even asked God to bless you. And you don't shake Mr. Hicocks's hand?"

"I don't necessarily remember every time I shake someone's hand."

"But you remember shaking his hand when he came into your house. You remember not shaking his hand as he left your house. You remember what Susannah was wearing. You remember what your wife was wearing. You remember what you were wearing. Your memory about handshakes and clothes does not seem deficient."

Butt was on his feet again, looking cross. Knight held up his hands and said, "Just one more question, Your Honour, about the lack of a handshake, and then I'll move on."

Judge Hornby acquiesced, "One more, then move on."

"Is it possible, Mr. Sinclair, that you did not shake hands with Mr. Hicocks because you had blood on your right hand?"

Murmurs rumbled across the courtroom. Judge Hornby quieted the court with warnings about interrupting the process of justice.

"Mr. Sinclair," continued Knight, "is it possible?"

"No," Sinclair's voice was on edge. "I didn't have blood on my hand."

"I promised to move on after that question. Now I want to ask about your trousers."

Butt launched to his feet again. "Your Honour, do we have to listen to my learned colleague ask if it is possible Mr. Sinclair's trousers committed the alleged offence?"

"Mr. Knight, Mr. Butt, approach the bench," ordered Judge Hornby.

The judge and the Q.C.s had a hushed conversation as the courtroom fell quiet. James located Rosamund, who was on the edge of her seat, her eyes unnervingly feral.

The Q.C.s returned to their places. Butt sat in a resigned way, and Sinclair understood that he had to answer questions about his trousers.

"Mr. Sinclair," began Knight, "Mr. Williams, the constable, investigated your home under warrant before you arrived home from work on January 31st. He searched your wardrobe for signs of blood on your clothes. He found none."

There was no question to answer. Sinclair glanced again at Butt and Judge Hornby, but he received no indication of what to do.

Knight waited a few additional seconds. "But something puzzles me, Mr. Sinclair. There was something odd about your wardrobe on January 31st."

Knight paused again. "What I can't figure out is why your brown trousers, the ones you wore on the 22nd, were not in your house on the 31st. Mr. Sinclair, what happened to your brown trousers between January 22nd and January 31st?"

Sinclair did not take his eyes off Knight. "I don't know. My wife takes care of my clothes. You'd have to ask her."

"Mr. Sinclair, your wife cannot testify at trial, so I must ask you. What happened to your brown trousers between January 22nd, when you testified you wore them, and January 31st, when they have, apparently, vanished?"

"I ... I don't know."

"You don't know?" Knight harshly asked. "Is it possible that you rid yourself of those trousers because they had blood on them, blood you wiped on them from your hand after you indecently assaulted Susannah?"

Murmurs surged again in the courtroom, which Judge Hornby had more difficulty tamping down.

Knight pounced when decorum was restored. "You don't have an extensive wardrobe. Most of your clothes are for work, but not those brown trousers. We must account for the trousers you wore on the day of the alleged assault, the day you're alleged to have a girl's blood on your hand. Where are the brown trousers, Mr. Sinclair?"

"I don't know."

"Have you worn your brown trousers since January 31st? Shall I ask Judge Hornby to send the constable to your house today to see if those trousers are back in your wardrobe?"

Sinclair did not answer.

"I have no further questions." Knight dramatically sat down at the prosecution table.

Judge Hornby set closing arguments for late morning the following day and adjourned the court. James caught up with Rosamund outside the court building. He asked what she thought so far of her first trial. She gave an unexpected answer.

"He's guilty," she stated, and James was struck by her raw anger.

"Because of the trousers?" James asked.

Rosamund's face went dark. "He's guilty. It's in his eyes. It's on his face. It's in the way he carries himself. I can see it."

James stood mute, and she became furious. "But the jury won't convict him. Not enough evidence for a prejudiced law to see a man's guilt. God, don't you understand the courage it took to do that? For her not to stay silent?"

James was not sure a girl as young as Susannah understood what she was doing in these circumstances, but he did not have the fortitude to do anything but stay silent.

Rosamund's fusillade continued. "Why did you put the poor child through this? Will a jury believe this girl? Or her mother? What were you heartless men thinking?"

James said nothing.

She walked away but twisted back to declare once more, "He's guilty."

Back in the court building, James ran into Frederick Guarracino, who said the message to Philip Francis had been sent and then added, "Telegraphic legal research—must be a first."

James smiled weakly but noticed over Frederick's shoulder that Mehmed was motioning for him, so he left Frederick and walked toward Mehmed. They went into the clerk's room. Mehmed shut the door.

James asked, "What is it?"

"Earlier today," Mehmed began, "there was a woman in Mr. Logie's office, when Mr. Logie wasn't there. She was upset, crying very hard, and was having trouble breathing."

"When?" James asked.

"After the girl, after the judge made the break, after I saw you in here."

"Do you know who it was?"

"No. I have only seen a woman cry that hard once in my life," Mehmed replied.

The girl's testimony had upset women in attendance. Many strained, James recalled, not to weep after what they heard. Rosamund, by contrast, had unleashed tearless ferocity.

"Can you tell me anything else about her?" James asked.

"I saw her only quickly. I turned away, then I tried to find you, but you were gone," Mehmed responded, before adding, "She is what Englishmen call beautiful."

Englishmen, James knew, called many women beautiful, and rarely for honourable reasons. Given everything else going on, James left the matter there.

—

James was in early the next morning to help Judge Hornby before the trial's final session. The judge showed James the telegraphic messages Philip Francis had sent. The case law was inconclusive. They re-read the messages, disappointed that the telegraph had not solved the problem. Edmund observed that Francis's research reinforced his sense that he had to send the case to the jury rather than rule, as a matter of law, that the Crown failed to meet its evidentiary burden.

The court reconvened for closing arguments. James was sure Rosamund would be there, but he was too busy with last minute things to scan the assembling audience. Judge Hornby called the court to order and instructed Sebastian Knight to close the Crown's case.

"Gentlemen, this case is disturbing. The crime is shocking. The consequences are grave. As you—members of the jury—no doubt understand, the challenge of establishing the facts of what happened, the truth of those fateful moments, is considerable. The Crown must convince you of the accused's guilt, and we believe the facts support his conviction for this crime.

"I have years of experience in criminal cases. I've seen it all. Until this case. As you know, English law disfavours the participation of children in criminal cases, unless justice requires it. The Crown and counsel for the defence agreed that the testimony of Susannah Hicocks was essential in the search for truth. Under law, you must consider Susannah's testimony as seriously as you would testimony from an adult.

"What is remarkable is the purity of the consistency in what Susannah said happened on January 22nd. It has all been the same. What she told her mother after the incident; what she told the police during the investigation; and what she told this court yesterday. Asked repeatedly what befell her, she has, in circumstances that would shake the nerve of grown men and women, provided the same account, time and again.

"But don't take my word for it. Please note that defence counsel has identified no discrepancies in Susannah's account. His theory, supported only by insinuations, is that the Hicocks engaged in a conspiracy to gain advantages given their unfortunate circumstances. Yet counsel for the defence has no evidence, none, to support this speculation.

"As the Crown has demonstrated, the truth is far simpler. Something happened to Susannah. She told her mother; she told the police; and she told you what happened to her. The accused is guilty of committing indecent assault against an innocent eleven-year-old girl."

Maurice Butt was on his feet as soon as Knight finished. "Members of the jury, the Crown must satisfy its burden that the person accused committed the crime in question. Mr. Sinclair is an Englishman, and he has full rights to the protection of English law. Under English law, the Crown must establish guilt with facts. In this case, the Crown has failed to do so.

"The Crown has provided no facts to support the accusation against Mr. Sinclair. We have no witnesses. We have no evidence that Susannah was bleeding on January 22nd. We have no evidence that Mr. and Mrs. Hicocks behaved in a manner on January 22nd consistent with their daughter being indecently assaulted. We have no evidence that Mr. Sinclair has, in the past, demonstrated any behaviour suggesting he would commit such an act against a young girl. We have no evidence of what motive Mr. Sinclair would have for committing the alleged act against a child in his house, in a room with two of his own children present. Without any evidence, the Crown has concocted speculation about handshakes and trousers.

"Cases decided by English courts involving similar facts demonstrate the inadequacy of the Crown's case. Recently, Baron Alderson forced the Crown to withdraw a case in Newcastle-upon-Tyne because the claim was made too many days after the alleged assault. The delay compromised the ability to discover the truth. Here, Mr. and Mrs. Hicocks do not approach the police until nine days have lapsed—a delay that makes uncovering the truth impossible.

"I can see in your faces, members of the jury, puzzlement about what, then, happened on January 22nd. Remember, we have no evidence that the acts Mr. Sinclair is accused of committing caused the alleged bleeding. I established with Dr. Hoyland that other plausible explanations exist—she unexpectedly started her courses or, more likely, her romping with Mr. Sinclair's boys broke the hymen, resulting in the bleeding. Poor Susannah doesn't understand what is happening. She is scared, embarrassed, and in distress. Her mother asks suggestive, leading questions that allow the frightened child to blame Mr. Sinclair—an accusation that proves beneficial for the family's fortunes at a dark time in their lives, if the family keeps the story straight."

"So yes, the decision you need to make is simple. You cannot find Mr. Sinclair guilty based on no evidence. Such an act would run counter to English law and justice."

With closing arguments finished, Judge Hornby asked for quiet as whispers began. The judge gave the jury its instructions, and he reviewed the burden of proof that the Crown had to satisfy for the jury to hand down a guilty verdict. Hornby also told the jury that decisions of English courts on the effect of delays on the Crown's burden of proof drew no clear lines for this case, meaning that he had to send it to the jury for its decision.

The dismissal of the jury was followed by a noisy scene, with people talking loudly as they left the courtroom. The commotion prevented James from finding Rosamund. He made his way to the court's offices, where he heard Judge Hornby yelling for him. Edmund wanted James to organise his notes for preparing a report. Whatever the verdict, Edmund anticipated the trial would produce demands from the Foreign Office for an explanation. He instructed James to work on this task until the jury returned. James collected his papers and sat at the clerk's table. As he bent over his notes, he feared that, despite everything, the truth evaded everyone. Without the truth, how could there be justice, despite all the law and legal proceedings?

James was surprised when less than an hour passed before Donald popped his head in to tell James that the jury was ready to deliver its verdict. The quick decision suggested that the jury agreed with the defence that the Crown had not satisfied its evidentiary burden. James reached the courtroom as fast as he could, a journey made arduous by people returning to witness the verdict. Judge Hornby had difficulty bringing the courtroom to order, and he instructed Williams and Guarracino to close the doors. Once the courtroom settled down, the jury re-entered.

"Foreman of the jury, have you reached a verdict?" Judge Hornby asked.

"Yes, Your Honour," replied the foreman.

"What is your verdict?"

"Your Honour, we find the accused guilty."

Chapter 8
The Lord's Work

Normally obliging, Bones became cantankerous on the Saturday afternoon ride to Rosamund's. James had chosen a new route, but it was not difficult and would not explain his horse's behaviour. Bones stopped between two curves on the path, tossed his head, and sniffed the air in an exaggerated manner. James dismounted to inspect his horse, but he found nothing amiss. He rubbed the horse's forelock, but Bones turned away, rejecting something he typically welcomed.

"What's wrong, boy?" James asked.

Then he smelled it. Jasmine, flowering nearby.

February had barely become March. February had enjoyed unseasonably warm patches, but, still, it was too early. James searched along the path and found the white flowers. He picked the freshest ones and inhaled. Her scent. He walked back to Bones, remembering how the horse had often nuzzled her neck and hair. Bones gave the flowers a sniff before trying to eat them. James put the flowers under his own nose again. Not quite her. She had worn jasmine perfume, but what he remembered was more than what these flowers gifted to the air. It was how jasmine smelled on her. He should have placed some petals on her coffin, but she died in December, when there was no jasmine. He let the flowers fall to the ground.

James gathered himself and steadied his horse to remount. Bones shifted again in agitation. James cursed but then saw two men coming around the curve ahead. The older one was in religious garb. The younger one's neck was ringed with an iron collar, from which ran a chain held by the older man. The man in the collar was muttering and gesticulating with tremulous hands. The man holding the chain took offence at the reaction on James's face.

"What, never seen a lunatic?" he barked in accented English.

James had, in fact, never seen a lunatic, but it was the collar and chain that disturbed him.

"Why?" James asked.

The question brought the older man to a stop, who hissed in Greek to halt his companion. He wiped his forehead with a sleeve of his cassock and then pointed west toward the Sea of Marmora. "On the mountain in the sea, at the monastery, I will chain this wretch to the wall so that he can look upon the face that cures madness."

"The face that cures madness?" James's surprise sounded like sarcasm, which produced a scowl from the man holding the chain.

"The icon, the holy face circled by silver, the sacred visage possessed with healing powers." The man pointed at the collared unfortunate.

"The face of Jesus?" James, not unreasonably, ventured.

The man yanked the chain and began to walk. "No, unbeliever, the face of St. George. There are different kinds of dragons."

James watched them disappear around the next bend in the path. Distracted by what he had just experienced, he had trouble mounting a still uncooperative Bones. Only with difficulty did he refrain from applying his riding crop aggressively.

He was anxious, and possibly late, for tea with Rosamund—the first time he would see her after *R v. Sinclair*. He had not visited Rosamund on the Saturday following the trial. On that afternoon, he had shivered in a drizzle with Judge Hornby, Consul-General Cumberbatch, and embassy staff outside Sancta Sophia in the old part of Constantinople. There was a ceremony that involved cannons firing across the Bosphorus and the Sultan arriving to do something in St. Sophia the purpose and significance of which no one had explained.

As her fury during the trial demonstrated, the case had affected Rosamund, but he was unsure how to talk to her about it, even nearly a fortnight later. The verdict had divided the British community, as had Judge Hornby's sentence of six months with hard labour. James could not forget Mrs. Sinclair's grief when the jury rendered its decision.

As the judge predicted, news and criticism about the case reached London. The Foreign Office requested a report, which did not bother Hornby. Something else agitated him.

"The punishment," the judge had confided to James, "should have been more severe."

Once within the Colborne residence, the butler walked James to a different room where, to his surprise, Rosamund sat on an ornate chair with her father and mother standing well apart from her and each other. Rosamund welcomed James as if nothing was unusual, and he greeted Mr. and Mrs. Colborne.

"You must be pleased that awful case is over," Mrs. Colborne said as she poured tea.

"Thank you," James received the cup and saucer. "But it might be appealed."

"Lawyers," grumbled Mr. Colborne. "A necessary evil. Too often an unnecessary one. Always expensive."

James smiled awkwardly and glanced at Rosamund, who sipped tea without expression. James knew Hugh Colborne was a leading merchant in Constantinople and that merchants had little affection for lawyers. And from the tension he sensed in the room, it was not clear that much affection existed among the members of the Colborne family, either.

"But," Mr. Colborne's voice brightened, "we'll soon have Sir Henry Bulwer as ambassador. He'll tame Hornby's enthusiasm for rules and fees. Hornby's run circles around that fossil Stratford."

Mr. Colborne set his cup down, stared at James, and finally said, "Bingham, with me."

James looked at Rosamund as he placed his cup and saucer on the tea tray. She met his eyes but said nothing. He turned to follow Mr. Colborne into his study.

"Bingham, what are your intentions?" Hugh poured himself whiskey.

"Sir?" James did not anticipate being interrogated about his intentions.

"Here, in your profession?" Hugh's reply did not clarify what the merchant intended.

"Well, I hope my time here makes me a better lawyer and a better man." James immediately disliked the treacly response.

"And you want to return to London and resume your practice there?" queried Hugh.

James hesitated. He had not thought about returning to London. Hugh raised an eyebrow at the hesitation, which caused James to affirm that, at some point, he would return to London.

"My daughter talks to my wife about you." Hugh's pronunciation of "my daughter" demonstrated his displeasure with her. "And you aren't here for the conversation."

"I didn't know your daughter talks about me." James's unguarded honesty produced an odd look from Hugh.

"I have contacts in London with members of the Bar." Hugh swigged some whiskey. "I have influence with barristers given the fees my businesses generate. I keep my lawyers on their toes, so they don't take me for granted."

James's confusion deepened, but Hugh continued. "Of late, I've become concerned that some barristers have been less attentive than they should be."

Hugh paused to ensure he had James's full attention. "At the moment, I'm not pleased with one in particular—Cranford Pennington."

Although James did not react, Hugh saw in the young man's eyes that he had hit his target.

"Stratford isn't the only one with ferrets," Hugh remarked, referring to the ambassador's many spies and informants.

James then realised what Hugh Colborne intended. Take Rosamund off his hands in exchange for help in returning to the Bar in England and achieving revenge on Pennington. Hugh could tell that James understood the bargain.

"Think on it, but I'm not a patient man," Hugh began to walk away. "And don't betray my confidence—to anyone."

James remained in the study, trying to fathom this development. The eagerness of parents to marry off daughters was not unknown to him. Emma's parents had been desperate for someone to wed her. For Colborne, the transaction would rid him of a troublesome daughter and put in his pocket an indebted barrister son-in-law conversant with the law in London and the Levant.

For James, however, what mattered most was the one thing independent from such calculations—Rosamund talked about him with her mother. James put his hands in his pockets and smiled.

Mrs. Colborne appeared to say that Rosamund would like to talk. She departed, leaving James to find his way back to Rosamund.

"You're looking rather pleased with yourself," Rosamund commented. "What did you talk about with my father?"

James dissembled, "He asked if I knew a certain barrister in London. It seems important to his business."

Rosamund looked as if she did not believe him, but said with resignation, "With him, it's always about him."

James changed the subject. "Well, interesting times of late."

"Yes," Rosamund arched her eyebrows. "Justice was done, astonishingly, and, also to my surprise, there was an attempt at reconciliation."

James looked confused, so she continued. "I told you he was guilty. I didn't believe a jury of men would convict based on a girl's testimony, but perhaps law and justice are not perpetual strangers. I berated you during the trial, but I never asked what you thought about the case as it unfolded. Did you think he was guilty, before the verdict?"

"I didn't think the jury would convict because the Crown didn't produce sufficient evidence for a guilty verdict," James replied.

Rosamund frowned. "That's a lawyer's answer. I'm asking you, as a man, what you thought about the accused, about what that girl said. In your heart, in your sense of right and wrong, did you think he was guilty? Putting faith in legal rules alone is not enough, Mr. Bingham. That's not how to turn water into wine."

"You said something about reconciliation," James changed the subject again. "Between the Hicocks and the Sinclairs?"

"No, that's not going to happen. I hear Mohammedan cases involve measures that seek reconciliation between disputing parties," Rosamund said.

"I'll ask Mehmed," James responded.

"Who?"

"A Turkish lawyer working with the consular court."

Rosamund was incredulous. "You have a Turk, a Mohammedan, working for the court?"

"Yes, but you said something about reconciliation," James tried again.

"No doubt you've heard that I rejected Henry Wattling," she began, her quizzical look about the Turkish lawyer only slowly dissipating. "Allegedly, my rejection caused the dissolute life he subsequently led."

James nodded. He had heard the stories but had never laid eyes on Wattling.

"This Thursday past, Henry appeared here. He apologised for his behaviour and any hurt he caused me. He told me that he has found Christ, that Jesus has forgiven him, and that, born again, he's a changed man. He's back in Constantinople to do the Lord's work, and he hopes that I can forgive him," Rosamund said matter of factly.

"What did he mean?" James probed, masking how disagreeable he found Wattling's return.

"I don't know. Religiosity makes me nervous."

"Do you forgive him?" The impertinent question provoked a harsh look from Rosamund.

She then changed course, noting that the *Sinclair* case made her more interested in what the court did. She asked about other cases. He told her that, after *R v. Sinclair*, he and Mehmed needed to get back to developing a code of criminal procedure that blended general principles of English law with rules and procedures reflecting the Turkish context. She seemed sceptical and asked how far they had progressed. He explained that every time he and Mehmed thought they would advance the project, something interrupted their plans. She pursed her lips and said that the project sounded about as easy as turning Bones into a unicorn.

Rosamund glanced at the clock and insisted that James return next Saturday afternoon. She accompanied him out the front door, waited until his horse was brought around and, with hands on hips, shook her head at the sight of Bones.

After returning to Judge Hornby's residence, a servant appeared at his room and told him to join the judge in the study. When he arrived, Edmund was in animated conversation with Henry Wroth and Donald Logie. Henry signalled for James to come over.

"James," began Edmund, "can you find Mehmed, right now?"

James had to admit that he did not know where Mehmed lived. The judge instructed Donald to find Frederick Guarracino and tell him to locate Hasan, the *mufti* who had facilitated Mehmed's clerkship with the court. He tasked Henry to go to the embassy and brief the ambassador's staff. He ordered James to find Mehmed.

"Why do you want Mehmed? What do I tell him if I find him?" asked James.

"Tell him," Edmund's frustration barely under control, "that we need his help. We've learned that some missionaries are planning a demonstration tomorrow at St. Sophia to condemn Mahomet as a false prophet. If we don't intervene, Mahomedans might attack them and, perhaps, the British community as well. Take Halil, my *cavass*. He's somewhere about the residence. It might already be dangerous out there."

James found Halil in the stables grooming his horse and told him the mission. Halil asked where Mehmed lived, and James said that he did not know. Halil laughed and had the stable hands saddle his mount and Bones. When the horses were ready, Halil described Mehmed to the stable hands. They exchanged a few words and then replied that Mehmed occasionally visited the residence. One said that, when Mehmed arrived, his horse was not sweaty or thirsty. Even James understood what that meant. Mehmed lived on the European side of the Bosphorus and not far from the Hornby residence. Halil asked the stable hands from what direction Mehmed came and went, and they pointed the same way. Halil led, seeming to have some notion of where to search.

After unhelpful interactions with young Turkish men, Halil spoke with the proprietor of a coffee house and received helpful information. They rode down narrow streets into an adjoining neighbourhood, stopping in front of a large, well-kept property. Halil dismounted and entered; James secured their horses in front. After a few minutes, Halil emerged to tell James to come in. They climbed some back stairs to a landing with a wooden rail that looked down on a room where about fifteen people sat, some in chairs and some on floor cushions. Mehmed was near the front, writing. James had never been with Mehmed in any setting other than the consular court, and he had never seen Mehmed dressed in anything but European clothes.

With difficulty, James took his eyes off Mehmed to look at Halil. The *cavass* explained that a *kadi*—a *sharia* judge—was deciding a case. Halil listened, and after a few minutes, he started translating. The case involved an alleged assault, with one man accusing another of ripping his beard, hitting his face, and beating his head with a cane. The *kadi*, whose turban and beard were pure white, was summarising the case. According to the *kadi*, the evidence presented by the victim did not satisfy the requirements for finding the accused guilty.

"Which ones are the lawyers?" James whispered.

"The what?" Halil asked while trying to follow the proceedings.

"The lawyers, like barristers at the court. Who is Mehmed representing?"

Halil gave James an irritated glance. "There are no lawyers in *sharia* cases. The two sides argue the case before the *kadi*, who makes a judgement."

"No lawyers?" James did not understand. "But isn't Mehmed a lawyer?"

Halil disengaged from the *kadi*'s summation. "We have other courts, other laws, beside *sharia*. Those courts, Ottoman courts, need lawyers. But in *sharia* courts, no lawyers."

James looked at Mehmed, who was rapidly writing down what the *kadi* was saying. "No lawyers? How do the parties argue legal cases if they are not legally trained or advised?"

"There are those who, for payment, help prepare cases, but these people don't have a great reputation," Halil replied.

"What do you mean?" James pressed.

"Are barristers liked by their clients?" Halil asked.

"No," James recalled Colborne's excoriation of lawyers earlier in the day.

"Same with us," Halil smiled. "Neither the civilised nor the uncivilised like your tribe."

"Now hush." Halil resumed translating, "The judge, he says that, because the accused refused to swear an oath on his innocence ... and because people in the community testified that the accused was a troublemaker ... the judge has decided to fine the accused."

Punishment without legal guilt? James did not understand and wanted to ask more questions, but the proceedings began to break up. Halil told James to stay upstairs, and he went down, reappearing minutes later with an agitated Mehmed.

"What are you doing here? You aren't supposed to be here. You're not welcome," Mehmed whispered harshly.

James ignored the anger, told Mehmed why he had come, and asked Mehmed to return with them to Judge Hornby's residence. Mehmed looked terrified.

"I can't help you," Mehmed fought his emotions. "I must warn the mosque. I must defend the mosque."

"No, Mehmed," pleaded James. "We need you to help us stop it. If we prevent it, the mosque needs no warning and won't require defending. Telling people now might cause violence. We don't even know whether what we heard is true. Think of the European retribution if Mohammedans attack Christians based on rumours."

Mehmed lashed out, "Why can't you leave us alone? Why don't you Christians, you Europeans, leave us in peace?"

James begged, "We don't agree with these people. We want to stop them. Help us."

"How much must I betray my religion and country for this court?" Mehmed was in crisis.

"Please, give Judge Hornby one hour, just one hour." James was desperate.

Mehmed went quiet, looked away, and then nodded.

"Is your horse outside?" asked Halil.

"Yes," answered Mehmed. "Bay horse, black saddle, in the back." Halil and James descended the stairs to collect the horses.

When the three entered the Hornby residence after a furious ride, they found the judge with two men around the dining room table. The older man, in an ill-fitting black suit, was standing, while the younger man and the judge were seated across from each other. Tea had been brought, but no one had touched it.

"Why are they here?" asked the older man, derision dripping off the pronoun.

"They work for me," Judge Hornby replied.

"We will speak the truth in God's kingdom, including in front of a mosque," the older man said. "You have no authority to stop us. We would commit no crime under English law."

"You know damn well St. Sophia isn't Speakers' Corner," Edmund chastised.

"Nor do Turks have jurisdiction," the man pointed at Mehmed and Halil. "The Turks have agreed not to apply the Koran to Christians, so our words before a mosque cannot be blasphemy. If the Turks arrest us, then you, Hornby, must decide the case with the Turkish judge. And you wouldn't dare convict Christians under infidel notions of heresy. Go, ahead, ask your Turkish lackeys over there if I'm right."

Mehmed stepped forward at the insult, held back when Halil forcefully grabbed his arm.

"The response to your acts will not happen in a court," Mehmed declared.

"Threatening us with violence, boy? With death at the hands of a rabid crowd? Like the Jewish rabble that killed Christ? We won't tremble at homicidal violence by a Mussulmen mob when we speak the Word of God in a land where Christ's disciples led people to salvation. The Bible proclaims that every knee shall bend at the name of Jesus, and every tongue shall confess that Jesus is Lord," the man bellowed.

This oration prompted an "Amen" from the younger missionary who, for emphasis, adjusted the cuffs of the white shirt extending just so from the sleeves of his tailored, charcoal suit.

The older missionary turned on Hornby. "You and your ilk have drained God from law, the divine from justice. You denigrate us as dangerous radicals, yet you silence us because Turks will attack us for voicing our beliefs. My God, man, one of your own—that Mussulman fanatic right there—threatens violence against Christians, and you condemn us."

Edmund put his elbow on the table and rubbed his temple and forehead with his fingers and thumb. In such tinderbox moments between religions, he knew neither side would accept responsibility, preferring always to blame the other. When gods justify ends and means, primitive things in men are unleashed.

In his experience, however, when trouble loomed with Christian missionaries in Ottoman domains, a compromise could usually be struck by giving them some of what they wanted to avoid greater problems. Turks hated the inroads that missionaries made through such bargains. Edmund found negotiating with missionaries distasteful but increasingly unavoidable.

"What do you want?" Edmund finally asked.

"We will do what God says must be done. We won't negotiate," the older man replied.

Edmund rubbed his forehead and temple again.

"Gentlemen," the older missionary said. "We have nothing more to say, and, it appears, neither do you. Henry, let's go."

As the missionaries began to leave, Thomas Williams, the police constable for the court, and his deputy emerged from an adjoining room. Edmund nodded, and Williams astonished the evangelicals by clapping them in irons, taking them into custody, and marching them off for the trip to the consular gaol. Edmund did not immediately follow. His temper was running too hot.

"Missionaries," Edmund paced the dining room, making the hardwood absorb his anger. "They utterly lack judgment and sympathy for the beliefs of others. What these gentlemen threaten is beyond the irresponsibility these people normally show. I can't permit their recklessness to end with innocent heads being staved in."

Once Edmund had cooled down, he asked Mehmed to find Hasan and tell the *mufti* that the agitators were in custody and to stay available in case help was needed with the leaders, the *imams,* of the great mosque. He ordered James to accompany him to the gaol, under the escort of Halil. Waiting outside the gaol was Frederick Guarracino, who had long, rolled papers in his hand. Inside, the missionaries were praying in their cell, but they stopped when the older one glimpsed Edmund coming in.

"This won't stop our denunciation. Tonight, others will place posters around St. Sophia announcing what will happen tomorrow," he declared.

"You mean these?" asked Edmund.

Frederick unrolled the papers to reveal posters announcing to the "Mussulmen of Constantinople" that tomorrow, on the steps of the mosque, English missionaries would denounce Mahomet as a false prophet.

The sight of the posters made the older man angry. "You've detained us illegally and violated our rights."

"Silas Benson," replied Edmund, "I'm sure I'll hear from you again, probably when your superiors at Exeter Hall lodge protests with the Foreign Office. However, I'll let you go if you can show me, in your Bible, the laws you claim protect you from my authority."

Benson did not reach for his Bible.

"No?" Edmund continued. "You announce that you and your fellow missionaries will cynically exploit English and Turkish law to escape the consequences of your dangerous behaviour. You condemn lawyers for taking God out of law. But when you believe you're treated unfairly, you want the laws that you manipulate and condemn to protect you. When you're in trouble, your religion needs my law. Why should I take you seriously on matters of either religion or justice?"

When he received no answer, he spoke to the younger missionary. "What about you, Henry? You've spent time in this gaol before, for drunkenness and fighting. At least then you were only a danger to yourself and a disappointment to your parents. Now you believe that Jesus wants you to incite religious violence. That's quite a conversion."

Edmund and James returned to the judge's residence and said goodnight to Halil, but James was uneasy. Edmund noticed and asked what was wrong. James explained that he did not know what law the missionaries had violated, or what law authorised their detention and the search of their property. With weariness, Edmund asked whether James thought his actions unjust.

"I'm confused. Earlier today, I saw a *kadi* fine a man who was not guilty of an alleged crime," James began.

"You saw what?" Edmund asked with surprise.

"We found Mehmed at a *sharia* trial," James explained. "And then you ordered a detention and search for actions that didn't, at least this evening, qualify as crimes under English law. Does the Foreign Jurisdiction Act provide the authority to do this?"

Edmund collected himself. "I exercised my authority as I thought right under the circumstances. Oft times, religious texts and legal codes provide no guidance when action is imperative. Sometimes we must find justice somewhere between our laws and our gods."

Chapter 9

St. George and the Druidess

James was not sure why she did it. He did not mind. She saved him from finding the nerve to ask. Not long after Sultan Abdul Mejid sent the invitations, James crossed paths with Mrs. Colborne, who embraced him, kissed his cheek, and whispered, "Thank you, James, thank you."

He thought she was expressing gratitude for his Saturday visits with Rosamund. James soon realised that something else was afoot. The day after his encounter with Mrs. Colborne, Judge Hornby came into the clerk's room to return some documents and said, "My wife saw Rosamund at the dressmakers. Well done, Bingham, well done."

Mehmed overheard the comment and, after the judge left, he asked why James was buying a dress for a woman. James replied testily that he was not buying any woman a dress. Mehmed grinned at James's awkwardness. "Who is this woman buying dresses? Is she what Englishmen call beautiful?"

James remembered that the Turk had used that phrase before, but Mehmed continued teasing, "Maybe you are not what Englishwomen call handsome."

It took, however, Henry Wroth and Donald Logie to clarify his chivalry. James went to discuss a thorny issue with Henry and found Donald already talking with him.

"Well, if it's not St. George himself," Henry said as James appeared in the office doorway, making Donald grin.

James looked at Henry and Donald, not comprehending why he was being likened to the patron saint of England.

"You're rescuing a damsel in distress," Henry offered.

Donald cocked his head. "Wait, didn't the damsel diddle the dragon for St. George?"

"There has to be a damsel to rescue if you're going to kill a dragon," Henry said.

"No, St. George killed the dragon to convert people to Christianity," Donald asserted.

"No, he rescued a princess whom a dragon was going to eat. Everybody knows that you must kill the dragon to rescue the damsel," Henry chastised. "James, help me out."

James did not want to be drawn in, but the debate was preferable to being teased. "St. George was, if I recall, a Roman soldier from Cappadocia martyred in Palestine for refusing to renounce Christianity. And his icon cures madness."

The banter stopped as Henry and Donald shared confused looks.

Not eager to return to work, Henry spoke first. "Did you hear that, Donald? James thinks St. George was Turkish."

"It's coming back to me now," Donald ignored Henry. "The dragon and George fight, and George asks the damsel to take off something, her corset maybe, to make a leash for the dragon. The princess then leads the dragon around with it. Now that's a damsel."

"They didn't have corsets back then. Chastity belts maybe, and, besides, he's a saint, so he's not asking a damsel to take off her clothes," Henry countered.

"It was a girdle," James interjected.

"A what?" Henry looked perplexed.

"A long leather or metal belt women wore in the Middle Ages," James explained.

Donald shook his head. "George only kills the dragon after the damsel has the beast under control. The girdle is as important as the spear. And George slays the dragon because, well, Jesus was always killing dragons."

"That's quite a legend," Henry laughed. "But, no, as patron saint of England, he kills the dragon, marries the damsel, and feasts on figgy pudding. That's in the Anglican Bible."

James smiled at the silliness and, forgetting why he was in the doorway of Henry's office, began to leave.

Henry would not let him go. "We're not done with you. Tell us about your damsel rescuing."

"What are you talking about?" James leaned against the door frame.

"You know, Henry," said Donald, "I've never thought of Rosamund Colborne as a damsel in distress. She's more like a dragon, what with those green eyes and wicked tongue of hers."

"Donald, that's not nice. I imagine James rather enjoys that wicked tongue and has no idea what colour her eyes are," Henry winked at Donald. "But escorting Miss Colborne to the Sultan's ball in honour of Lord Stratford achieves some rehabilitation after the trouble she's caused at home and in society. That's why James is St. George to Rosamund's damsel in distress."

"At least we know around whom Rosamund has her leash," Donald added.

"Bingham!" Judge Hornby's bellow rescued James from his colleagues.

James walked to Hornby's office, now doubting that, as he had believed, Rosamund's eyes were blue. As he entered, the judge motioned for him to close the door.

Edmund sat at his desk, rubbed his face, and began, "Thank you for the report on the *Sinclair* case. The Foreign Office seems to accept how we handled things, and Sinclair has not appealed."

James nodded to recognise the judge's gratitude.

"However," Edmund continued, "challenges continue to arise. As you know, Lord Stratford is leaving. He tells me British merchants in the Levant believe Sir Henry Bulwer will be a stronger ally as ambassador. They expect Bulwer to oppose our reforms. We've nearly completed our new rules for consular officials to follow. Already British merchants are expressing opposition to what will soon be required throughout the consular system in Ottoman domains."

"Why don't they want clear rules and procedures uniformly applied?" James asked.

"The Ottoman government is desperate to improve its finances and repay the money that it borrowed during the war. To bring in substantial sums, the Sublime Porte is selling rights to build railways, canals, mines, etcetera to the highest-bidding European enterprises. Merchants are pouring in to exploit this concession mania. Stratford has acted coldly toward them. I have no doubt that complaints from British merchants about Stratford's indifference contributed to the Government's decision to recall him.

"And I've been accused of taking British commerce in the Levant from 'no law to all law'—to quote Rosamund's father," Edmund observed. "The merchants want Bulwer to bring back 'no law.' But there's something else—an attack on Mehmed."

James furrowed his brow. Edmund explained that Silas Benson had accused the court of employing a "Mussulman fanatic" who threatens violence against Christians. It was no coincidence, the judge noted, that stories in *The Levant Herald* and, courtesy of Exeter Hall, in London newspapers used the same "Mussulman fanatic" appellation.

Edmund feared that missionaries, supported by merchants, wanted to undermine the court by slandering Mehmed. Questions from the Foreign Office and the Sublime Porte suggested that Mehmed's involvement with the court was becoming politically fraught. For his part, Mehmed was upset that he had been publicly called a violent, religious madman from the Pera district to Hyde Park.

"As if that isn't enough," the judge continued, "we must intervene with the Ottoman authorities about another criminal case involving someone who enjoys British protection under treaty law. I want your help on this case. With Donald going to Smyrna to implement our reforms at that consulate, I need you to play a larger role here."

James was surprised to be thought worthy of taking on more responsibility.

"Thank you, sir," James responded. "But what about the code of criminal procedure? With Mehmed's situation, and with me having an expanded role, what about the code?"

The code remained important, the judge said, because it was the only approach that would, in time, extricate the British and Ottoman governments from their feud over the treaty capitulations. He thought it best to have Mehmed focus on the code, which would keep his profile lower until the Mussulman fanatic problem blew over.

James felt rather chuffed as he rode to the Colborne residence the Saturday after learning he was attending the Sultan's ball with Rosamund and getting more responsibility at the court. But his sunny disposition could not keep one question at bay: Should he still ask her to the ball?

As Bones sauntered along, James pieced together something that he had not considered before. He had not discussed his visits with Rosamund, or what they talked about or did, with anyone. Yet British society in Constantinople seemed all too aware of the visits. The gossiping included details that could only have come from within the Colborne residence, such as when he and Rosamund strolled around the walled garden or in the open, meadowy area beyond the garden's gate. Further, their attendance at the Sultan's ball was known to various and sundry people before they had even talked about it. What did it mean? On this delightful afternoon, he decided that he did not care.

Tea was barely in his cup when Rosamund began peppering him with questions about the Mussulman fanatic. She had read the stories in *The Levant Herald* and heard the chatter in society. James had to admit that he did not know where the Turk had learned English, the number of times a day he prayed, whether he had memorised the Koran, or how many wives he had.

She stiffened her back. "How can you know so little about him?"

James shrugged.

Then she leaned forward. "Is he uncivilised, as we claim the Turks are?"

James did not answer, and Rosamund shook her head at his silence.

She then fixed her gaze on him, the intensity of her green eyes doubling his discomfort. "Sometimes I understand the Turks—deemed inferior, subjected to the power of others, and forced to suffer the consequences. And always expected to capitulate."

He wanted to escape her disapproval, so he made the only connection between Rosamund and Mehmed that he could conjure. "Mehmed once asked me whether Englishmen think you are beautiful."

"He asked what?" Rosamund's question was laden with displeasure.

James should have retreated but did not. "Mehmed talks about women whom Englishmen find beautiful."

"He talks about what?" her voice went cold.

James again failed to fall on his sword. "Once, he saw a woman at the court who was very upset, crying, struggling to breathe—and all he could say about her was that Englishmen would call her beautiful."

"He sees—" Rosamund stopped to collect herself. "He sees a woman weeping—after what the court just heard—and all he talks about is whether she is beautiful? God, you are all the same."

After what the court just heard? James wondered, for the first time, whether Mehmed had seen Rosamund that day during the *Sinclair* trial. Should he ask?

Rosamund gave him no time to decide. "What Englishmen?"

James knew the answer he should give, but he did not respond.

She looked away. "Mr. Bingham, sometimes I wonder whether you actually asked a woman to marry you."

The comment cut, just as when, at the embassy dinner, she had asked whether Emma actually loved him. Still, he said nothing.

Rosamund sighed. "Mr. Bingham, we're going to the Sultan's ball. Perhaps, just perhaps, you have wondered how this could be when we haven't spoken of it. I assumed you asked me in your way, and I accepted in my way. But I have to say, our ways don't converge easily."

James apologised for frustrating her and not asking her to the ball. But he did not tell her that she was, indeed, beautiful.

His ride home was uncomfortable. He wanted to be mad at her. But did she deserve it? It was not her fault that he stumbled into a searing memory of hers. Was she wrong to be exasperated with his failure to ask her to the ball or to show any initiative in the relationship?

It had been the same with Emma. That he finally asked for her hand was something of a miracle, coming at the last moment before Emma abandoned all hope in him. Her answer did not dispel his fear that Emma believed she had no choice, other than spinsterhood, by the time the question came. That haunted him as much or more than her death.

—

That same spring afternoon, Mehmed met Hasan at the *mufti*'s favourite coffee house. Mehmed had asked to talk because newspapers in Constantinople and London had described him as a fanatic who threatened Christians with violence. This warped perspective about the incident with the missionaries put him in a difficult position with the British and the Sublime Porte. Mehmed was also worried that the incident might hurt Hasan, who had recommended him to Fuad Pasha even though many Ottoman officials thought he was an arrogant troublemaker.

Hasan had his own concerns. He was educating a new generation of lawyers to navigate *sharia*, Ottoman legislation, and European demands for legal reform. The need for such lawyers was growing as disputes between the Ottoman government and Europeans increased because of the wave of concession contracts being awarded. The establishment of state tribunals separate from religious courts as part of legal reforms also fed demand for a new type of lawyer. But the proliferation of courts and secular law threatened to overwhelm the capabilities of the new law school, the processes of legal reform, and the development of modern forms of Ottoman justice.

In all this, the Mussulman fanatic controversy was a serious problem. It fed European prejudices and encouraged *imams* to criticise reforms for allowing foreign powers to threaten *sharia*. Initiatives, such as the joint development of a code of criminal procedure, were vulnerable, as were the people involved. With the Sublime Porte unhappy, Hasan could not predict how events would unfold for Mehmed or his own efforts to train Ottoman lawyers for a more complicated, dangerous world.

The coffee house was popular among Turks keen to argue about politics. Mehmed and the *mufti* knew their meeting would be observed. The Porte's spies had started watching Mehmed as soon as he went to the English court, with surveillance increasing after the missionary incident. They took a table where they could be seen but not, without difficulty, overheard.

Mehmed began in anger about the situation, but the *mufti* interrupted and asked Mehmed to put the controversy aside and talk about the English court. "Remember, I said you could learn from Hornby. What have you learned?"

The *mufti* could tell from Mehmed's reaction that the young man had not reflected on what he had learned. Mehmed replied that nothing had changed his view that the English exercise of jurisdiction in Ottoman lands was illegitimate.

"But," Hasan persisted, "you've watched the English now. How have they exercised their jurisdiction?"

When Mehmed did not reply, Hasan pushed. "Was Hornby's treatment of the missionaries lawful? Was it just?"

"The missionaries said Hornby had no right to detain them. Whether English law authorised what he did seems unclear. But there was no violence," Mehmed answered.

"What about the trial involving the girl? Was the conviction lawful? Was it just?"

"How do I know?" Mehmed replied. "I'm not an English lawyer."

"Don't give me a child's answer," the *mufti* chastised. "Tell me what you think."

"They took the law seriously, but I didn't understand everything, especially the decision by the jury," Mehmed said.

"And the verdict? Was it just?" the *mufti* pressed.

"Teacher, I don't know," Mehmed confessed. "The court followed the law, and the court produced a verdict, so in that sense, the verdict was just."

"But?" Hasan sensed that Mehmed had more to say.

"But I still wondered whether the man committed the crime, as did some of the English lawyers. Would a different jury have reached the same decision?" Mehmed responded.

"What have you learned about Ottoman law and justice working at the English court?" Hasan shifted the conversation.

"That the English constantly complain about it."

"About *sharia*?" the *mufti* wondered.

Mehmed paused. "No, about Ottoman courts and Ottoman law when British subjects are involved. Hornby complains about the failure of government courts to comply with the treaty capitulations, the lack of clear rules in these courts—especially in criminal cases—and the absence of trained Turkish lawyers and judges."

"Do you think Hornby is justified?"

"The complaints hinge on the capitulations, which are unjust, so his position is not legitimate," Mehmed answered.

"With *sharia*, do we have clear rules and trained experts?" probed Hasan.

When Mehmed did not respond, Hasan continued. "Why, then, is it illegitimate to expect the same when *sharia* does not govern in Turkish legal proceedings?"

Mehmed replied that foreign interference tainted reforms and that the capitulations were a coercive tool that Europeans used to dictate what the Ottoman government did.

"For example," Mehmed continued, "Hornby got upset last week about another case that he claims violated the capitulations. A Turkish judge tried for robbery some Ionian protected by the British under the capitulations. The judge found the evidence insufficient to support a conviction, and Hornby concurred as the treaty requires. But then, the Minister of Police referred the case to the Supreme Council at the request of the man convicted of the robbery. The Supreme Council banished the Ionian from Ottoman territory. There's not a single person in this case who is English, other than Hornby. British jurisdiction is a legal fiction imposed by a civilisation that believes itself superior."

The *mufti* ran his fingers over his beard. "What is your view of the case if the capitulations did not exist?"

"What do you mean?"

"Assume a Turkish judge finds that a person cannot be found guilty of a crime because of insufficient evidence. But the Minister of Police, at the request of the individual convicted of the crime, submits the case to the Supreme Council, which punishes the innocent man without evidence that he committed any crime. Does this seem just to you? In the case that you described, can you blame the English for what Turkish officials did? Doesn't the process and outcome in the case support Hornby's argument that the capitulations should remain in force?" Hasan explained.

The *mufti* held up his hand to let Mehmed know he did not need to respond, but he admonished Mehmed to do more than criticise the capitulations. Mehmed needed to see problems not caused by the extraterritorial jurisdiction that Europeans exercised in Ottoman domains. However, Hasan was worried that, after the missionary incident, Mehmed's position was precarious. His anger about the capitulations could worsen his standing with the English, and his criticism of Ottoman behaviour could expose him to retribution by the government. The purpose of having Mehmed at the English court—to advance his training as a new kind of lawyer—was in jeopardy. He advised Mehmed to avoid situations that could make things worse.

"Teacher," Mehmed replied, "the court's staff, including me, has been invited to the Sultan's ball to bid farewell to Stratford. Not attending could be seen as an insult to the Sultan, but my presence might agitate members of the English community who believe I'm a violent lunatic."

Hasan advised Mehmed to attend, but after his presence was observed, to make himself inconspicuous until the ball was over. Mehmed was preparing to thank Hasan when a bearded face loomed over the table. It was Ali, from the law school.

Ali grinned as he looked from Hasan to Mehmed. "Who would have thought? Mehmed, the fanatical scourge of Christianity."

Hasan motioned for Ali to join them, but Ali declined because he was late for something.

"You haven't been attending, Ali," said Hasan.

"I'm not coming back. I've found more productive uses for my time," Ali replied.

"Such as?" Mehmed's tone was sarcastic.

Ali did not answer, preferring to give Mehmed a long, sideways stare. Then, his smile becoming a sneer, Ali finally responded loud enough for those nearby to hear, "Let's just say that I'm not licking the boots of British barristers."

Ali laughed loudly as he walked away. Mehmed wanted to confront him, but Hasan put his hand on Mehmed's forearm, keeping him seated at the table.

"I don't know what that boy is doing," Hasan's voice became hushed. "But I'm afraid for him. This is a dangerous time when extremism seeps into angry men like water seeking gravity."

They sat in silence sipping tepid coffee before Hasan whispered, "Be careful."

—

A fortnight before the ball, Halil alerted James that, the previous night, an English and a Turkish vessel had collided on the Bosphorus. Ali Ghalib Pasha, the Sultan's nephew, had drowned. Apparently, the pasha and his crew were drunk when the collision happened. The Ottoman official with legal authority over the strait, called Mushaver Pasha, was a former Royal Navy commander, Sir Aldolphus Slade. With the British government's permission, Admiral Slade had joined the Ottoman navy during the Crimean war and remained in its service afterwards. James learned that Slade had hastily established a commission that assigned responsibility for the collision to the English ship. By treaty, the British had exclusive jurisdiction over English vessels in Turkish ports and waters, so the commission could not exercise legal authority over any English vessel without the consent of Her Majesty's Government.

With Mehmed, James reported this news to Judge Hornby at his residence while the judge was having afternoon tea with his wife. The young lawyers shared a glance when they sensed that the judge and his wife had exchanged harsh words. The judge welcomed the interruption. Edmund listened, but he made it clear he did not care for a British naval officer "going native" and working for a foreign government.

Emelia defended Slade, reminding Edmund that Slade laboured for a British ally, and thus for British interests. Slade's efforts were why Her Majesty made him K.C.B. last year. "There is more," she said, clinking her teacup down. Slade had also facilitated the translation of English instructional books for mothers on the care of infants into Turkish. Sir Aldolphus lamented the unnecessary infant mortality that British physicians believed were caused by Turkish women's lack of education on child rearing.

"Tell me, Edmund," she said tartly. "How does your court help Turkish mothers keep their babies alive?"

Edmund did not respond, but his eyes hinted that his wife's words hurt. Having lived in the residence for some time, James knew that all was not well between husband and wife. Mehmed silently sipped his tea, undecided about what was more comical—the judge's caricature of Slade, Mrs. Hornby's dressing down of her husband, English condescension about Turkish mothers, or Ottoman dependence on a British naval officer.

Judge Hornby was furious with Slade, but Mehmed persuaded him that Slade threaded a difficult needle—having a Turkish determination of responsibility, which avoided an intoxication scandal involving the Sultan's nephew, without holding the English crew criminally liable, which prevented a diplomatic crisis. Hornby decided not to press the matter, but it was, he said, such Turkish contortion of legal rules and processes that deepened his commitment to the capitulations. Mehmed held his tongue, deciding not to compare Slade's response with Hornby's actions against the English missionaries.

On the Saturday before the Sultan's ball, James described the Mushaver Pasha affair to Rosamund. She suppressed a yawn during the tale and, when it ended, she turned immediately to discussing the ball. She knew James had no experience with such things, and she wanted to make sure he understood what to expect, and what she expected from him. She told him the ball was being held at *Dolma Batche*, the Sultan's newest palace, on the European side of the city. She had not been inside this palace, but she had, on being rowed back-and-forth across the strait in *caiques*, seen its snow-white reflection in the dark blue Bosphorus. Those who had been within swore that its opulence was spectacular and enchanting, especially the gold-gilded ceilings and the English-crystal chandelier that illuminated the glass-domed ceremonial hall through hundreds of gas jets.

Rosamund emphasised that he should remain with her all evening. She intended to stay with her parents. He could make acquaintances with important people and expand his contacts among merchants. Rosamund insisted that he meet Geoffrey Hancock, her father's partner, who had a soft spot for her because she had been best friends with his daughter, Margaret. Mr. Hancock, she said, had quarrelled with her father after she rejected Henry Wattling because he agreed with her that Wattling was a wastrel.

James had no plans for the ball, so he had no reason to object to her instructions. Never leave her. Stay close to her parents. Meet important people with her; meet people important to her. Make a good impression on Mr. Hancock. It seemed a little calculating, but it could only have one purpose, so he would do her bidding.

When the tutorial ended, James, not wanting their time together to end, asked Rosamund to describe the ball that she remembered most from her time at Constantinople.

She did not expect the question, and she looked away before answering. "The costume ball that Lord Stratford gave at the

British embassy after the war ended. I was seventeen. It wasn't my favourite ball, but it's the one I most remember."

"Because of the costumes?" James probed.

"No—well, the costumes were memorable. There was an African king with a tattooed chest, animal-bone necklace, and feather headdress. Two men dressed as devils, in black velvet with faces painted red and forked tails wrapped like snakes around their arms. My best friend, Maggie, went as Mary Queen of Scots. I was a Druidess, in white robes and an oak-leaf crown."

"A Druidess?" James stifled a laugh.

"Yes, a Druidess," Rosamund gave his reaction a look of mock disapproval. "Before the event, Maggie said my costume might be the most intriguing—"

Rosamund stopped mid-sentence, and James sensed melancholy come over her.

"Maggie," Rosamund said quietly, "we shared just about everything together."

James did not know what to say, but Rosamund relieved him of the need to be sensitive. "My costume generated conversations, but Maggie's prediction was wrong. Mine was not the most memorable costume."

James sat back with his tea, and Rosamund continued. "There was a Turkish woman at the ball. She wore a cream *yashmak* veil and a blue *feridjee* cloak adorned with an ivory velvet collar and ornamented with red and yellow embroidery. My, those clothes were beautiful, exquisite in combining traditional styling and vibrant colours."

James nodded, as if he appreciated why the woman's attire had left such an impression.

"She was walking alone amidst the guests, causing a sensation, and prompting whispers about who she was and what she was doing alone at the ball. Mr. Hancock wondered whether she was one of the Sultan's wives or mistresses permitted to walk about without a chaperone and witness a rare celebration involving Mohammedans and Christians. Maggie and I followed her at a discreet distance. She walked up to men, both Turkish and European, and spoke to them in their native tongues. That was amazing to hear—a woman fluent in so many languages."

James stopped himself from nodding again but failed to produce any other gesture to demonstrate that he, too, was impressed.

The timbre of Rosamund's voice changed, "After inserting herself into a circle of English military officers, she touched and caressed the medals on their tunics with her gloved hands. Then, in English, she declared, 'You see me. We are coming out now. No more cages for us. No more foolish rags over our heads. No more symbols of slavery over our faces. We are entering the world to judge things for ourselves, and to love whom we want.'"

Rosamund went quiet, staring at her hands in her lap.

James remarked that the account was, indeed, memorable. Rosamund replied that she had not reached the most memorable part. James arched his eyebrows in anticipation.

"The uncomfortable officers didn't know how to respond to such a declaration from a Turkish woman. I was thrilled to hear any woman proclaim such things. The veiled figure then nestled against the senior officer—it was such a suggestive move—and asked if he would like to kiss and play at St. George. The officer's face melted into pure trepidation. Then, with one dramatic motion, the figure removed the *yashmak* to reveal a man, Percy

Smythe, an attaché at the embassy. The jest produced no end of laughing and backslapping amongst the men."

James could tell that the moment was memorable because of the pain it had caused Rosamund. For James, Smythe's performance smacked too much of Drury Lane pantomime to merit such emotional pain. They sat in silence. Rosamund turned her head so that he could not fully see her face. Deeply uncomfortable, James tried to end the awkwardness.

"Where's Maggie now?"

Rosamund turned her tear-filled eyes to James. "Where's Maggie? That's what you have to say?"

Rosamund again looked away. She dabbed the corners of her eyes with her wrists, sniffed, and focused her gaze on the mantel clock.

"Malta. Wife of a naval lieutenant. Expecting," Rosamund said flatly.

James set his teacup and saucer down as quietly as he could. Without breaking eye contact with the clock, Rosamund sniffed again and indicated that she had to take care of matters relating to the ball. She did not—as she had always done—escort him to the front entrance and wait until Bones was brought around.

As he plodded away, James distracted himself from the way his time with Rosamund had ended by remembering when he and Emma went to social functions. They never had invitations to anything like the soirées of Constantinople, and they never had ambitions such as those Rosamund had for the Sultan's ball. Emma stayed on his arm during such affairs because, she said, she liked it. When they talked with people, she moved her thumb slowly up and down the inside of his upper arm. It was a small thing. No one could see her do it. It was just for them.

A horse trotting up from behind spoiled his vignette.

Hugh Colborne brought his horse close to Bones and gave James's mount a derisory look. "Bingham, stop."

"Good afternoon." James reined up, anticipating the salutation would end the pleasantries.

"Bingham," Hugh had to regain control of his horse, which bumped into Bones, before he commanded, "After the ball. You ask her the day after the ball."

James feigned ignorance. "Ask what?"

Hugh leaned forward, saddle leather creaking under his weight. "Even you can't be that stupid. But, in case you are, you ask her to marry you the day after the ball."

James said nothing and showed no reaction.

"Do I make myself clear?" Hugh asked with irritation. "Say it."

"After the ball, sir, the day after the ball," James complied.

Hugh relaxed in his saddle and anticipated James's question. "She won't. She wouldn't have entertained you, of all people, for this long and been this disciplined about it. She's come to her senses. She's yielding. But, just in case, I'll ensure there's no escape."

James patted Bones on the neck as "there's no escape" lingered in the air.

"After the ball, boy. The day right after the ball." Hugh turned his horse for home.

Part II

Cross-Examination

Hearing.

328. The prosecutor shall be at liberty to conduct the charge and to have witnesses examined and cross-examined by counsel or attorney on his behalf.

329. The accused shall be admitted to make his full answer and defence to the charge, and to have the witnesses examined and cross-examined by counsel or attorney on his behalf ... — *Rules of Her Britannic Majesty's Supreme Consular Court and other Consular Courts in the Dominions of the Sublime Ottoman Porte, 1860.*

Chapter 10
The Sultan's Ball

The avenue approaching the *Dolma Batche* palace was exceptionally smooth, with elegant gas lamp posts along each side. James rode with Rosamund and her parents, and the air hinted that rain might fall later in the evening. At the avenue's end, on a beautiful white gateway, *Abdul Mejid* and *Victoria*, spelled out by paper lanterns suspended in the air—as if by magic—greeted arriving guests.

After their carriage passed through the gateway, the blue Bosphorus appeared on one side and, along the luminous palace, finely dressed Turkish officers sat tall on magnificent horses. After stepping from the carriage, James helped Rosamund down. As she shifted from holding his hand to taking his arm, he felt blessed, an emotion that life had rarely bestowed on him. The sensation went beyond the honour of escorting Rosamund, who, in a white gown of gossamer simplicity, was breathtaking. It went beyond the grandeur of the palace and the elegance and élan of the other guests. It took him to a place of liberation.

In the arriving swirl, James and Rosamund lost touch with her parents. In moving toward the entrance, they heard the languages of many nations—Turkish, French, Spanish, Greek, Arabic, German, Russian, and the flat English of Americans. After entering the palace and being announced, they descended a small flight of stairs and walked into the ceremonial hall, where James spotted Mr. and Mrs. Colborne. As James and Rosamund fell into step with one another in walking toward her parents, a voice called out, "There, Pup."

James suddenly stopped, and Rosamund did likewise. She saw that James was looking at something and smiling with astonished joy. Before Rosamund could speak, he put his hand on the small of her back and redirected her. To her great surprise, she welcomed the strong and spontaneous touch.

James led Rosamund toward George and Jemmy. He embraced them first before introducing her. "George and Jemmy Oakeston, let me introduce Rosamund Colborne, a merchant's daughter."

James and the Oakestons laughed together, and the smile on James's face expanded. Rosamund tried to look amused but did not know what was so humorous.

"Well, look at you," Jemmy inspected Rosamund. "I say, James, you must have remembered Caroline," which triggered more laughter from James and the Oakestons.

"Who's Caroline?" Rosamund was bewildered by all the joviality.

"Don't worry, Miss Colborne," Jemmy touched Rosamund's arm, "just things we share with James."

James explained that he had kept company with the Oakestons on his voyage to Constantinople, but he turned back to George and Jemmy. "It's good to see you, but I thought you were bound for India."

"We are, but business kept us here longer than expected," George replied.

"You've been here and didn't send word?" James could not hide his disappointment.

"Our apologies," answered George. "But we, like you, have been busy. And your schedule needed time for this young lady, who must be better company than old George and Jemmy."

James began to reply, but George cut him off. "Pup, we didn't expect to meet you tonight, but it has warmed our hearts. However, we wish to bid farewell to a dear old friend, tonight's guest of honour, so we must find him before the evening becomes too ceremonial."

"Lord Stratford? You're friends with the ambassador?" James was surprised.

George smiled but did not answer. He shook James's hand and kissed Rosamund's.

Jemmy embraced James, holding him tight for an extra moment. "She's a bright and shiny thing. Is she real?"

Before James could react, Jemmy let go, took Rosamund's hands, and leaned in very close to whisper, "He's a good man. Make sure he remains one when you're done with him."

James saw a curious flicker in Rosamund's eyes.

"Are we not allowed to know what you're whispering?" James asked in what he hoped was a playful tone.

Jemmy released Rosamund's hands. "Well, Miss Colborne, Mr. Bingham still has much to learn about women. But James, if you must know, I advised her to buy a green dress."

George laughed, and Jemmy hugged James again and kissed his cheek. The Oakestons took their leave. James offered his arm to Rosamund, but she was oblivious to the gesture.

"Rosamund, is anything wrong?" He sensed something amiss in her demeanour.

She shook her head unconvincingly. "Did Caroline have a green dress? Was she—?"

Rosamund did not finish the question. She realised that, after months with James, she did not know his late fiancée's name. She had never bothered to ask. She suddenly felt cold.

"Was she what?" James enquired.

Rosamund waved her hand to deflect the question. She smoothed her gown and turned to James, "Your arm, please."

They located her parents and took up positions among the people conversing with them. James's mind kept returning to the great fortune of seeing George and Jemmy again. The presence of Hugh Colborne next to him ended the warm feeling.

As Rosamund began answering a question, Hugh stepped closer. "Interested in an early payment?"

James looked blankly at Hugh, not understanding the question. Hugh interrupted to say he was taking James and Rosamund to meet someone. James offered Rosamund his arm, and they followed Mr. Colborne. As they walked, James could hear that, somewhere in the palace, music was playing. As they passed through a long hall punctuated with small, windowed alcoves, James spied Mehmed alone in one hunched over a book. He did not stop but shot Mehmed a look intended to get his colleague to join the festivities. Mehmed did not lift his eyes from his reading. James smiled and left the Turk to whatever he was doing by himself amidst a grand ball.

They navigated through a small room before emerging into a larger salon. And there he was, in the middle of the salon, chatting with other guests. The tall, lanky frame; the walking stick. A few more steps, and, yes, that baritone.

"My God," James said under his breath, "Cranford Pennington."

Rosamund heard and whispered, "Who's Cranford Penning-ton?"

Rosamund could not believe that another person from James's past had appeared at the Sultan's ball—it was certainly not something she had factored into the evening's purpose.

Hugh set up the approach perfectly, shielding James from Pennington's view. "Cranford, my good fellow, let me introduce my daughter, Rosamund," and Pennington kissed her hand. "And, with her tonight," Hugh shifted to clear the line of sight, "Mr. James Bingham."

For the first time that evening, an introduction of the couple did not result in eyes focusing on Rosamund. Pennington locked eyes with Bingham, and James returned the favour. The tense silence that followed prompted Rosamund to gaze back and forth between the two, wondering what was going on. Then, unusually, James timed his moment well.

"Mr. Pennington," he pronounced every syllable clearly as he extended his hand.

Pennington hesitated and shot a sideways glance at Colborne, before raising his hand in a pained manner. The handshake was firm but perfunctory, with neither man eager to prolong contact. Hugh turned the knife a bit more.

"Don't they make a handsome couple," he observed, causing Pennington to look at Rosamund. "James is one of the diplomatic service's finest young lawyers, who may, in short order and with my admiration, return to the Bar in London. James, Mr. Pennington is a barrister in England, who handled some of my legal affairs. I'm surprised your paths never crossed."

For James, standing before Pennington without feeling the need to confront or embarrass the man was sufficient revenge.

In that moment, he marvelled at Colborne's machinations. In one encounter, Hugh had created a debt that James would feel obliged to repay, had put Pennington on notice that the barrister could not take his business for granted, and had sent a clear signal to Rosamund.

Pennington had no idea that Colborne was playing with him, or that Bingham was in on it. Colborne's introduction must mean that Bingham had not spoken of what had happened—and Bingham was not taking this opportunity to divulge anything about it. The boy at least had discretion, a virtue that provided Pennington with an opening.

"Well, Mr. Bingham, I see life at Constantinople is full of promise and potential. A beautiful woman at your side; the admiration of a merchant influential across empires; and the stature to be invited by the Sultan to this event. It would, perhaps, be hard to imagine the same happening to a young barrister in London, would it not?" Pennington savoured each word.

"Perhaps," was James's reply, enough to acknowledge Pennington's repartee while taking nothing away from how he had handled coerced exile.

Hugh did not want the encounter to linger but would not end it without one more twist of the blade. "It was good to see you, Cranford, but I must take this young couple to meet some important people. Excuse us."

As they returned to the ceremonial hall, James sensed a change in Rosamund. She was distant and muddled when he tried to engage her in conversation. Feeling good after the encounter with Pennington, he tried to lighten the mood, assuring her that she need not buy a green dress. She nodded vacantly, but whatever preoccupied her did not lift.

James had never mentioned a Cranford Pennington, so Rosamund could not fathom why what she had witnessed was so peculiar. But that was not her primary worry. No, she had just watched her father all but betroth her to James and send them back to England. *Handsome couple. One of the diplomatic service's finest young lawyers. Return to London with my admiration.*

She swallowed against dryness in her throat. She had been so fixated on creating room for serendipity that she failed to anticipate her father's moves. She never intended to fill the space she was trying to create through James Bingham with James Bingham. Until this evening, his behaviour had reinforced her belief that he would never ask her to marry him. But what message did James receive tonight other than that the Colbornes, and especially her, would welcome a marriage proposal?

Stay with my parents. The gown. *Make acquaintances with important people.* The hair. *Expand your contacts.* The jewellery. *Meet Mr. Hancock.* The perfume. *Remain with me all evening.* The charade.

A sour queasiness spread through her. George and Jemmy, Caroline, Pennington—she did not know James; she had not even deigned to understand him. He showed true emotion with George and Jemmy that she had not seen before, and that, maybe, she did not stir in him. He showed something with Pennington—stoic dignity perhaps—that she did not think him capable of having. And his firm hand, touching her, taking her toward what he wanted. Perhaps there was a real man in James Bingham after all.

She stole a look at James as they approached the ceremonial hall, a glimpse that, for the first time, revealed him as something other than a means to an end. A good man. The glance made her light-headed, breached her defences, and routed every excuse.

Rosamund remained subdued as they re-entered the hall. They took glasses of champagne from silver trays carried by servants, and James offered a toast to Lord Stratford. Hugh Colborne asked them to raise their glasses for Sir Henry Bulwer, the incoming ambassador. "Finally, a diplomat," he added, "who understands business."

After the toasts, Hugh motioned for James to follow him. Rosamund, with reluctance, released his arm, unsure what her father was doing now.

James followed Hugh back into the hallway with the windowed alcoves. He did not see Mehmed in the alcove farther down. Hugh went to stand by the closest window. James joined him. Hugh said nothing. James peered out and saw distant lightning in the sky.

"Do it now, not tomorrow," Hugh finally said.

"Ask her to marry me?" James was taken aback.

"You accepted early payment on our deal. So, with payment taken tonight, you must honour your part of the bargain, now. Or put more bluntly, revenge comes with a price."

"Your revenge or mine?" James shot back.

The retort made Hugh give James an unblinking look. "The law provides remedies for a breach of contract. Your acceptance of payment tonight sealed our contract. If you don't honour the contract when performance is due, the remedy is for Rosamund to learn that you cut a secret deal with me. She'll believe that I'm capable of it, but the fury you'll face will make her cat o' nine whipping of Henry Wattling look like a tender kiss."

Before James could react, he heard pounding footsteps. From the other end of the hallway, he saw Mehmed running toward him. James stepped out to meet his colleague. An out-of-breath Mehmed huffed to James that Judge Hornby needed him. There was a murder at the Galata docks and a request for British assistance. The judge required James immediately. Hugh had followed James and overheard what Mehmed said.

"Mehmed, please come with me." James began to move in the direction of the ceremonial hall.

"Bingham," Hugh planted his hand on James's chest, "our contract."

"Sir, there's been a murder. I'm needed on Her Majesty's business." James then used his barrister voice, "Performance tonight is excused because of unforeseen circumstances."

"What are you talking about?" Hugh pushed hard against James's chest.

"James," Mehmed interrupted, "the matter is urgent. You must go."

"Sir, I am not your lawyer." James pushed roughly past Hugh.

As they walked toward the ceremonial hall, James asked Mehmed to remain with Rosamund for the rest of the ball.

"No, I cannot." Mehmed reacted badly to the request.

"I need you to do this. I don't want her left alone." James touched Mehmed's elbow.

Mehmed pulled his arm away. "She is not alone. Her parents are here."

"No, I don't have time to explain. Please stay with her. How hard can that be?"

"For me, it will be hard. You forget—I'm the Mussulman fanatic."

The two stopped. James had given no thought to Mehmed's situation.

"That's why—" James began to say.

"I've kept to myself tonight," Mehmed finished the statement.

James anxiously ran his hand through his hair. "Perhaps the best response for a Mussulman fanatic is to do a chivalrous favour at the Sultan's ball for a desperate Englishman."

Mehmed put his hands on his hips. "Why are you desperate? What's wrong with you? What's wrong with that woman?"

"Please," James begged.

Mehmed cast his eyes down at the floor. "Do I have to dance with her?"

James embraced his colleague, nearly sending Mehmed tumbling backwards.

When they reached the ceremonial hall, James saw that Hugh Colborne had not returned. He pointed at Rosamund, whose back was turned, so that Mehmed would know who she was and asked him to wait until he was gone. James went to Rosamund and took her aside.

"What did my father want?" She tried to hide her nerves.

"He wanted to talk about contracts," James replied, half-looking over his shoulder.

"He wanted to talk about business? Tonight?"

"In a manner of speaking," James answered, before telling her about the murder and Judge Hornby's order that he leave immediately for the docks.

Rosamund was not pleased, but after one protest, she surrendered to the impossibility of him remaining at the ball.

"Mehmed agreed to be with you for the rest of the night," James said.

"The Turkish lawyer?" Her question was thick with incredulity.

"Yes, I begged him to do so," James explained.

"I can take care of myself. I don't need male supervision." Her eyes flashed with annoyance.

"My concern," James leaned close, "is not you. Do you understand?"

She nodded, but in the moment, she did not understand. She acquiesced because it mattered to James, and she felt a duty, for once, to support him. James kissed her hand, something he had never done. Surprised by the gentle gesture, she wanted him to stay but had to watch him leave.

In an emotional daze, her designs for the evening in tatters, she turned to locate her mother only to find standing before her a young Turkish man she had never seen before. His eyes went wide in astonished recognition. He did not move for some moments before he tentatively offered his arm.

"Miss Colborne?" Mehmed thought that he might have breached protocol, with the young woman so still that she seemed not to breathe.

Rosamund finally spoke, "You must be the Mussulman fanatic."

"At your service, Miss Colborne," he bowed.

She took his arm. "No, you shall call me Miss Rosamund."

"As you wish," he said as they began to walk.

"Did I hear correctly from James that you talk about beautiful women?" She noticed people in the ceremonial hall were already starting to stare.

He smiled. "Miss Rosamund, I have only talked about one woman that Englishmen call beautiful."

She felt no need to ask the next question.

Chapter 11
Law and Order

Resplendent in attire donned for the Sultan's ball, British and Turkish officials started arriving by horse at the Galata docks with their security escorts. James could not keep pace with Judge Hornby, who was determined to be the first from the palace to reach the docks. James was riding a creature of more mass and muscle than Bones, and he struggled to control its power. But others had taken up Hornby's challenge, including someone James thought was Aldolphus Slade.

Milling about and emerging from a wooden sailing ship were sailors looking every inch like men who had spent weeks at sea. Angry Ionian dockworkers were appearing, armed with clubs and staves. The *cavasses* escorting the British and Turkish officials dampened any enthusiasm that the sailors or Ionians might have for an immediate melee, but the potential for violence remained palpable.

James trotted his horse through the cordon that the *cavasses* had created to keep the sailors and the dockworkers apart, and he dismounted inelegantly. He quick-marched to where Hornby and Slade were talking with a ship's captain. Although he missed the start of the conversation, James grasped the situation.

There had been a murder on a Swedish ship *en route* to Constantinople. The captain had the alleged perpetrator, an Ionian sailor, under guard below deck. After the ship had docked, word reached Ionians drinking nearby that a compatriot was in trouble on the vessel. The captain believed that he could no longer keep the sailor safe onboard from retribution by angry crew members with more time and alcohol at hand. And now he feared that he could not protect the ship and its crew from the Ionian dockworkers. The ship needed refitting and could not anchor offshore. The captain also claimed that the Swedish legation at Constantinople did not have a secure place or police staff to detain someone accused of homicide. The captain wanted the British consulate to take custody and detain the suspect in its gaol until he could be taken to Sweden for trial.

A wild-eyed representative from the Ionians elbowed in to argue that only an Ionian court could try their man, warning that his countrymen would not permit him to remain under Swedish control. As the ranking Turkish authority on the scene, Slade told the captain that the Ottoman government had jurisdiction. The Swedish ship was in Turkish waters and docked at a Turkish port, with its captain intending to land the suspect on Turkish soil. With a dismissive wave, Slade added that there was no reason to involve the British.

As this discussion unfolded, tempers flared and insults flew among the Swedish sailors, the Ionian dockworkers, and the Turkish *cavasses*. The air at the docks was oppressive. Lightning shot eerie illuminations across the deteriorating situation. Hornby sensed that it was time to act.

"The suspect is Ionian," Hornby cut off the captain's response to Slade. "Under our treaty with the Ottoman government, he is a protected person and falls within the jurisdiction of Her Majesty's Government."

Slade reacted angrily, "The British government has no jurisdiction. The capitulations give you rights when Ionians have committed crimes in Ottoman dominions. This murder was not committed in Turkey. Under international law, Sweden has exclusive jurisdiction over crimes committed on its vessels sailing the high seas."

The captain nodded. "And Sweden has a treaty with Turkey that accords us exclusive jurisdiction over our vessels in Turkish ports and waters. So, I want the British to assist me in exercising Sweden's rights until I arrange for the suspect's transport to Sweden for trial."

Slade was not deterred. "I'm not challenging your exclusive jurisdiction over the crime or over your vessel. But you want to land this man on Turkish territory, where you don't have exclusive jurisdiction. Neither you nor the British have any rights to dictate what happens to this person once he disembarks your vessel. The Turks are civilised enough to detain this individual until you're ready to take him to Sweden for trial."

Commotion interrupted this debate when Ionians began throwing bottles and rocks at the Swedish crew, who began arming themselves with sharp and stout instruments.

"Mr. Williams," Hornby called his police constable forward. "Go on the ship, arrest the suspect, take him into custody, and detain him in our gaol. Go, now!"

Williams and his deputy went onboard. Slade began to protest, but the judge pre-empted him, "You have no jurisdiction on the Swedish ship. I'm arresting the suspect on the ship. You have no authority to dictate what happens here."

Hornby gestured for Slade to lean in and continued in a lowered voice, "The Ionians will not attack if I take custody. They have too much to lose because we protect them under the capitulations. If I take custody, the Swedish crew will not riot. If you prevail, we'll have violence."

Before Slade could respond, Hornby broke off to speak to the representative of the Ionian dockworkers. The captain told his crew what was happening. The explosive atmosphere cooled, with the Ionians ceasing provocations and the Swedish crew retreating to their quarters.

As Williams led the suspect from the ship, Slade rasped at Hornby, "This is not over."

As far as the judge was concerned, it was over. Violence and bloodshed had been avoided. Slade would make the incident a problem between the British and Ottoman governments, but Edmund was content to leave it for diplomats, rather than sailors and ruffians, to square off in bloodless manoeuvring.

Edmund told James that he was returning to the ball, but he ordered James to stay and interview the captain and crew about what had happened on the vessel in connection with the murder. He had ordered a man's arrest to diffuse a dangerous situation, but the order was based solely on what the captain alleged took place. A better record was needed to justify the arrest and prepare for the recriminations likely to come from the Sublime Porte.

James did not protest, even though he wanted to return to the palace to see whether Hugh Colborne had pursued his remedy for breach of contract and destroyed what he and Rosamund had, with difficulty, developed. And if the damage was done, what could he say to her? What could he claim that was true? That he had behaved honourably? That he had acted out of love?

James realised that the elation he felt arriving at the ball had been a delusion built on a deception that he had been too weak to reject when the poisoned chalice was first offered. Despondent, he boarded the ship and descended below deck.

Chapter 12

Glove with a Pearl Button

When? Mehmed rummaged in his memory. When was the last time?

Rosamund's hand on his arm had unsmiling faces following them across the ceremonial hall. Her touch warmed his skin as though he wore no clothes. The nearness of her body telling him that it was wrong, all so very wrong.

When? He could not stop the question. When did a woman last touch me?

Her hand shifted their course through the islands and streams of the Sultan's guests.

It was not the woman his father had arranged for him to marry. It was before that.

A waft of her perfume passed when she moved closer as the crowd swelled around them.

It must have been that night. When his mother had woken him. When she had embraced him fiercely. When she buried her hand in the hair on the back of his head. When she smelled of salt and metal.

She laughed, but he could not tell what, in the sea of gowns and suits, caused her mirth.

She released him and had vanished. The salt and metal lingered. His hair felt wet. He lit a candle. He ran fingers across the back of his head and brought them into the candlelight. Shiny, red, blood. From his mother's hand. From her revenge. From her goodbye.

"Over there," she ordered, and with navigational precision, he changed headings.

That was the last time. The night of her justice. The night of his shame.

"That way," she pointed. "My mother's over there."

They halted as a flood of people passed between them and Rosamund's mother.

"Your mother? Which one?" Mehmed asked to settle himself as the surge continued.

"The taller one, with the white feather in her hair."

Over the ebbing tide of women and men, Mehmed saw the feather dancing. They stepped into the now-empty space between them and Rosamund's mother. Glimpsing Rosamund approaching, Katherine moved to greet her daughter. Her smile collapsed when she saw her dear girl arriving with a Turk. Rosamund saw the reaction and stopped short, forcing Mehmed to manoeuvre inelegantly to retain his balance.

Only a few paces separated Rosamund and Mehmed from Katherine, a distance filled only with the blue marble floor. Before words, good or ill, were exchanged, Hugh Colborne emerged, planted himself before his wife, and squared his shoulders at Mehmed, who aligned his body to the challenge. Hugh's movements, and Mehmed's response, left those pretending not to watch with little doubt that drama was nigh.

"Be gone, boy," Hugh barked, his emotions already raw from James's defiance.

The ultimatum prompted people to line up along both borders of the cerulean gap between Hugh and Mehmed.

Mehmed did not move. "Who invited you here tonight?"

The question deflected Hugh's insult, making the merchant look like a peevish bully.

"Are you deaf and dumb? Be gone, Turk." Hugh's anger was building toward an unpredictable storm.

Mehmed had the advantage—and he knew it. He arched his eyebrows theatrically. "Perhaps you did not hear or understand me, Englishman. Who invited you to this ball?"

Hugh's shoulders began to appear less fully squared.

"The Sultan invited me, Osman Mehmed," the tone and volume of Mehmed's voice modulated to reach across the little gathering. "The Sultan invited you, Hugh Colborne, as well. We are here as equals. Not as man and boy. Not as master and servant. Not as civilised and uncivilised."

"Get away from my daughter," Hugh howled.

Rosamund coiled to curse her father, but Mehmed was quicker. "Do you, Mr. Colborne, keep the promises that you make to Englishmen?"

"What?" Hugh finally grasped that he had lost the initiative.

"Do you keep your promises? Is your word your bond among the English?"

Hugh did not answer. He did not know how to retreat.

"Mr. Colborne prefers giving orders to answering questions. So, let me ask you, sir," Mehmed pointed at a beefy British man standing nearby. "Do you keep the promises that you make to Englishmen?"

"Why, of course," came the meaty reply.

"As do I," Mehmed emphasised each word. "And I will keep the promise I made to an Englishman, Mr. James Bingham, of Her Britannic Majesty's Supreme Consular Court. A promise to escort Miss Rosamund Colborne for the rest of the Sultan's ball while Mr. Bingham conducts urgent business on Her Majesty's Service."

With Mehmed's words hanging in the air, the spectators turned toward Hugh, who realised that this declaration—especially how it wrapped James in Her Majesty's authority—had captured the sympathies of those entertained by the confrontation.

Struggling to control his anger, Hugh turned on Rosamund. "Get rid of that Mussulman fanatic."

Rosamund slipped her hand from Mehmed's arm and stepped into the gap. "I, too, made a promise to an Englishman. To a gentleman. To James Bingham. I shall honour that promise."

Rosamund's proclamation of fidelity appeared to generate approbation among the encircling crowd. But Hugh ostentatiously re-squared his shoulders—a signal to all that he had not been bested. Rosamund's little performance confirmed that she had, as Hugh suspected, thrown in her lot with James. The moment and the setting were serendipitous but perfect for the destruction he had painstakingly prepared for this night.

"You made a promise to James Bingham, did you? A gentleman, is he?" Hugh's sudden laughter transformed the scene. "Shall I tell you about the promise that Mr. Bingham, the gentleman you so honour, made to me?"

Rosamund tried to be stoic, but her father had unsettled her.

Hugh pounced. "A promise about you that sealed a bargain with me. Behind your back. Did you not know? Do you understand me now, little girl?"

The surrounding faces, even more enthralled after this dramatic twist, turned on Rosamund. Feeling once again trapped by her father and judged by society, she closed her eyes against them. She slowly ran the back of her fingers down her right cheek to remember why. But his firm touch on her body. That woman's whisper. The kiss on her hand. Her fury and shame collided and combusted.

Rosamund's eyes blazed open and her voice was scorching, "You made a bargain about me with James Bingham, did you? You manipulated him, did you? Just as I have done. Behind his back. Behind your back. Did you not know? Do you understand me now, old man?"

Confused murmurs rose all around as Hugh, confounded by his daughter's outburst, said nothing. The thrumming dissipated as Hugh's face changed from discomposure into comprehending rage.

"You bitch, you scheming bitch!" Hugh moved aggressively toward her.

Sounds of shock from the crowd swept over a frightened Rosamund as she lunged behind Mehmed. The desperation in her retreat stopped Hugh cold, a mere arms-length away. Mehmed did not flinch, confront Hugh, or comfort Rosamund, even though she steadied herself with a trembling hand on his back. He lowered his chin, searching Hugh's blood-ripened face. He shifted to look at Rosamund, showing his back to the merchant. He lifted her resisting chin to see her eyes, but she turned away as tears welled over. A woman nearby scowled at Mehmed, put a comforting arm around Rosamund, and pulled her into a protective embrace. Mehmed slowly turned back to Hugh, a movement that hushed the assemblage.

"Sir," Mehmed addressed the beefy Englishman again. "You were man enough to answer my question earlier. May I ask another favour? Can you lend me one of your dress gloves? Just one, please."

Mehmed accepted the large, white glove and wrapped his hand around its fingers. He lowered the glove against his side. The chandelier light in the ceremonial hall flashed off a big, round pearl clasping button on the wrist of the glove. Without warning, a white blur connected the button and the glove with Hugh's face.

"That," Mehmed shouted, "is for insulting your daughter."

Amidst gasps from the crowd, a second slash struck Hugh's cheek. "That is for insulting James Bingham."

A third blur smacked into flesh. "That is for making your daughter afraid."

Mehmed heard, but did not acknowledge, the ensuing commotion. He returned the glove to its astounded owner and went to Rosamund, who was stunned like everyone else.

Mehmed held out his arm. "Miss Rosamund, it is time to dance."

Chapter 13
Perchance

With pen, ink, and paper from the captain, James completed the interviews on the Swedish ship. Multiple crew members had witnessed the murder. The captain had preserved as much evidence as he could, including stuffing the victim's body in a barrel of vinegar. Proving the guilt of the accused at trial would not be difficult. But the accused's guilt was not the issue that would cause trouble for Judge Hornby in the wake of the near violence and heated disagreements over jurisdiction.

James climbed to the ship's deck. The crowded, noisy, oppressive, and volatile docks from earlier were now empty, silent, dark, and wet. It had started to rain while he was below deck, and, as he disembarked, a deluge began. He had no coat. The horse he rode to the docks was gone. As best he could, he protected his notes from the torrent before trudging into the night. Upon arriving at the Hornby residence, he peeled off his saturated clothes, struggled his clammy skin and shivering bones into a nightshirt, and crawled under cold covers to sleep.

—

"In the drawing room?" Emelia Hornby turned the butler's statement into an astonished question.

"Yes, in the drawing room," confirmed Giovanni.

Why, Emelia wondered, as she readied herself for unexpected company, was Rosamund Colborne in the drawing room? Only a few days had passed since the Sultan's ball. She remembered Rosamund and James looking quite the couple at the palace. Rosamund was a woman who improved the cut of any man standing next to her, but Emelia thought James, unusually, had his own aura that night. "My God," she mumbled as she fumbled with clothes. "Did he ask her to marry him?"

She had heard whispers before the ball that something might happen between the two after the event. The chatter, and the behaviour of the gossips, had the whiff of premeditation. James would not start a whispering campaign, nor Rosamund, unless she had transitioned from manoeuvring to marrying. Rosamund's mother did not have the nerve for this game. The source had to be Hugh Colborne. Emelia did not know what to make of it, including whether Rosamund was aware of the rumours.

Anxious to hear what Miss Colborne had to say, Emelia arrived short of her normal standards for receiving visitors. Rosamund appeared not to notice as Emelia shuffled in with haphazard attire and hair askew. What Rosamund had to say rendered social etiquette nugatory.

"Cut off? Back to England?" Emelia summarised with disbelief when Rosamund had finished.

Emelia's next emotion, left unexpressed, was envy—of Rosamund being able to return to England. There were just too many times during her years at Constantinople, and especially after they had returned for Edmund to establish the court, when she wanted nothing more than to be living again in the Weybridge cottage. Where she had started married life. Where she had delighted in walking her terriers down country lanes bordered by hedgerows and ferns glistening after a rain. Where her children remained with her mother because Edmund refused to bring them East, fearing oriental diseases would kill them. Where she would not have to endure the tears and loneliness that this strange place and her husband's relentless responsibilities and endless absences wrung from her. Where Edmund had conversed with her as a companion and a lover rather than treating her as just another functionary in Her Majesty's Service.

"How does he expect you to live?" Emelia forced herself to focus on Rosamund. "What does he expect you to do?"

Rosamund did not know. Her father had simply announced his decision to cut her off financially and had placed a chit on the table to exchange for a one-way ticket to England.

"Is he forcing you to leave right away?"

"A deadline for my departure was not specified—an outcome, I suspect, of my mother begging for the banishment not to be immediate."

Emelia failed to hide her confusion. "Did he hint at this before or during the ball?"

"Until James left with your husband, I sensed that my father was using the ball to make it impossible for me not to marry James."

"That's consistent with what I heard beforehand," Emelia said.

"What did you hear?" The query suggested that Rosamund had not heard the whispers.

Emelia explained the gossiping and her suspicion that Rosamund's father had enabled it. Rosamund did not react because the information confirmed her father's behaviour at the ball.

"What happened after James left?" Emelia asked.

Rosamund was stunned that Mrs. Hornby did not know. Everyone, Rosamund said, was still talking about it. Emelia indicated that she only stayed at the ball after Edmund departed until the storm hit. After the ball, with Edmund off somewhere without saying goodbye, she had cocooned at home. Rosamund said that her father had a confrontation with Mehmed. When Emelia appeared more confused, Rosamund became less cryptic.

"James asked Mehmed to stand in for him for the rest of the ball. Why James was desperate to have Mehmed do so remains unclear," Rosamund explained.

"Have you talked with James since the ball to find out why?" Emelia interjected.

"No."

"You can ask him when we're done if he's still in his room," Emelia said.

"He lives here?" Rosamund was genuinely surprised.

"Where did you think he lived?" Emelia was incredulously surprised.

Rosamund shrugged at another example of the lack of interest in James she had perfected before the ball.

Emelia wanted to return to what happened at the palace. "Back to the ball, go on."

Rosamund provided a condensed account of the confrontation between Mehmed and her father, or as wags about town were calling it, the "bitch-and-slap affair." She included the accusation that James had made clandestine promises with her father, and she told Emelia that she did not believe it. But she left out what she said about James in her response to her father. Astonished by the tale, Emelia wanted to know what Rosamund's father had done after being publicly humiliated.

"I don't know," Rosamund admitted. "Mehmed slapped my father, turned around, and said 'it's time to dance.' So we went to dance, which he does not do well. Then that storm arrived, blowing open doors and windows, extinguishing candles, and exposing everything to wind and rain. Lightning struck the palace, frightening people, sowing confusion, and causing the premature end of the festivities. Mehmed borrowed a horse—well, in truth, he pinched it—and we rode that stallion home. We were both sopping and laughing at the end."

Emelia agreed the storm and lightning had ruined what was left of the evening, an outcome made ridiculous by speculations among guests about the tempest's meaning. Did it confirm the Ottoman empire's decline? Was Allah displeased with Mahommedans for celebrating with Christians? It was at this point that she had left the ball—but certainly not dressed only in an evening gown and mounted on a stolen horse while mirthfully clinging to a young Turkish man during a torrential storm. Emelia fought the urge to ask more questions about the wet ride home to focus on Rosamund's predicament. Did she, Emelia asked, want Edmund to intervene? Or someone else to whom her father might listen; Mr. Hancock, perhaps?

Rosamund pondered the question. Her initial reaction to her father's decision had been a sense of liberation. She declined Emelia's offer of intercession.

"But what are you going to do?" Emelia was worried Rosamund had not thought things through.

"I don't know," Rosamund began. "Perhaps today I can dream. Perhaps tomorrow I can learn what freedom means."

"Freedom? My dear girl, you've been cut off financially and exiled from family. You show no signs of wanting to marry James. You have no practical training to support yourself. You have no other marriage prospects, a situation not improved by what's just happened. And do not tell anyone else about how you got home from the ball, or your reputation will be utterly ruined. Your situation is precarious." Emelia did not hold back.

Rosamund suddenly shifted the conversation. "I haven't been fair to James. Someone at the ball said something."

"Said what?" the admission intrigued Emelia.

"It's still too raw," Rosamund replied. "But can you believe it? After all the time I've spent with him, I don't know the name of the woman he wanted to marry."

Emelia did not know the name either.

"Was she Caroline?" Rosamund asked, more to herself than Emelia.

"But your father—" Emelia stopped before finishing the statement.

"I don't need his approval. If I please, I can marry James, or someone else. If I read James correctly, his interest in me has never been about my father's money and influence."

"Do you actually love him?" Emelia bluntly asked.

Rosamund avoided the question. "I'll continue to see James, but now, I won't use him—as you put it—to create space for things just to happen, so that my father's sins and money don't dictate my fate."

Emelia studied Rosamund's face. Did the poor girl not realise that her father, with all his trespasses and sterling, had determined her fate? No money, no familial support, and no protection from how England rips apart women in penury abandoned by family and society. Whatever freedom Rosamund had should not be used for idle dreaming or assuaging remorse about how she had treated James.

"What is it?" Rosamund was unsure what Emelia was thinking.

"Child, guilt doesn't lead to love."

Rosamund bristled. "Neither will fear. You say my position is precarious. I cannot deny it. Whether I act from guilt or fear doesn't matter. I must approach marriage as a cold, calculating transaction. Just as my father always wanted. Even in his humiliation I am defeated. In your union, you have love—a love that sustains you in trying times. But can I—a woman without skills, banished from her family without a penny—expect love? Poverty, and what it forces a desperate woman to do, is a poor source of sustenance and serendipity."

—

Mrs. Hornby instructed the maid to empty the bowl into which she had wrung the sweat mopped from the young man's body. Dr. Hoyland had come and gone, diagnosing a fever of unknown origin. All that could be done was to keep the boy comfortable until the sickness burned out. The malady had a thorough grip, and the doctor had cautioned that the patient might exhibit delirium until the fever broke.

Emelia had nursed her share of fevers, but in her experience, the patient had not suffered alone for as long as James apparently had. She only learned he was ill when she went to talk to him after Rosamund's unexpected visit. He was in a frightful condition—prostrate on the floor, with only a sweat-soaked nightshirt and threadbare blanket covering his shivering body. She had no idea how much time he had been in such a bad way. She had cleaned him up and started applying cold cloths to his forehead and keeping him, his nightshirt, and the sheets as dry as possible. The young man appeared to have no idea what was happening. In fitful sleeping, he mumbled as if dreaming, but she could make no sense of the gibberish. It was again late, and with no more to be done until morning, she went to bed.

His throat was parched. James needed water but wanted warmth. Get up, he urged himself, get a drink. No, stay under the covers. Stay with her. All night. With her warm hand, her green eyes. Is she real? Who's Caroline? Tonight, or cat o' nine tails. Where is she? Down this hallway, past those alcove windows. Out in the night, lightning, no thunder. Follow the music. There. Alone, in that gown. Say what to her? Her back is turned. Touch it. Her hair is down. Feel it. But it's not dark. It's not hers. Can't see her face. It cures madness. She laughs. That soft laugh. Say what to her? Jasmine petals falling. Did she?

A spasm jolted James awake. Cold, drenched, and trembling, he forced himself onto the edge of the bed, blanket straining around his shoulders, stone tiles frigid against his bare feet. He struggled to breathe. He crashed to the floor, the sorrow unrelenting.

Chapter 14
For What?

"And all for what?" Geoffrey Hancock pleaded. "Hugh, why are you ruining your daughter?"

"It's none of your business." Hugh Colborne did not care for the inquisition.

"You've wronged her," Geoffrey was going to air his distemper. "She didn't send Bingham away. She didn't ask that Turk to humiliate you. Good God, man, in front of everyone, you called your daughter a bitch. I'm glad the Turk slapped you. Someone needed to."

Silence descended between the two men. They had been business partners for as long as either of them could remember. Neither came from privilege. They shared a visceral dislike of the aristocracy and a passion to hasten its death. The one irritant in their relationship was how Hugh treated his wife and daughter.

Geoffrey had played the surrogate uncle for Rosamund after he and Hugh had moved to Constantinople to expand the business when Rosamund and Margaret were young. He had enjoyed bringing Rosamund gifts, joking with her, and, as she grew older, being another adult with whom she could talk. Hugh and Katherine, he had commented to his wife before she died, treated Rosamund—and each other—with inexplicable indifference. Rosamund was a wonderful companion for Margaret. Katherine had shown fortitude and compassion as a nurse during the war. But something about the mother and daughter vexed the father.

As Rosamund grew older, Katherine had become withdrawn, almost reclusive at times. The haste with which Hugh had wanted Rosamund to marry when the time came, and Katherine's apathy about it, was distasteful, especially that ugliness with Henry Wattling.

"Hugh, she wants to continue seeing Bingham," Geoffrey ended the silence. "And I suspect you were, before the ball, bribing the boy to marry her. But now you're cutting her off, casting her out. Don't you realise what that will do to her prospects for a respectable marriage? Bingham is at least in the realm of the respectable."

"Bingham's a fool," Hugh struggled to control himself. "And my daughter played him for one. You heard her at the ball. Now she appears to be playing you for a fool, too."

"Rosamund did not ask me to talk to you," Geoffrey brushed off the insult before going deeper into where he was not welcome. "Why is Rosamund afraid of you? I saw her jump. Everyone did. The Turk, too. He gave you that last slap for it. Why's she afraid of you?"

"Afraid of me?" Hugh laughed. "Geoffrey, you more than anybody have witnessed the disrespect she has heaped on me for years. That's not the behaviour of someone who's afraid of me. Being soft of head and heart, you think she's a spirited, intelligent young woman. But you don't know what you're talking about."

"Hugh," Geoffrey moderated his tone, "she's your only child. What are you doing?"

"Letting her go. Letting her determine her own fate."

"It's cruel," Geoffrey picked up his hat and cane. "But perhaps this will register with you. It's not good for business to call your daughter a bitch in society and discard her to a fate that women rightfully dread. Who wants to do business with such a man?"

"Plenty of people," Hugh mumbled as Geoffrey departed. "Plenty of people."

Hugh went to the window of his study, crossed his arms, and looked across the garden toward the meadow and trees beyond. Geoffrey was indispensable with the finances of the business, but he failed to see the entire game, think strategically, and execute the decisive moves required for victory.

Empire, he had repeatedly told Geoffrey, unfolds in predictable and profitable patterns. Either military power gains a foothold and fosters commerce, or commerce develops and draws in military power. From these military-economic cycles empire sinks roots. Jurists and religionists arrive to bless and justify enough of what soldiers and merchants do for empire to pretend to have some higher purpose. British arms secured victory in the Crimean war. The commercial wave in Ottoman lands was surging toward a lucrative crest. Lawyers and missionaries were arriving in greater numbers to excuse the exercise of military and economic power. This was not old-style empire, but it was still imperial in cloaking raw power in the raiment of civilisation.

Hugh believed that other merchants would not risk profits over how a powerful merchant in the good graces of the British and Ottoman empires parented an unruly daughter who was—it would be simple to promulgate through the gossips—becoming hysterical. He had often seen her from this window, walking in that wilder space outside his property. She had strolled across that meadow and among those trees before the Sultan's ball, often with that dim barrister—and he was not finished dealing with that ponce either. But her walks alone in that place had increased after the ball, perhaps to ponder a future she had not anticipated.

He clenched his crossed arms and pressed them against his chest. He saw opportunity before most. He took risks when many hesitated. He exploited his setbacks while others licked their wounds. At times, it was too easy. He could herd people like sheep to get what he wanted, all without the advantages that heredity and tradition provided the degenerate gentry. His instinct and discipline ensured that his machinations almost always produced wealth—and the opportunity for more. In the gladiatorial contests that he waged across empires, law was a weapon and justice a ruse. In his world, blessed were the ruthless.

A growl grew deep in his throat to keep his demons down. Dark things that disturbed and disrupted his power. He was stalked by a primal anger that could savage his cold, steely calculations. A primitive wrath that became dangerous when he was confronted with a refusal to bend to his will. He hated being defied, and when he was, his rage was vengeful and rapacious.

He had tried to reason with Katherine. He attempted to persuade her not to do it. He emphasised her responsibilities as a mother. He explained why it was not fitting for the wife of a man of his stature in society. He lectured her that he knew best how she should serve Queen and country. He mocked her for believing that she could help because she was a woman without wit, wiles, or worldliness. He commanded her not to do it because he was her husband and master. He had warned her that there would be consequences. But she had defied him. She had gone to the military hospital. He hated being defied.

—

With James still weak after the fever, Emelia kept the world away to facilitate his recuperation, which included stopping her husband from bothering the boy with work. But today she made an exception. While he slept into the late morning, she put the envelope on his nightstand, propped up so that he would see it when he woke.

She returned in the early afternoon, knocked on the door, and entered without knowing whether James was awake. She found him sitting on the edge of the bed, and she saw that he had opened the envelope.

"Have I thanked you for nursing me through my illness?" James asked. "I can't remember from one day to the next whether I have."

"Yes, you have done so sufficiently and need not do so again," Emelia responded before pointing at the envelope on the nightstand. "Please forgive me, but what did Miss Colborne say?"

"What?" James sounded very tired.

"What did Rosamund say in her note? It's none of my business, but she came here and was concerned about you." Emelia embellished Rosamund's unexpected visit.

"It's an invitation for tea on Saturday." James was parched and weary.

"Come to tea for what?" Emelia pressed.

"For tea." James suddenly wondered whether Mrs. Hornby knew what the invitation truly portended. "Did you expect Rosamund to say something else?"

When Mrs. Hornby did not respond, he continued. "She knows, doesn't she?"

"Knows what?" Emelia was perplexed.

Now James was confused. "Do you have something to tell me about Rosamund?"

Emelia sat down opposite James on the creaky chair by his small window. She told him what had happened at the ball after he had left to deal with the murder on the ship. She repeated Rosamund's telling of the events, but given James's still weak condition, she did not mention Mr. Colborne's claim that James had made a secret bargain with him concerning Rosamund.

When the young man did not react, she said, "There's more."

"More?" James had not absorbed what he had just heard.

She nodded, but she told James that he would have to hear the rest from Rosamund.

James dropped his head and stared at the floor. "I guess I'll get more than tea."

———

With Donald departed for Smyrna, James ill, and Mehmed absent without explanation, the court had fallen behind on cases and correspondence when Edmund and Henry met on Friday afternoon to see what had accumulated during the week after the Sultan's ball. After reading through the pile, Edmund and Henry sat in silence staring at three unsettling documents.

The first was an expensively printed petition from something called the "English Committee of Constantinople" that contained a declaration of grievances from British merchants against the Supreme Consular Court and a call for Parliament to abolish it. The second was a despatch from the Foreign Office enclosing a formal demand from the Law Officers of the Crown that Judge

Hornby explain his arrest and detention of a person on a Swedish ship—actions, the Law Officers asserted, the judge had no authority to take. The third was a note from Cevdet Ahmed, the Ottoman Minister of Justice. Ahmed Pasha informed the court that a Turkish military vessel had removed the crew of an English tugboat, the *Enoch Wright*, from a Greek ship grounded by a storm and detained them, over the protests of the tug's Austrian captain, for committing "piratical acts" in violation of Turkish waterway and port regulations.

Edmund and Henry had not expected to find the court—within a single week—attacked in Parliament by British merchants, challenged by Her Majesty's Government, and confronted by a brazen Ottoman violation of treaty law. Worse, they knew that Ambassador Bulwer must have facilitated the petition to Parliament and the complaints about the Swedish ship incident. Bulwer and British merchants had launched a coordinated political offensive in Constantinople and London against the court's authority, legitimacy, and existence.

"How," a bewildered Henry asked, "did we not know about this?"

"We have no spies," Edmund replied. "Apparently Lord Stratford's ferrets did not know either, or he would have informed us, as he did about other skulduggery. And we did not read the signs right in front of us—merchant opposition to our reforms, Bulwer's support for British commerce, and political protection for the court leaving with Stratford."

Henry picked up the petition from the English Committee of Constantinople and the demand from the Law Officers of the Crown. "God, this is devious. Bulwer and the merchants have colluded to have the Government damage you and Parliament destroy the court."

Edmund nodded, realising that Bulwer could also manipulate the *Enoch Wright* incident in this assault on the court. Bulwer could claim, and perhaps already had, that such a blatant Ottoman violation of the treaty showed how little influence he, as head of the consular court, had with the Sublime Porte. And worse, he retained a Turkish law clerk—a Mussulman fanatic who had confronted Christians and slapped an Englishman—and was expending resources of Her Majesty's Treasury on a legal code for an ungrateful and still-uncivilised Ottoman empire.

Henry saw that the judge knew things were in a bad way. "I'm sorry, Edmund, after all you've done, and for what you've sacrificed to improve law and justice in two empires."

A knock on the door pre-empted Edmund's response, and Frederick Guarracino stepped into the office. "Judge, the Minister of Police is here."

"Safveti Rifat?" Edmund was taken aback.

"Rifat Pasha," Frederick confirmed. "He wouldn't tell me why he's here."

Frederick served Turkish coffee while Edmund and Rifat Pasha engaged in ritual greetings and pleasantries. With the coffee imbibed, the minister asked for Judge Hornby's help in locating Mehmed. The Ministry of Police needed to question him in investigating a crime that Hugh Colborne claimed Mehmed had committed at the Sultan's ball.

Edmund lifted his eyes from the dregs in his cup. "Hugh Colborne brought a criminal complaint to the Ministry of Police against Mehmed for what happened at the ball?"

"Yes, for assault," Rifat responded. "We were surprised because it showed that a prominent Englishman has confidence in our justice system."

Edmund struggled with how to respond. Colborne had no respect for Ottoman law, but the merchant's scheme with this manoeuvre was not immediately clear.

"Can you help us find Mehmed?" Rifat Pasha asked.

Edmund held up his hand to gain a few moments for his confusion to clear. Gradually, Colborne's gambit surfaced—gain more concession contracts by flattering the Ottomans and force him to protect a Turk who had humiliated an Englishman in the Sultan's palace at a ball honouring the British ambassador.

Backed into a corner, Edmund decided to fight. "Your Excellency, I don't know where Mehmed is, but his whereabouts are not the critical issue."

Rifat Pasha looked perplexed. "We must find him to investigate and, if necessary, detain and try him. It is the critical issue."

"No, Your Excellency, you don't have jurisdiction," Edmund countered.

"He's Turkish. He is accused of committing a crime in the Sultan's palace. We have jurisdiction. Even the English merchant recognises this," responded Rifat.

"Your Excellency, Mehmed is a person protected under the capitulations while he is a clerk with the court. The Foreign Minister approved this status. Thus, you don't have jurisdiction to investigate, detain, or prosecute a crime allegedly committed against a British subject by a person under the legal protection of Her Majesty's Government," Edmund explained.

The Minister of Police did not know what to say. The capitulations had never come up in the ministry's discussions about

Colborne's claim. The talk had focused on the implications of an Englishman bringing a legal complaint to Turkish authorities—especially the lack of confidence in the English court that the complaint exposed. Indeed, the complaint's political importance was discussed beyond the Ministry of Police.

Edmund let the silence linger for a few moments more before saying, in a tone bordering on the belligerent, "Tell Colborne to bring his claim to me."

After Rifat Pasha left, Edmund asked his *cavass*, Halil, to find Mehmed. Halil reported back later that he could not locate him, but he did learn that Mehmed had apparently escaped the clutches of some violent miscreants. Halil suspected they were rogues hired to attack Mehmed for what had taken place at the ball. With the Ottoman police and thugs hunting for him, Edmund was afraid for Mehmed's safety and his future.

—

Hasan took steps to ensure that the men assigned to follow him did not know where he was going. He lost them easily, which meant they were not particularly skilled. Tasking men to track him meant that the police, now two weeks past the Sultan's ball, faced mounting pressure to find Mehmed—and for reasons unrelated to the English merchant's complaint.

On the first weekend following the ball, radicals had disseminated a pamphlet around Constantinople criticising the "spineless and supine Sultan, sovereign only in his flaccid dreams." The pamphlet excoriated European oppression of Turkish sovereignty and incited patriotic Turks to "Slap an Englishman Today." The pamphlet was signed by "The Mussulman Fanatic."

Immediately after the pamphlet appeared, young Turkish men wielding dress gloves began slapping Englishmen in the streets of Constantinople. The new British ambassador was fulminating to the Sublime Porte about these "uncivilised outrages." *The Levant Herald* made matters worse by translating the pamphlet and claiming that the author was the Turk who worked for Judge Hornby.

Hasan knew Mehmed was not involved, but the radicals had given the Ottoman authorities reason to link him with seditious material. That Mehmed was hiding indicated the young man was, unlike at the Sultan's ball, letting calculation prevail over impulse. Many believed that hiding signified guilt, and Hasan was sure that Mehmed wanted nothing more than to face and rout his accusers. But the boy was showing guile in staying beyond the reach of the police.

However, he wanted to slap Mehmed for not following his advice to remain inconspicuous at the ball. Nothing important was at stake in a petty spat between a pompous father and a petulant daughter, neither of whom Mehmed had even met before that night. Now the boy had enemies at the palace, the Sublime Porte, and the English colony.

Hasan found Mehmed as arranged. Mehmed was in good spirits, considering the circumstances. They dispensed with pleasantries to address the critical issues. Mehmed said that he had yet to have any encounters with the police. He had a safe, and ironic, place to hide. No easy way to escape his predicament had occurred to him, other than to continue to hide until something happened to reduce the danger. The *mufti* wanted to make sure an ironic hiding place was, in fact, safe. But he put that worry aside to offer his best idea for Mehmed to come out of hiding.

"Agree with Hornby. Accept that you are a protected person under the capitulations," Hasan said. "Then, the merchant's assault claim against you must be brought in the English court. Any Turkish proceeding against you related to the pamphlet must involve Hornby, and any judgement by a Turkish tribunal must have his consent."

"Save myself by hiding behind the capitulations?" Mehmed was disgusted.

"The Foreign Minister agreed that you would be a protected person while you worked at the court. Hornby is demanding that the merchant's claim be brought in the English court because you are protected by the capitulations," Hasan argued.

"What I did at the ball, and what I'm accused of writing in that pamphlet, are beyond my duties at the court and fall outside my status as a protected person." Mehmed recalled the tutorial he had received from Hornby during the *Sinclair* case.

"But," Hasan stroked his beard anxiously, "you can't hide forever. There are too many spies and informants about. If you don't accept English protection, either you surrender to the police, which I don't recommend, or you leave Turkey—exile yourself—as soon as possible."

Mehmed began glancing around. "We shouldn't stay here any longer."

Hasan grabbed Mehmed's arm. "They have Ali. He's in the *Bagnio*."

Mehmed's eyes flashed with the fear that any mention of the infamous prison incited. "Ali's involved with the pamphlet?"

"I don't know," Hasan whispered. "But you saw his anger. He might have fallen in with dangerous people."

Hasan gripped Mehmed's arm tighter. "They'll torture him. He'll say anything to make it stop. He'll say you were involved because that's what they want to hear."

Mehmed wrenched his arm free. "Torture is banned. By law. The ban is absolute. And Ali wouldn't break. For all our disagreements, Ali has honour. He has courage."

Hasan put his hand on the back of Mehmed's neck and brought their foreheads together. "Listen to me. The alleged crimes are crimes against the Sultan. They'll torture him. He'll tell them anything. They'll find you. They'll torture you. You'll say anything to make it stop. Accept English protection or go into exile. Do you hear me?"

Mehmed shut his eyes, shaken by his teacher's conviction that the law meant nothing, and that torture would destroy a man.

"Do you hear me?" Hasan whispered, his voice fearful.

"Yes," Mehmed disengaged from Hasan. "But there must be another way."

Hasan watched Mehmed disappear into the bustle of the street.

"And all for what?" the *mufti* angrily muttered, pulling his cloak tight and disappearing into an alleyway, while guilt devoured his hope.

Chapter 15
Stone Turbans

She should leave. Lingering served no purpose. She lived close by—proximity that made this place so advantageous. Still, she hesitated and looked about. Her eyes fell upon what, in nervously executing her task, she had not taken in—the cypress trees populating the cemetery.

She entered the shade of a fine specimen, retrieved a handkerchief, and—in a manner as ladylike as she could manage—swabbed an unladylike amount of perspiration from her forehead. The cool of the shade enabled some physical and mental easing, but she did not want the frisson of the deed to dissipate entirely. "When are you going to start living?" Maggie had incessantly asked her. Well, perhaps today.

In the cypress shadow, Rosamund thought about Maggie. As girls, they had been inseparable. As young women, they had drifted apart. Maggie had navigated society's expectations of a marriageable virgin without hesitation or illusions, never playing the victim of patriarchal conspiracy. Once old enough to marry, Maggie patrolled the soirées of Constantinople like a privateer empowered with a letter of marque from Her Majesty to chase down bachelors and sink, burn, or take a prize. Maggie mocked the priggish advice in the marriage guidebook maternally placed in her bedroom. Margaret Elizabeth Hancock had a sense of herself, possessed, in her own words, of "a woman's desires and a lady's common sense." She wanted "a man in my bed, a husband in my house, and children in my life." Maggie was nearly there—several months wed to a strapping Royal Navy lieutenant and already with child.

She, in contrast, had refused to conform. Maggie grew exasperated and angry with her "holier-than-thou disdain" for society and how women lived. She demanded answers to questions that Maggie and others did not want to ask, let alone answer. Why, with transformation everywhere—sail giving way to steam, post to telegraph, local bazaars to free trade, landed gentry to professional men, dogma to science, uncivilised to civilised—did one thing remain unchanged and seemingly immutable? Why was a woman without a husband, family, or money made a wretched thing? But the longer her questions were ignored, the louder Maggie's admonition became: "A woman can live and love without answers."

She looked across the cemetery at various headstones topped with stone turbans. She left the shade, walked a few yards, and paused before a turban so finely chiselled that it seemed composed of swathes of silk. She traced a finger along its surface.

She stopped and withdrew her hand. The feel of the stone brought back a childhood memory—a picnic with Maggie and her parents somewhere near the Black Sea. While Mrs. Hancock prepared the meal, she and Maggie, followed by Mr. Hancock, had explored the environs. Over a ridge, they stumbled upon a graveyard. Almost to a headstone, the stone turbans had been bludgeoned off. Decapitated turbans lay scattered here and shattered there.

She and Maggie knelt to touch a lichen-covered, partially buried turban. Maggie asked, "Father, what happened?"

Mr. Hancock replied, "Hatred that would not let the dead rest in peace."

In that childhood moment, Rosamund did not understand. But now she knew that hate could deprive the living of peace. That wounds without scars fester most deeply.

But could she live without hate? For too long, her anger felt honourable and just because it illuminated right and wrong in the world without exposing the suffering that brought clarity. But the more her acting out in society proved of no consequence, the more it resembled an animus that banished all else from her heart and would not let her live in peace.

And all that past pique meant nothing now that her future was in her own hands. Being cut off and sent back to England was cruel, but strangely, she sensed the enmity was starting to seep away, permitting her, perhaps, to live and love without answers. This curious, unexpected shift opened an ambiguous space rather than a terrifying void.

Today, she had explored it. Not in another too-clever-by-half display of indignation that no one understood, but through a simple, silent, and solitary act for another. Could more quiet, tactile, and helping acts let her live in peace? Make her part of something else? Of someone else? Someone real rather than the mythical figments she conjured in her bed from an ancient age of heroes that had never been.

Other stone turbans nearby were plain, reflecting a lack of funds or an artistic disinclination to mimic cloth in stone. The most arresting featured only the elemental shape of a turban, the bare essence of the thing. These abstractions looked like inscrutable statues of an ancient people. Once, she recalled, James likened searching old, musty court decisions to what antiquarians did. After digging through centuries of sediment, the antiquarian discovered some dusty artefact but had no idea what importance it held in a vanished society. Was this potsherd the remnant of a sacred chalice or all that remained of a chamber pot?

The stone turbans were unknowable remnants of persons once alive. People still living remained abstractions to her, persons she had not dared to know. Katherine—the elemental shape of a woman whose life she did not know and had never asked her mother to share. James—the bare essence of a man in whom others saw goodness that she had lacked the decency to appreciate. Perhaps she was—to her mother, James, and others—an inscrutable abstraction with a head and heart of stone.

Farther down the cemetery she saw large, carved headstones that resembled the grand turbans that aged Turks wore in the old city. She loved the style, elegance, and boldness of those traditional turbans. They made a statement in silk about a people who had seen the new become the ancient many times across the centuries. But over the years, she saw fewer and fewer in her trips into old Stamboul. She recalled something that Lord Stratford said at an otherwise forgettable embassy function, "Change must come, but I cringe when Turks abandon the noble turban for the Parisian top hat."

As with almost everything that Stratford said, this quip was enigmatic, capable of multiple interpretations, leaving the crafty statesman to decide what meaning best served Her Majesty and the British empire at the decisive moment. For her at least, Stratford's regret about turbans and top hats meant that a civilisation could change without discarding what made it distinct—a sentiment lost in a world where the civilised hectored the uncivilised and, in such arrogance, never valued those wearing veils and bonnets.

She focused on one of the large stone turbans, and given the glare of the sun, she shaded her eyes with her hand. Suddenly, the turban and its headstone appeared to move. The pulse of surprise ebbed when the walking statue transfigured into a thin, bespectacled young man wearing a turban much too large for his head. She retreated into the shade of the cypress tree. She watched him stroll to a crumbling plinth standing amidst some long-neglected graves. He bent down, shifted a rock at the base of the plinth, and retrieved from the crevice the corded bundle that she had put there. She watched the large turban bob away as the young man continued his mission. She stepped from the shadow, popped open her parasol, and started her journey home.

Chapter 16

Forgiveness

It was so typical of his father. Rather than talk face-to-face, the coward wrote a note. His father's crabbed hand was as clear as his distaste for his son. He made the sign of the cross and opened the note.

Henry,

Hugh Colborne visited me, Tuesday past, to encourage me to advise you to call again on his daughter. He believes that she will receive you. If so, God does work in mysterious ways.

Garrett Wattling

He signed his full name? In a note to his son? Why did paternal disdain run so deep? Yes, he had failed as a soldier and in commerce, but he was then adrift, taken where British power cleared pathways for the next generation of young men. He went along, never questioning conventions, never challenging society's expectations, and never reflecting on the purpose of it all. He was not nobility, but he behaved like the sons of aristocrats. He treated privilege, derived from paternal wealth rather than ancestral blood, as a right to things rather than a responsibility.

But why did the father insult what saved the son from drunkenness, violence, and lechery? From what opened the son's eyes to a wasteful life? He did not expect his father, Anglican for appearances only, to have a road-to-Damascus reaction to his turn toward Christ. The peace he found in forgiveness was sublime, and beyond his ability to communicate to his father. But was some compassion for a son's resurrection from gin, gaols, and dollymops too much to ask? A kind word, a heartfelt handshake? Instead, his father spewed cold, cutting ridicule.

His irritation almost made him miss the nub—"she will receive you." He read the note again, focusing on the information about Rosamund. "Call again upon his daughter." He still felt it, painfully reminding him that, despite his prayers and penance, it had not smouldered into ash.

His courtship of Rosamund had been traditional, logical, liturgical—handsome son of wealthy merchant should marry beautiful daughter of wealthy merchant with the blessing of family, society, industry, church, and empire—amen. But the woman proved unconventional. He had not noticed that Rosamund was different until it was too late. He blamed his blindness on the embarrassment of bungling his stint in the army and his father's withering impatience during his time as a merchant. But his excuses, he knew, were deluded. The truth was uglier. He had simply assumed that she was his to have. He performed the pageantry of courtship but did not treat her as a person. Lust was the deepest feeling he had when courting her. Like the unsparing mirror, her rejection reflected his depravity.

"She will receive you." He had gone earlier in the year to apologise and witness Christ's role in his new life, but she had not been receptive. He had accepted responsibility for his failings. He had asked for forgiveness, but her response had left him tormented.

She did not forgive him as expected. He had convinced himself that she would heed the Christian duty to forgive those who trespass against us. At the very least, forgiving him would have been good manners, a polite formality no matter how devoid of sincerity. Instead, she had demanded to know why, with God's forgiveness, she had to excuse his drinking, violence, and whoring.

Before he could reply, she had coldly said, "You just apologised for your behaviour after I refused you—*after.*"

He recalled stammering that he feared he had hurt her because of his sins. That her forgiveness would be a blessing. That he had changed with Christ's help.

She gave him a sharp look before emphasising, again, that the sins for which he wanted forgiveness happened after she had rejected him. She had to remind him that her rejection had nothing to do with transgressions not yet committed. She was not upset when he went around drinking, gambling, and fighting. She was not hurt when he put his cock into prostitutes. He should, she had added for good measure, ask them to forgive those trespasses.

He also remembered that she had to pause to collect herself before passing final judgement. "You don't need my forgiveness for your trespasses against others. Jesus can handle the sins you committed before and after we parted."

And she was correct. But deep inside, he could not abide the justness of her rejection and her refusal to forgive him. He did not, and still had not, apologised for his behaviour before she ended the courtship.

He read the note from his father again. Why does Hugh Colborne believe Rosamund will receive him now? Colborne had wanted Rosamund to marry him and was apoplectic when she refused. Does Colborne know something that might make Rosamund receptive? Was the merchant signalling that he would make it worthwhile for Henry to rescue a disinherited, desperate Rosamund? Or had she committed carnal sins with that toady barrister that made her need a husband who could put Christ into her life?

Henry's unexpected appearance at the Colborne residence caused confusion among the servants, but Rosamund escorted him into the library, where they sat opposite each other across a small, round table. She was irritated that this part of her past had reappeared again.

She spoke first, "Tell me why you're here."

"It has come to my attention that you wished me to call on you," Henry nervously began.

Her head pulled back in surprise. "It has come to your attention? Is God speaking to you again, Henry? Like when God told you to denounce Mohammed before a mosque?"

Henry faltered, and she continued, "Who brought it to your attention?"

"I received a note that said you would receive me." Henry's voice almost broke.

"You received a note? Did I send you a note?" Rosamund demanded.

Henry hesitated, and Rosamund turned the screws. "Receive you? I didn't ask to receive anything from you. Do you want to sprinkle me with holy water? What do you want?"

Henry retreated. "My father gave me a note."

"Your father gave you a note? Henry, why are you here?" Rosamund was exasperated.

"Your father told my father that you would receive me."

"My father told your father?" she asked with surprise, having believed that, in cutting her off from family and money, her father had finished with ruining her life.

"I didn't know whether your father approached my father because you were no longer courting that barrister, given what happened at the ball," Henry lamely offered.

"That barrister? Oh, Henry, tell me that you're not jealous." Rosamund's ire was rising.

Henry did not answer.

"You thought that I'd receive you as a suitor? Have you forgotten why I refused you? After being drummed out of the army, you strutted around as a pretend merchant in tailored finery purchased with profits you couldn't earn on your own. Despite your military and commercial failures, you assumed aristocratic airs while blind to your parasitical existence. You constantly tried to kiss and touch me, forcing your unwelcome hands and body on me. You treated me like sexual property our predatory patriarchy bestows upon its sons. And you thought that I'd receive you because you've found religion? Because, like when the British empire runs out of excuses for its predations, God is on your side?"

"I've changed, Rosamund. I acknowledge my sins. What happened was my fault. I have asked for your forgiveness, which you withhold out of spite for a man who no longer exists," Henry became agitated. "And you shouldn't see that barrister anymore. Given what has happened, no one believes that you'll marry him, except that fool."

Henry did not attend the ball and had only heard the tittle-tattle about the bitch-and-slap affair, including the gossiping about Rosamund's manipulation of James. He expected Rosamund to lash out again, but she did not. She went mute as those stinging words at the ball rushed back—"When you're done with him." When Rosamund did not speak, Henry sensed that he had drawn blood.

"We both know, everyone knows, that you must marry given the fate you face. I love you, and, with God's help, I can make you happy." Henry reached his hand toward Rosamund.

She leaned back, away from his touch, and laughed sardonically. "What every girl wants to hear—a man needs a god to make her happy."

Henry's hand retreated as if singed. "Why do you condemn me, mock my beliefs, and loathe my feelings for you? Is there no empathy in your heart for what human frailty can do to a man?"

"I mock beliefs that hate other faiths. I condemn any man—frail or not—who professes love while preying on a woman wronged," she shot back.

Before he could speak, she was on her feet. "Your feelings? Did God the Father tell my father to tell your father to tell you to have feelings for me? Or has it come to your attention in some lurid or self-abusive way that you have feelings for me?"

"I'll pray that our sins are forgiven." Henry stood to leave.

"Pray for yourself," she answered. "Get out."

Chapter 17
Freely

James again sent his regrets to Rosamund concerning another invitation to tea. He blamed his continuing recovery from the fever, but in truth, he was not ready to see her. He wondered whether she would be offended, especially given that she apparently had things to tell him. However, another invitation soon arrived for tea on the Saturday next. Her note came with no sympathy about his recuperation, no harsh words about the declined invitations, and nothing to enlighten him about what Rosamund had to say about events following the Sultan's ball.

Despite Mrs. Hornby's efforts to keep her husband away, the judge managed to cajole James to work in his room. He asked James to analyse the Swedish ship incident. Edmund provided the despatch in which the Law Officers of the Crown asserted that he had no authority to arrest and detain the suspect. He also tasked James to untangle the issues raised by the *Enoch Wright* affair. Edmund made it clear that he would not retreat from the positions that he had already staked out—the Law Officers were wrong about the Swedish ship episode and the Ottomans had blatantly violated the treaty concerning the *Enoch Wright*. Any retreat, he advised James, would weaken his authority and credibility—something he could not do with the court under attack in Constantinople and London. Surprised, James wanted to know about the attack, but Edmund ordered James to find support for his positions and leave the law and politics to him.

James found the work therapeutic in ending bodily malaise and burning away mental fogginess. But his improving physical vigour and cognitive clarity created tension concerning what the judge had ordered him to do. The deeper he ploughed into his tasks, the more he felt that his role as a subordinate officer at the court required less subordination. "Bingham, write it, as instructed," had been the judge's parting words. Based on his study of the incidents, he believed that the judge was wrong about the law and the politics and needed to be set straight.

After working in his room for a few days, James finally felt sturdy enough to ride Bones to the court to present his analyses to Judge Hornby, but Edmund was not there. Henry Wroth greeted James, "It's about time, Mr. Bingham."

Henry had James sit in his office, where James apologised for his absence and enquired after Mehmed. Henry shrugged. Henry acknowledged that the illness was not James's fault but lamented that it had come at a bad time. He explained the court's travails after the Sultan's ball and the pressure the judge was under from Ambassador Bulwer, British merchants, the Foreign Office, the Law Officers of the Crown, Parliament, the Sublime Porte, and Englishmen slapped in the streets.

"Englishmen slapped in the streets?" James reacted to this peculiar item in the parade of problems.

Henry described the "Slap an Englishman Today" pamphlet and how many people, including the Sublime Porte, linked Mehmed with it, which probably explained why no one knew where the Turk was. James thought the notion that Mehmed was involved in sedition absurd, but he grasped that his colleague was in trouble.

"What can I do?" James asked.

"Get back to work."

"How about now?" James offered.

Henry clapped and rubbed his hands together. "There's our St. George."

He asked to see what James had produced on the Swedish ship incident, and James handed over his draft. Henry's countenance hardened as he read it.

"This isn't what Edmund instructed you to do," Henry said with concern. "Do you want me to brief the judge on this?"

"No," James responded firmly. "I need to do it. Given how the Law Officers reacted, he should re-think the justification he gave, even if he rejects what I recommend."

Henry nodded tentatively. "Are we wrong on the *Enoch Wright* as well?"

James shook his head. "Not necessarily. The *Enoch Wright* incident is more complicated, and more political, so we should discuss the issues more before deciding what to do."

After the judge returned to the court, James met with him and explained that he agreed with the Law Officers that the consular court did not have legal authority to arrest and detain the suspect on the Swedish ship.

Edmund was not pleased. "My actions saved lives—a just outcome. The dockworkers only stood down because the British government took jurisdiction to arrest and detain the suspect as a person protected under the capitulations."

James had been present that night and knew that Edmund's decisiveness had averted violence, but the outcome did not answer whether the law authorised what the judge did.

"Sir," James replied, "we have no jurisdiction over any sailor, even a British one, for crimes committed on a foreign vessel

navigating the high seas. We have no jurisdiction to board foreign vessels in Turkish ports to arrest and detain any person, including a British subject, for committing such crimes. And after the arrest, we didn't act as if we had authority over the suspect. We didn't conduct a preliminary examination, charge the
suspect, or start judicial proceedings as required by the court's
new rules. We simply handed him back when the Swedish legation informed us that a ship was ready to transport the suspect to
Stockholm for trial."

"What would you have me do?" Edmund complained. "Admit that I was wrong from beginning to end, just as the court
faces ferocious opposition here and in London?"

"No," James had a different approach in mind. "Explain to
the Law Officers that you engaged in an act of comity. You supported Sweden's exercise of its jurisdiction over the crime and
the suspect. Apologise for any confusion that might have arisen
between you and the Law Officers about your actions given the
volatile circumstances that night. Sweden won't protest. It has
physical custody of the suspect, so it doesn't care whether English law authorised your actions. The Law Officers will probably
close the matter, removing it as a source of friction between you
and the Government. The Sublime Porte has picked a much bigger fight over the *Enoch Wright* and has no reason to prolong the
Swedish ship controversy if you take the comity approach."

Edmund nervously fingered the document that James had
prepared. He sensed that he would not win the argument with
the Law Officers unless he changed course. If he remained stub-
born, his credibility could be damaged, perhaps irreparably in
the present circumstances. To his credit, James had found a way
out of this tight spot. But what James suggested did not reflect

what he did on that difficult night to avoid violence. The political need to devise a legal fiction to explain a just outcome made him uncomfortable.

"Prepare a draft despatch for my review," Edmund gruffly concluded.

James nodded.

Edmund then stared at James for several moments before adding, "Perhaps you should get deathly ill more often."

James drafted the despatch and spent the rest of the week at the court analysing the *Enoch Wright* case and processing routine legal work. Though often tired, he suffered no relapse. Late Friday morning, James decided to stretch his legs after a long session at the clerk's table.

He had not gone far when he heard someone call out, "Bingham, James Bingham!"

He turned to see Henry Wattling—finely dressed and sporting a well-trimmed beard—on a handsome chestnut horse. James nodded politely, but Henry was not in the mood for pleasantries. He walked his horse aggressively up to James but did not dismount.

"Forget," Henry leaned over his saddle to speak down at James, "about Rosamund Colborne."

James's only prior encounter with Wattling had been when Judge Hornby detained him and Silas Benson to prevent them from denouncing Mahomet at St. Sophia. In that event, Henry was passive—a demeanour inconsistent with the tales James had heard about the rake's penchant for whiskey, fisticuffs, and whores. But today, Henry's handling of his horse and intimidation from the saddle unsettled James.

Hugh Colborne had bullied him. His failure to stand his ground had stained his character and, perhaps, ruined his relationship with Rosamund. He wanted no quarrel with Wattling. But the taste of defeat and dishonour was still bitter, and he wanted no more retreats.

"Thank you, Mr. Wattling. Duly noted." The clipped reply summarily dismissed Henry, and James resumed his walk.

Henry blocked James's progress with his horse, which bumped into James.

"You don't seem to understand, Bingham. Don't see that woman anymore, to preserve your dignity."

James stroked the horse's neck, calming the creature and himself, while pondering how to respond to an evangelical's thuggish display of interest in his dignity.

"Tell me, Mr. Wattling," James finally replied. "Do you intend to continue your missionary work at Constantinople?"

The question caught Henry off guard.

"Bingham, temptation will lead you into sin. Think about what you have already done to have her. If you don't care about your dignity, attend to your soul." He reined his horse away from by being stroked by James.

James went cold and wanted to probe whether Henry knew about his contract with Colborne, but the desire to end this conversation prevailed.

"Mr. Wattling, you want something from me concerning Rosamund. I'm not sure what you want, or why it's appropriate for you to speak to me in this manner."

"You're a fool, and you're the only one who can't see it."

"Why do you care if I am a fool?"

"Because I was a fool. I was tempted. I was selfish. I failed as a man. As a Christian, I don't wish any other man to fall into sin as I did when I was weak."

"If I am a fool, then shame on me. If I am a weak, I will commit different sins from the ones you did," James jabbed back.

Henry did not appreciate the retort, twitching his riding crop as if tempted to thrash James with it. James asked again whether Henry planned to remain in the city doing the Lord's work, less interested in Henry's plans than whether he would have more such encounters in the future.

Henry backed his horse away from James. "Mr. Benson thinks it best if I do the Lord's work elsewhere. Missionaries are now needed in Africa and distant Asia more than here."

James considered mentioning Caroline, likely now in Africa, but he decided to keep that memory for himself. "When will you have your new calling?"

"Soon. But the decision is not mine."

"Will you be taking a wife?"

"What?" Henry did not anticipate the question.

"Have you found a woman to be your wife, who'll go with you to Africa or the Far East?"

"With God's help," Henry said through gritted teeth.

The odd way Henry made this declaration suggested that the conversation was over. Henry nudged his horse into a walk down the street, turning back to glower at James, as if to remind the barrister to preserve his dignity and save his soul.

On Saturday afternoon, James saddled Bones for his ride to the Colborne residence. He let Bones set a languid pace because he had left in plenty of time to arrive at the appointed hour. The amble provided him ample opportunity to ponder what might transpire over tea. Did Rosamund know what he had, in the words of Henry Wattling, "already done to have her"? Had Colborne pursued his remedy for breach of contract? What remained, if anything, between them? What about that recurring dream when he was ill, when he searched for Rosamund in the Sultan's palace but found Emma instead?

The dream did not answer whether Emma had actually loved him. That he would never know. It meant that he had loved her, but, through weakness, had been unable to admit and embrace that love when she lived. Could it all have been different? He hated the question, but he had to face his failures as a man. If he had asked for her hand earlier, when he was at so many moments on the cusp of the question, could he have set in motion events that might somehow have prevented her death?

Rosamund greeted him as she always did, with no indication that they met under transformed circumstances. Her outward demeanour was the same, but James sensed there was something different about her. She said he looked recovered and assumed he was back at the court. James replied that he had started work again. He shared that he was sorting out legal issues created by the actions of a former British naval officer employed as an Ottoman official concerning an English tugboat piloted by an Austrian captain that was in Turkish waters towing a Greek ship. The problem, Rosamund opined, had the makings of a joke, with the Turks least likely to laugh.

Tea arrived, and James, unusually, advanced the conversation past preliminaries. "You have something to tell me about what happened after the ball."

Rosamund did not hesitate. "My father has cut me off financially, is casting me out of the family, and is forcing me to return to England alone and penniless."

"What? Why?" James was shocked.

"In his eyes, I defied him three times that night. By not breaking my promise to you. By not stopping Mehmed from humiliating him. And by staying with Mehmed afterwards."

James did not know what to say. He never expected such disturbing news. His mind went to the dilemma that Rosamund faced, but he did not want his first reaction to focus on her dire future.

Rosamund continued, "My defiance confirmed my lack of respect for him, which I have often demonstrated, especially in my rejection of Henry Wattling and my performance at Lord Stratford's dinner. He apparently believed that my efforts with you were me bending to his will."

"He wanted you to marry me?" James sought to move the conversation toward whether Rosamund knew about the secret deal.

"He wanted to get rid of me. You were simply a means to an end," Rosamund replied, deciding not to admit her equivalent culpability.

James leaned back in his chair, perplexed. Had Hugh Colborne really said nothing to Rosamund about the contract? Should he tell her? Should he be honourable and acknowledge what he had done? Or did she know but could not flog him because he might be her only way to avoid a grim fate?

"When do you have to return to England?" he asked instead.

"My mother managed to have the deadline vaguely set some weeks hence. In the meantime, I intend to make choices freely, something women rarely do."

The sentiment was noble, James thought, but what choices would she have without money, family, skills, or a husband? He knew what his mother had suffered after his father absconded from marital responsibility. Should he ask for her hand and prevent a similar fate for Rosamund?

Rosamund partly read his mind. "You have practical concerns. How will I survive? Where will I get money? What kind of life can I have alone? Can a woman be free and fully alive?"

James nodded.

"Well," she continued earnestly. "I plan to become a prostitute to earn money that will set me up for other endeavours. But I need to practice first, and you can help me with that."

What she saw in his face made her laugh and clap her hands. "That reaction, Mr. James Bingham, is why I freely choose to see you. That reaction tells me you don't doubt my resolve."

James smiled with some embarrassment at the jest. Rosamund wanted to start over, casting aside the past and moving beyond the malign interference of others. Just the two of them. In that moment, he was not sure what he wanted, but he had an unexpected chance to find out.

"I choose the same," James said.

Chapter 18
Untouchable

The Foreign Minister was impressed. The suspect's whereabouts were never discovered. How the fugitive had influenced a community of people to communicate with different Ottoman officials remained undetected. But the same message emerged in missives and meetings—moving against him would cause trouble. It was an orchestrated campaign, and only one person knew how all the pieces fit together. It was not just the strategy's brilliance; it was also the nerve it took to execute the plan under duress.

The task of determining what to do with Mehmed once the police had detained him fell to Fuad Pasha. The Foreign Minister, after all, had sponsored Mehmed to work with the British court, so the Sultan decided Fuad Pasha, rather than the Minister of Justice, should clean up the mess. Like everyone else, the Foreign Minister had assumed the police, with their legion of agents and informants, would find and detain Mehmed for his alleged collaboration with radicals on producing and distributing seditious material.

The palace considered the "Slap an Englishman Today" pamphlet, with its criticism of the Sultan, as incitement for Turks to take up arms against the government, a crime punishable by death. The Imperial Criminal Code also made distributing written material inciting violence against the government punishable by death. In the aftermath of the pamphlet's dissemination, the pressure to punish those involved was intense. Few Ottoman officials believed that Mehmed was not somehow involved.

But the police could not locate Mehmed. Interrogation of other suspects produced little, if anything, linking Mehmed to the pamphlet. Several detained persons did not know who Mehmed was. Others knew Mehmed by reputation but claimed never to have interacted with him. The paucity of information created a desire within the police and at the Sublime Porte for more productive interrogations. With one exception, Rifat Pasha, the Minister of Police, quashed this desire by reminding everyone that, in the Imperial Criminal Code, the Sultan had prohibited the use of physical coercion to obtain evidence in criminal cases.

The argument that hiding proved Mehmed's guilt wore thin as the police found nothing proving his participation in the drafting or distribution of the pamphlet. The police matched the paper used to print the pamphlet with paper produced in Aleppo, suggesting that it was printed there and smuggled into Constantinople. A police raid on a printing press in Aleppo found copies of *The Levant Herald* that contained the Mussulman fanatic story and the English translation of the offending pamphlet. Surveillance before the Sultan's ball meant that the police had recorded Mehmed's movements. The records, which were complete for the period in question, provided no indication that Mehmed had met with radicals, handed anything to anyone, or left the city. His ability to escape surveillance after the ball suggested that Mehmed knew he was being watched beforehand and had made no effort to hide what he was doing.

As the fervour to capture Mehmed cooled, different Ottoman officials heard from various contacts that Mehmed was

not guilty and that continued efforts to find, detain, and interrogate him would create problems for the government. Initially, Fuad Pasha did not notice the similarities in the messages
being communicated to Ottoman officials. He started to sense
the strategy after the Sultan's chief religious advisor, the *Sheik
al-Islam,* sent him a note describing the support Mehmed had
among religious leaders because of his actions when faced with
the Christian missionaries' plan to denounce the Prophet, Peace
Be Upon Him. Ahmed Pasha, the Minister of Justice, received a
similar message from groups that disavowed radicalism but embraced nationalism as a way to achieve greater domestic stability and international security. These groups perceived Mehmed's
actions at the ball favourably—as those of a Turk standing up
to European bullying. Fuad rolled his eyes at Mehmed's behaviour being described as Turkish nationalism, but did the Sublime
Porte want to anger sensible nationalists?

Other Ottoman officials heard from persons involved in re-
formist movements tolerated by the government. Here, the message also cautioned the Porte not to proceed against Mehmed
without clear evidence of guilt. Convicting Mehmed for political
reasons, reformists argued, would provide the European powers
with ammunition to keep the capitulations. For reformists,
Mehmed's efforts at the British court demonstrated that he was
no radical but was training to help the Ottoman government regain sovereignty through changes that the government needed
to make.

The police interrogated persons associated with Ottoman legal reform, including Hasan. To the surprise of the police, Hasan
admitted to meeting with Mehmed, which meant the *mufti* did
not believe his student was involved with the seditious material.

The *mufti* emphasised that the British government protected Mehmed under the capitulations, which elevated the scrutiny of how Ottoman authorities handled him. Hasan informed the police that Mehmed, while working at the English court, had continued his studies in *sharia*, a choice incompatible with collaborating with radicals hostile to the Ottoman government and Islam's role in Turkish life.

Fuad had no way to prove that Mehmed had coordinated the same message through different sources. But it could be no coincidence that Islamists, nationalists, and reformists sought to protect him. Mehmed could not have undertaken this effort without supporters, people who provided Mehmed with places to hide and assistance with correspondence. The police never found out where he was, who was helping him, or how he managed such an extensive network. It was all impressive.

The Foreign Minister knew that the palace had reached a different conclusion. Even if innocent, Mehmed had challenged the power and authority of the Sublime Porte and the Sultan. Clever and well-connected, Mehmed had outwitted the police and coordinated a campaign to protect himself from the government. Fuad believed that the Sultan would not overrule his decision to stop investigating Mehmed. But the palace was unnerved. The truth about the pamphlet, whatever it was, could not explain how a hunted man had made himself untouchable. The palace still considered Mehmed dangerous; he was someone the palace would not let escape the next time.

Fuad knew he had to go to the *Bagnio*. Not to punish the perpetrators, who were in custody. He had to face the victim, a former law student, who was recovering from injuries suffered during *bastinado*. In the prison's makeshift medical ward, he found Ali on his blackened feet trying to walk, but it was clear that the pain was excruciating. Fuad sat in a chair at a small table near Ali's cot. Despite Fuad's entreaties, Ali would not sit. Fuad informed Ali that Mehmed was no longer under investigation. He apologised for what had happened and promised that those guilty would be punished according to the law.

"The law." The young man's voice was deep with derision.

Ali shifted his weight to balance the pain in his feet. "Who gave the order? You know that those who tortured me didn't act on their own. Tell me, great reformer, will the law punish those who gave the order? Will the law—will you—even ask that question? And what would the law have done had I given the Sultan an innocent head on a guilty plate?"

Fuad did not answer.

Ali hobbled to the nearest wall and leaned his back against it. Lightly, he began tapping his head on the wall, as if to dislodge something trapped by the pain.

"They didn't even ask about real threats to the Sultan. It really is incompetence from the *seraglio* to the *Bagnio*. Mehmed, a security threat? You are bigger fools than he is."

Ali paused tapping his head and shifted to equalise the agony in his feet. "Have you ever seen a man tortured?"

Fuad did not reply.

Ali resumed the tapping. "I am bruised and disoriented from being interrogated. Light streams in from a barred window near the top of a wall. It enters at such an angle that it expands within the cell. I close my eyes and tilt my head to catch warmth on my face. From behind me, someone enters and says, 'Kiss the stones, traitor. Kiss the stones you've pissed on.' The voice is new, and the command lacks conviction. It comes with reluctance, resentment, or perhaps fear."

Ali glanced at the Foreign Minister, who averted his eyes.

"Then something strikes the back of my knees, and I crumple into a kneeling position. I am kicked in the back, and I slam onto the floor. 'Kiss the stones, traitor. Kiss the stones before you shit on them.' Ropes tighten around my wrists and ankles, and my arms and legs are pulled so that I am stretched across the floor. Like the god of the Christians. My knees bend as my feet are lifted and lashed between boards, the bare soles facing up, as if in supplication. Someone kneels on my neck and back, and I can't breathe. 'Names,' he yells. I squirm under the weight to get my breath, and he strikes my head. 'Names,' comes a foul whisper. 'Give us names, and all this goes away. Just one name. You know who, then we don't hurt you. You walk away—untouched.'"

Ali shut his eyes and stopped tapping his head on the wall.

"The first blow came without warning. The pain," Ali's closed eyes tightened, "exploded."

The young man stayed still before continuing. "Two whips striking in cadence, pausing occasionally to let the cruelty spread, like poison, everywhere."

Fuad said nothing.

Ali rested his head against the wall for a few moments, then looked at Fuad, a grim smile breaking open the darkness of his filthy, matted beard. "Mehmed is free, and I am crippled. Your Excellency, what will the law do when I have my revenge and my justice?"

Fuad returned to the Sublime Porte and communicated his decision to the Sultan. Shortly thereafter, the police reported

that Mehmed was riding his horse on the streets of Constantinople.

Chapter 19
The Gift

James could see the pain in Edmund's face. He handed over the document that the judge had to read to the accused, as required by the nearly finalised Rules of Her Britannic Majesty's Supreme Consular Court and other Consular Courts in the Dominions of the Sublime Ottoman Porte.

Judge Hornby stared at the paper before lifting his head to speak. "Having heard the evidence, do you, Osman Mehmed, wish to say anything in answer to the charge?"

Edmund had to clear his throat before continuing. "You are not obliged to say anything unless you desire to do so, but whatever you say will be taken down in writing and may be given in evidence against you on your trial. And I give you clearly to understand that you have nothing to hope from any promise of favour, and nothing to fear from any threat, that may have been held out to you to induce you to make any admission or confession of your guilt, but whatever you now say may be given in evidence against you upon your trial, notwithstanding such promise or threat."

Mehmed stood. "I wish to say, again, that this court lacks jurisdiction."

"Mehmed," Edmund scratched his beard with frustration. "I have ruled that this court has jurisdiction. You are a person protected under the treaty between the British and Ottoman governments. Objecting to the court's jurisdiction again will not change that ruling. So, do you have anything to say in answer to the charges against you?"

Edmund's frustration had sources beyond Mehmed's obstinacy in rejecting the court's jurisdiction. When he had rebuffed the Ottoman Minister of Police and claimed jurisdiction over Hugh Colborne's assault charge against Mehmed, he did not believe that Colborne would bring a criminal claim before the court. However, Hugh had called Edmund's bluff. And Hugh had done so in ways suggesting that he wanted to hurt the court more than punish Mehmed. The merchant was not insisting on a jury trial, which put the case in Judge Hornby's hands rather than before a jury of Hugh's peers. Nor did Hugh want Edmund to recuse himself because Mehmed was a clerk at the court. These preferences appeared to benefit Mehmed—they meant no jury of British subjects sympathetic to an Englishman humiliated by a Turk and a judge partial to the accused. Edmund realised too late that Hugh wanted him to preside because Hugh believed that the trial could damage the court.

Henry Wroth deciphered the stratagem. Under English law, Colborne's claim translated into the charge that Mehmed committed the crime of common assault by intentionally applying unlawful force. As a matter of law, Mehmed had intentionally applied force, but Mehmed had no defences against the charge. Statements from witnesses under oath during the preliminary examination contained nothing to support the position that Mehmed applied force against Colborne lawfully as, for example, in defence of a person threatened by unlawful force. Justifications based on honour would not sway a judge bound to apply the law. These facts put the Crown and Judge Hornby in a difficult position as custodians of the law—a position vulnerable to the political pressure that Colborne was creating to force the law to be applied.

The sentence for a conviction of common assault was, at the court's discretion, imprisonment not exceeding one year, with or without hard labour. Under its new draft rules, the court could require the convicted person to pay the prosecution's just and reasonable costs. Colborne encouraged counsel for the Crown, Sebastian Knight, to take statements from as many witnesses as possible, ostensibly to ensure fairness but, in reality, to inflate the prosecution's costs. If Judge Hornby did not impose a serious sentence and costs on Mehmed, then Colborne would exploit that exercise of discretion on behalf of a Turkish criminal in the campaign, led by the English Committee of Constantinople, against the court.

This strategy to damage the court would find fertile ground. Mehmed's humiliation of Hugh and the "Slap an Englishman Today" fiasco infuriated the British community at Constantinople. Further, the trial created more problems for the court with the Sublime Porte because Turks viewed the prosecution of Mehmed under the capitulations as unlawful and punishing him under criminal law as unjust.

As the case's implications clarified, Edmund sensed that he had walked into a trap. The way out was to rule that the court did not have jurisdiction—something Edmund believed was impossible for him to do. Mehmed saw the conundrum and gave the judge one last chance. Worse, Colborne knew the judge had figured out the scheme too late. "It's too bad," Hugh remarked as the case progressed, "that the advocates of justice are blind."

When Mehmed did not answer, Judge Hornby repeated, "Do you have anything to say in answer to the charges against you?"

Mehmed shook his head. Judge Hornby set the trial date for three weeks hence. Under the court's new rules, the trial had to be open to the public—another way in which Colborne could exploit the case. The judge admitted Mehmed to bail, but Mehmed would not provide the surety required, his only meaningful property being his bay horse and black saddle, which he refused to produce for this purpose. Edmund committed Mehmed to the consular gaol until trial.

James accompanied Mehmed as Thomas Williams, the constable, led him to the gaol. Mehmed showed no interest in conversing with James as he entered his cell. As he left Mehmed, James shook his head at how depressing it all was. The outcome at trial seemed clear, with Mehmed being convicted and imprisoned for some period. A conviction would end Mehmed's position with the court. But the trial would really be political theatre—a farce—rather than a judicial enquiry in which the truth leavens the law for a just end. For James, the episode had become one of those moments when, to borrow from Mr. Bumble, the law—and, in this case, the consular court—was an ass.

James also knew that Mehmed's relationship with the court was disintegrating. When he returned after being cleared of sedition, Mehmed was elated with the Sublime Porte's stand on the *Enoch Wright* affair. For Mehmed, the incident highlighted everything wrong with the capitulations. He opposed the positions that the judge had decided to take, most of which James also did not think advisable. James had proposed a diplomatic rather than a legal solution—create better cooperation between

the Ottoman government and European legations at Constantinople on salvage rules for vessels abandoned in the Bosphorus.
Such an agreement could diffuse the tensions around the *Enoch
Wright* incident and produce ways to avoid similar controversies
in the future.

Instead, the judge took an expansive, uncompromising
stance on jurisdiction and escalated the dispute. Edmund argued
that Her Majesty's Government had exclusive jurisdiction over
the tug's crew, meaning the Ottoman government could not act
against them under law for any reason. The judge also claimed
that the Sublime Porte had never promulgated rules for navigation in the Bosphorus. He permitted the *Enoch Wright's* owners to file a claim in the Supreme Consular Court against Aldolphus Slade personally for damages to compensate the owners for
losing the salvage value of the Greek ship. These positions made
Mehmed livid, and he went on the offensive against the court.

"Slade ordered Turkish naval officers to act against activities
occurring on a Greek vessel. The English do not have exclusive
jurisdiction over Greek ships. Your position does not match the
facts." Mehmed challenged James.

"It was an English crew." James described the nationality of
the crew rather than the location of their acts.

"Exclusive jurisdiction over English crews on English vessels
does not apply when English sailors are not on English ships,"
Mehmed replied. "Nor do the capitulations permit captains and
crews of English vessels to do what they please on ships flagged
to other countries. The actions that violated Ottoman regulations took place on a Greek ship, not an English one."

"But there are no regulations." James retreated to the next argument.

"What do you mean there are no regulations?" Mehmed leaned hard on the table.

"There's no written code of Ottoman regulations for ports and coastal waters, so Slade can't claim that the crew engaged in illegal activities."

"Where does the treaty require Ottoman laws and regulations be in written codes before they have legal effect in our dominions?" Mehmed demanded. "Hundreds of ships travel everyday through the Bosphorus following rules concerning navigation and other issues."

James knew that the treaty had no such requirement. "But it's better to have written laws."

Mehmed shook his head in disbelief. "This from an English barrister? Who applies unwritten law—common law—here and in England? Who insists that foreigners in England are subject to the common law and an unwritten constitution?"

When James did not respond, Mehmed continued. "So everything would be fine if the Ottoman government promulgated a written code of regulations for ports and coastal waters?"

"Britain and the other European powers would have to approve the code," James replied, restating the position staked out by the legations of the European powers at Constantinople in response to the *Enoch Wright* incident.

"Where do the treaties require that the European powers approve legislation applicable in the sovereign domains of the Ottoman empire?" Mehmed was even more incensed.

"The capitulations provide Britain and other European powers exclusive jurisdiction over their vessels in Turkish waters." James fell back on something incontrovertible but not on point.

"Such jurisdiction doesn't give Britain the power to approve or reject Ottoman laws that apply in sovereign waters. It means that the Ottoman government cannot, without British consent, enforce its laws against English vessels for actions on English ships," Mehmed countered.

James fell silent, and Mehmed exploded. "You claim legal powers found nowhere in the treaties. You claim jurisdiction over English crews when they're not on English vessels. You claim that Britain can veto legislation applicable where the Ottoman government is sovereign. And unsupported by anything in law, this court permits Englishmen to sue an Ottoman official for actions he took as a government agent."

"Slade is a British subject, and under the capitulations, disputes entirely between British subjects, as is the case in the suit for the loss of salvage value, fall under this court's jurisdiction." James used Judge Hornby's rationale for allowing the suit against Slade to proceed.

Mehmed threw his hands up in exasperation. "Slade acted on behalf of the Ottoman government, not in his personal capacity. Does English law allow Hornby to be sued personally for damages related to official actions taken as the Supreme English Judge? Of course not. But he is subjecting Slade to English law for actions he took as an Ottoman official concerning a Greek vessel in Turkish sovereign waters. Is there no end to what you think the capitulations permit? Have you no shame in what you claim treaty law justifies? When did justice become whatever Englishmen think is most convenient for the English?"

Much to Judge Hornby's consternation, Mehmed expanded his battle by criticising the court's rules being finished by court staff. Judge Hornby explained that the new rules connected law and justice in ways not seen before in Her Majesty's Service and served as an example for Ottoman law and justice.

Mehmed was not impressed. "You have developed 353 rules and 58 standard forms, all to improve how your law applies in the sovereign territory of another nation. The more you improve the application of English law, the less willing you are to end the capitulations—and the more insistent you are that uncivilised countries conform to your rules. These improvements do not achieve justice. They are merely the exercise of imperial power."

James sensed that Mehmed's vehemence meant that he had decided to chart a different course. Given the Ministry of Justice's stand on the *Enoch Wright*, and Mehmed's relentless attacks on British legal positions, James suspected that Mehmed would join the ministry, a departure delayed—and perhaps ruined—by his trial for common assault.

At their next Saturday afternoon tea, Rosamund asked James if she could visit Mehmed at the gaol. It was a curious request, but James saw no harm in it. To ensure that those in charge of the gaol would not summarily reject the request, he asked, "What should I say is the reason?"

Rosamund waited some moments before responding. "I want to express my regret that he faces conviction and imprisonment. I feel responsible for any suffering that he might endure."

James understood Rosamund's desire. He too had apologised for putting Mehmed in the situation at the ball that led to the incident with Colborne. The Turk would deliver the same response to Rosamund—that he alone was responsible for his actions. James organised her visit.

Otherwise, time with Rosamund proved troubling. She seemed oblivious to being financially cut off, cast out from family, and soon forced back to England. Their talks focused on cases and issues that he was handling at the court. Like a clever student, she pressed him with questions, looking for how the law did or did not produce justice. For him, she provided information on perceptions in the British community about the court, especially Mehmed's pending trial. Though mutually beneficial, these reciprocal tutorials were not forging bonds of affection.

He held back from probing more personal matters. He had been present when she gave her statement in the preliminary examination of the charge against Mehmed. The examination focused on what had happened at the ball, but she appeared to want to go beyond that limited purpose. He did not know why, and he did not ask her.

She too seemed wary to discover more about him. In one awkward moment, she had asked him the name of his deceased fiancée. She merely repeated, "Emma," and asked no more questions—and he did not volunteer anything about Emma that would provide Rosamund with insights into his life.

Nor did their time together engender hints of desire for intimacy. In social situations, she would take his arm, but otherwise, they did not hold hands, exchange small touches, or appropriately kiss when greeting or saying goodbye—as was customary for courting couples. With Emma, she had initiated such rapport. On walks in the countryside, if he stopped to observe something, Emma sidled up behind him, took his hand, leaned her body against his, and peered over his shoulder at whatever was of interest. During chats alone by the fire, if he ran out of things to say, Emma placed her hand on his cheek and gave him a kiss beyond the appropriate, which did not encourage loquaciousness. James believed that Rosamund deserved the same prerogative. She seemed uninterested in the right that he chivalrously accorded her.

As the calendar crept toward Mehmed's trial date, factions opposed to the court began a campaign in the press against it, in keeping with Colborne's political exploitation of the trial. Stories and commentary in *The Levant Herald* hammered Judge Hornby's employment of a "Turkish criminal" and the trial's exorbitant costs caused by "thousands of Hornby Rules." With English law and the Turk's guilt clear, one writer opined, justice should be swift and severe. Instead, the pundit claimed, Hornby made justice glacial, the process expensive, the rules lenient for the uncivilised, and the court an unfair burden on law-abiding British subjects.

A rare bit of levity came from an opinion piece in another publication. A pseudonymous author, Sir Hareld Lavent, argued that swift and severe judicial punishment for "a Turk so malevolent, so malign, so misanthropic, and so manly" was woefully insufficient. Instead, Sir Hareld proposed that:

> This sinister and savage—but rather good looking—Oriental should be pinioned in evening attire (top hat and tails, of course) to an executioner's post in front of the British embassy. There, Her Britannic Majesty's most imperial, noble, supreme, Christian, gossipy, and inebriated subjects could—in their righteous fury, drunken stupor, or domestic boredom—slap that cheeky miscreant's lovely cheeks with a gentleman's dress glove until he perishes, or until the glove is not so crisply white, or until people come to their senses.

Rosamund's visit to Mehmed was scheduled for the late afternoon of the day before his trial would begin. James met her at the court's entrance and escorted her to the gaol. She wanted to speak to Mehmed alone and give him a gift, and she retrieved from her reticule a small, square item wrapped in white cloth and tied with a blue ribbon. James did not think speaking to Mehmed would be a problem but said that Thomas Williams, the constable, might inspect the gift to ensure that it did not contain contraband. Williams was not present, and his deputy showed no interest in the package before wandering off to smoke.

James left Rosamund outside Mehmed's cell and sat at Williams's scuffed desk to toil over trial-related documents. He could not hear the two, but he occasionally glanced over. He saw Rosamund hand her gift to Mehmed through the bars of the cell, and he, curiously, handed her a small stack of foolscap pages folded to quarters. Another look over saw them in animated and intense conversation, with Mehmed shaking his head at whatever Rosamund was communicating with voice and hands—consistent with her desire to apologise, and his rejection of any need for her to express remorse.

Frederick Guarracino came into the gaol to collect a document. James rifled through his pile to find it. As Frederick left, James noticed that Rosamund was no longer with Mehmed. He looked outside the gaol, in the court building, and on the street in front of it, but to no avail. With evening approaching, James strolled to a shop and bought the crisp almond cakes dotted with pistachio nuts that Mehmed liked. He returned to the gaol to give them to Mehmed before heading home. Williams opened Mehmed's cell for James to enter.

"Thank you," Mehmed said as he received the cakes, sat on his bunk, and began his meal.

As he ate, Mehmed asked whether there had been any developments on the last day before the trial. James indicated that the only thing of note was that Judge Hornby had convinced counsel for the Crown and the defence to limit the number of witnesses who would appear in court. The preliminary examinations showed no differences among the witnesses about what happened, so it served no purpose to have every witness testify at trial. Sebastian Knight selected Bartholomew Warren for the Crown, and counsel for the defence, Maurice Butt, chose Rosamund. Hornby approved and retained discretion to allow the Crown or the defence to call Hugh or Mehmed after Mr. Warren and Miss Colborne had testified.

"Did Miss Colborne tell you that she would be testifying?" James went into what was none of his business.

Mehmed tilted his head to look at James but did not answer.

"This time, can I ask you for a favour?" Mehmed enquired, reminding James of the favour that he had done for the Englishman at the Sultan's ball.

"Yes, of course."

Mehmed lifted from his bunk the gift from Rosamund. Mehmed had unwrapped it, and, to the best of his ability, rewrapped it.

"Keep it for me until this is over," Mehmed's voice went soft.

"Yes," James accepted the small package. "I'll keep it safe."

"The last time I received a gift," Mehmed suddenly said, looking at the far wall of his cell, "was when Hira sent me a gift before our wedding."

"I'm sorry, Mehmed, I didn't know that you are married." James tried to hide his embarrassment about not knowing Mehmed's marital status.

"I'm not. Never have been."

"What happened?" James blurted out, immediately fearing the question inappropriate.

Mehmed stared at the wall and did not move for many seconds.

"I don't want to talk about it," he eventually said as his eyes found the floor.

James did not know how to react. Should he talk about the death of his fiancée?

Instead, Mehmed caught James unprepared. "Are you going to marry her? Miss Rosamund? Everyone thinks you should."

I don't want to talk about it, was James's first thought. The reaction unsettled him.

"Not everyone," James replied, recalling his encounter with Henry Wattling and his own doubts about Rosamund's views on the matter.

Mehmed looked toward James but focused on a point beyond where the barrister stood.

"My father arranged the marriage." Mehmed directed his voice where his gaze was fixed. "The war destroyed our lives. My sister was dead. My mother was probably dead. We fled to Constantinople to escape the fighting. My father shovelled horse shit for money, but it did not secure shelter or keep hunger away. I roamed the streets stealing food and picking pockets. I had a talent for it and never got caught. I learned how to use the city to move, steal, escape, hide, and survive. But my father was ashamed. He forced me to take a position cleaning away dishes, dirt, and dregs for a coffee house. The shit shoveler had difficulty arranging a marriage for his coffee-house boy."

James wanted to pry, but he hesitated.

"I didn't know Hira," Mehmed continued. "We weren't allowed to meet before or after the marriage contract was concluded. That wasn't normal, which made me anxious. I made enquiries, but all I learned was that Hira's family had repeatedly failed to arrange a marriage for her. Ours was to be a marriage between two people no one else would have."

Mehmed turned and dropped his head so that his face was over the floor. James did not know whether Mehmed would say anything more.

"My thoughts," Mehmed started again, "went to foolish places. Was she a widow? Divorced? Blind? Deaf? Disfigured? A lunatic?"

Mehmed let a small smile surface, a rebuke for his mind having run wild.

"But then," he was still gazing at the floor, "she sent me a gift. The girl who delivered it—perhaps a sister—wanted me to know the gift came from Hira, not her parents. The girl refused to answer my questions and kept saying 'open it' when I pleaded for something about the woman I was to marry. Hira tried to tell me something, perhaps about herself, perhaps about what she wanted us to be."

Mehmed's head lifted so that he again saw the wall opposite him.

"What did she try to tell you?" James again risked going where he was not welcome.

Mehmed rotated to face James, and he looked blankly at the barrister before staring again at the wall. "I don't know. She died.

I heard rumours that she died in childbirth, but those who whisper like to wound people just for the pleasure of it. I don't know why she died. No one would say. I didn't know what the gift meant. She reached out to me, but I couldn't figure out what she was trying to say. I didn't know the sound of her voice, how she laughed, if her eyes danced when she was happy. How could I know what she was trying to tell me?"

"Perhaps reaching out, from a woman to her future husband, was the message," James offered, remembering how Emma had wanted certain things—sometimes even little, silly things—kept just between them.

Mehmed remained still. "My mother once told me that every woman is a mystery. She made me promise that, when I married, I would marvel at the mystery and not try to reason with it, not attempt to command it. I had no idea what she meant. I still have no idea. With that gift, Hira became a mystery."

Mehmed spoke more quietly, "I gave the gift to her parents, to be buried with her, as an act of respect for their loss."

James reached out to touch Mehmed, but he stopped when Mehmed continued speaking.

"After Hira was buried, I passed her father's market stall. He sold cheap things, trinkets and the like. That man was poor, like my father. But there, among his wares, was Hira's gift to me."

Before James could ask whether he bought it, Mehmed went a different direction. "Hira's gift was about a future that never had a past. Miss Colborne's gift is about a present that promises a difficult future. She might be ruined. Perhaps your doubts about her are my fault because she has been cast out. I'll be convicted, and my future damaged. But I feel no regret. What's wrong with me?"

James wanted to assure Mehmed that there was nothing wrong with him, but Mehmed spoke first, "Is she a mystery to you?"

"Who?" James replied as he heard Emma's soft laugh.

"Who do you think?" Mehmed shot James an incredulous look.

James was not able to respond.

"James?" Mehmed sensed his colleague tensing up.

As James struggled for a response, Williams walked up to announce that it was time for the gaol to be secured for the night. Mehmed stared at James for a moment, then laid down, putting a forearm over his eyes.

"Until tomorrow," James said as he left.

Chapter 20
R v. Osman Mehmed

Interest in the trial was considerable. But after managing the throng during the *Sinclair* trial, Williams and Guarracino had a plan and filled the courtroom smoothly. Without facts or law in dispute, the trial would be short, perhaps lasting less than the morning. James scurried into the courtroom and took his place near the judge's bench. He was in a foul mood. He believed that, although the law would be applied, justice would not be done.

Judge Hornby began the proceedings and informed those present that the Crown and defence had agreed that the trial should have no jury and that opening statements should be waived. The judge asked Sebastian Knight, for the Crown, to call Bartholomew Warren to the witness box. Knight's questions led Warren to describe what he had witnessed at the ball, which contained the essential facts that no one disputed. In concluding, Knight posed questions intended to show that Mehmed had no legal defences.

"Was the accused acting in self-defence—that is, in response to a reasonable fear that Mr. Colborne would use force against him?" asked Knight.

"No," replied Warren.

"Was the accused acting to defend anyone else who had a reasonable fear that Mr. Colborne would use force against them?" Knight continued.

"No."

"Do you recall anything that would provide the accused with a reason to use force against Mr. Colborne?" Knight issued his last question and prepared to sit at the prosecution table.

Bartholomew failed to respond in keeping with the question's purpose. "He used a flimsy dress glove. I wouldn't call that using force."

Knight stopped himself from sitting, stiffened to his full height, and stared at the witness. "Mr. Warren, what constitutes force is a legal question about which your opinion is not relevant. Neither the defence nor Judge Hornby contest that, under English law, the accused used force. And to be clear for all concerned, the accused bruised Mr. Colborne's face. So, let me ask you again, do you recall anything about the incident that would provide the accused with a lawful reason to use force against Mr. Colborne?"

"He called his daughter a bitch, in front of everyone," Bartholomew replied.

Knight put his hands on his hips, regretting his decision to ask one last question. "Mr. Warren, we have established what Mr. Colborne said. The question is whether the accused had a justification for using force in response to such a statement."

Warren persisted. "He called his daughter a bitch, a scheming bitch. I would have used my fist, not some silly glove, if anyone had said that to my daughter."

"Mr. Warren," Knight did not want to reveal his exasperation. "Miss Colborne is not the accused's daughter."

"I would've punched in the face any man who so insulted the woman I was escorting at a social function, as would any honourable gentleman." Bartholomew stood his ground.

Knight sighed, knowing what he had to do.

"Mr. Warren, is it correct to say that Mr. Colborne's actions offended you, as an honourable gentleman?"

"Yes, as any honourable gentleman would have been offended."

"Would you say there were many honourable gentlemen who witnessed what Mr. Colborne did?" Knight probed.

"Yes, many."

"As an honourable gentleman, what did you do in response to what offended you?"

Bartholomew appeared confused.

"Mr. Warren, you say that you are an honourable gentleman. You say that the accused behaved as any honourable gentleman would have behaved in the circumstances. You say that you were offended. So, what did you do, as an honourable gentleman, in response to the dishonourable behaviour you witnessed?"

Bartholomew did not answer, and Knight continued. "Did any honourable Englishman do anything against the dishonourable behaviour that all those honourable Englishmen witnessed?"

Warren did not respond.

"Mr. Warren, are you suggesting, with your silence, that the accused was the only honourable gentleman present, for he is the only one who did anything in response to such offensive, dishonourable behaviour?"

Bartholomew looked at Judge Hornby, who instructed him to answer the question.

Sensing his momentum, Knight did not wait for a response. "Could it be, Mr. Warren, that all the honourable Englishmen present decided not to violate the law in response to what they witnessed, however much they felt honour offended? Is it possi-

ble that only the accused believed he was above the law in striking Mr. Colborne, not once, not twice, but three times?"

Bartholomew examined his hands.

"No more questions." Knight sat down to murmurs in the
crowd about the Crown's dressing down of Warren.

Judge Hornby did not order the murmurs to cease as he
waited for Maurice Butt to cross-examine Warren. Butt rose and
looked at the table in front of him. Warren's testimony was never
important to the defence. It contained the facts that the defence
did not challenge. Butt never intended to raise honour as a justification for Mehmed's actions, so Warren's foray into questions
of honour was not damaging. However, Knight's demolition of
Warren forced Butt to alter the strategy that he had planned to
take with this witness.

"Mr. Butt, do you have questions for the witness?" Judge
Hornby interrupted Butt's reformulation of his interrogatories.

"Mr. Warren, did you, or anyone else, act to stop Mehmed?"
Butt began.

"No," Bartholomew replied.

"So, no one intervened despite, according to the prosecution, Mehmed being clearly engaged in obvious criminal activity
under English law?"

"I don't think anyone thought of the law at the time. It was
only later when Mr. Colborne brought his claim that people realised the incident might have legal implications," Bartholomew
said.

Knight stood. "Your Honour, the witness is speculating
about things not relevant to this case."

Mr. Butt responded before the judge could speak. "Your Honour, the Crown questioned the witness on matters of honour.

Am I not permitted to explore, as the Crown did, the context in which the alleged offence occurred?"

"Proceed, Mr. Butt," Judge Hornby ruled.

"You have testified that you believed Mr. Colborne's words and behaviour constituted serious provocation, especially for the person escorting Miss Colborne. You have testified that Mehmed used, in your words, a 'flimsy, silly dress glove' in response to serious provocation. You have testified that no one, including yourself, spoke or acted against Mr. Colborne or Mehmed during the episode. Would it be fair to say that you and others present considered Mehmed's response proportionate to the provocation?"

Knight protested again. "Your Honour, counsel for the defence is asking the witness to speculate about what other people might have thought, which should not be allowed."

"Mr. Butt, confine your questions to what the witness can answer," instructed Judge Hornby.

"My apologies, Your Honour. Let me rephrase my question. Mr. Warren, would it be fair to say that you considered Mehmed's response proportionate to the provocation?"

Bartholomew did not hesitate. "Yes. I mean, Mr. Colborne calls his daughter a bitch, goes at her, she hides behind the Turk—and people are shocked by this. I heard women gasp. But the Turk, he doesn't punch or strike Mr. Colborne. He makes his point with a dress glove. I suspect no one thought, in those moments, that he had committed a crime."

Knight was up again, "Your Honour—"

"Please sit down, Mr. Knight. There's no jury. You don't need to act as if there is one," Judge Hornby reprimanded counsel for the Crown.

Butt did not want to lose momentum. "Mr. Warren, let's return to the provocation. We've focused on what Mr. Colborne said to his daughter. But what did Mr. Colborne say to Mehmed before he called his daughter a bitch and moved aggressively at her?"

"Your Honour, I protest," Knight interjected. "Counsel for defence is turning this into cheap theatre."

"Under the law," Judge Hornby replied, "the defence must establish that the accused had a lawful reason to use force, and that the force applied was proportionate. Mr. Butt appears to be addressing what the law requires defence counsel to do, and I—not you, not the crowd—decide whether he succeeds on behalf of the accused. Mr. Butt, proceed."

"Mr. Warren, shall I repeat the question?" Butt asked the witness, who shook his head.

"Mr. Colborne ordered Mehmed to go away, as if he were a servant," Warren replied.

"Did anyone else, any other British subject, treat Mehmed like a servant?"

"No. Many Turks were there. It was the Sultan's ball. Turks mingled with the English."

"Do you believe Mr. Colborne would have ordered James Bingham to leave his daughter's side, as if Mr. Bingham was a servant, had he remained at the ball?"

"No."

"Did Mr. Colborne act with prejudice toward Mehmed because he's Turkish?"

"He would not have talked to an Englishman in the arrogant way he did to the Turk."

"How did Mehmed respond to Mr. Colborne's command to be gone?" Butt enquired.

"He ignored it and said that, as two people invited by the Sultan to the ball, they met as equals, not as master and servant."

"So, Mr. Colborne insulted not just his daughter but also Mehmed?"

"Yes."

"Did Mehmed slap Mr. Colborne for insulting him?"

"No."

"Mehmed acted on behalf of others—Miss Colborne and Mr. Bingham—and not himself, is that right?"

"Yes."

"What did Miss Colborne say before her father called her a bitch?"

"She said that she would not dismiss Mehmed because she made a promise to Mr. Bingham, who brought her to the ball but had to leave. Mr. Colborne asked her whether she wanted to know about promises that Mr. Bingham made to him. She said she wasn't interested. Then he called her a bitch and went at her."

"Do you think we would be here today if Mr. Bingham had slapped Mr. Colborne with a dress glove?"

"No. I think that it would have been considered, among the British community, a matter of honour and not a matter of criminal law."

"No more questions," Mr. Butt stayed on his feet. "The defence calls Rosamund Colborne."

As Rosamund made her way to the witness box, the crowd became noisy, which prompted Judge Hornby to call for order. For James, the questioning of Bartholomew Warren had gone as expected—the Crown focused on the applicable law, with the defence raising mitigating factors that, if nothing else, might permit Judge Hornby to exercise leniency in sentencing. But the part about "promises Mr. Bingham made" was not something James had heard before concerning the incident, and he swallowed hard. He tried to catch Rosamund's eye once she was in the box, but she looked at no one other than Butt.

"During your preliminary examination," Butt began, "you stated that you flinched, moved behind Mehmed, and began to tremble after your father called you a bitch and stepped toward you. Your statement is consistent with those made by others. What other witnesses cannot explain is why you were afraid, sought protection, and started trembling."

Knight rose, "Your Honour, this case concerns Mehmed's actions, not Miss Colborne's emotions, which no one else, including the accused, could have understood during this incident."

Judge Hornby nodded, "Mr. Butt, explain your purpose."

"Your Honour, Miss Colborne reacted in a fearful way. Her fear is the proximate cause of what followed. If she had laughed at her father, or slapped him herself, we wouldn't be here. She's the only one who can enlighten us on this issue," Butt replied.

Knight grew animated. "Your Honour, the reasons why Miss Colborne exhibited fear would have arisen before the acts on trial today. They cannot possibly have legal relevance for explaining, let alone justifying, what the accused did."

The courtroom went quiet. Judge Hornby leaned forward to announce his decision. He did not get a chance to speak.

"Something happened." Rosamund's voice found every corner of the courtroom.

"Something happened," she repeated, her voice still loud but starting to quiver.

Confusion spread among the crowd. "What did she say?" from one part of the courtroom was followed by "Oh my God!" from another. Noise everywhere in the courtroom overwhelmed the proceedings, with Judge Hornby motionless behind the bench. Above the din, a declaration began to be heard, "I plead guilty, Your Honour, I plead guilty!"

Mehmed was on his feet in the dock shouting at Judge Hornby. James had not taken his eyes from Rosamund until Mehmed's voice cut through the maelstrom. He turned to see Mehmed standing and shouting with all the force he could muster. James scanned the courtroom to locate Hugh Colborne but could not see him. The banging of Judge Hornby's fist on the bench refocused James on Rosamund, and the judge's commands began to contain the clamour.

"Everyone be quiet," Judge Hornby ordered. "Everyone sit and be quiet."

Mehmed remained standing, staring at Judge Hornby, making sure that he would be the judge's priority when order was restored.

"Your Honour," Mehmed said as quiet returned to the courtroom. "I change my plea. I plead guilty."

Judge Hornby was incredulous. "You plead guilty? Now?"

"Yes, I plead guilty. No more testimony. Enough of this."

Noise built to another crescendo before Judge Hornby's calls for order prevailed. He motioned Knight and Butt to the bench. James glanced at Rosamund, who was in tears in the witness box and was being helped down and comforted by Mrs. Hornby. He caught Henry Wroth's eye, and Henry shook his head and shrugged to indicate that he had never seen anything like this.

Knight and Butt returned to their respective tables. Mehmed remained standing.

"Mehmed," the judge's voice silenced the courtroom. "You have decided to plead guilty to the charge of common assault. The Crown accepts your plea, which obviates the need for more testimony. All witnesses are dismissed. The only matter that remains is sentencing. I'll issue my ruling and inform the Crown and the accused. This trial is over, and the court is adjourned."

James remained in the courtroom long after it was empty, listening for what was left unsaid.

Part III
Verdict

Decision.

335. The Court having heard what each party has to say as afore-said, and the witnesses and the evidence adduced, shall consider the whole matter and finally determine the same, and shall convict the accused or dismiss the charge. — *Rules of Her Britannic Majesty's Supreme Consular Court and other Consular Courts in the Dominions of the Sublime Ottoman Porte, 1860.*

Chapter 21
Secret Ruin

Up again before the muezzin's first morning call to prayer, James brewed coffee in his room. Rosamund liked to rise at dawn. Perhaps he should ride by the Colborne residence, just to say good morning. Perhaps not. He had an early meeting with Judge Hornby and Mehmed to discuss the unfinished code of criminal procedure. Mehmed had been released from gaol yesterday, having completed his sentence for common assault. Still, a quick good morning with Rosamund sounded enticing. Emma had responded warmly, and always with a kiss, when he had appeared unexpectedly to spend time with her.

Sipping coffee produced sobriety. Whether Rosamund would welcome a spontaneous visit was not clear. Her life was in even more turmoil. Her interrupted testimony at Mehmed's trial stimulated speculation about what exactly happened and to whom. Rosamund's refusal to say anything more made the ambiguity too tempting. Salacious accusations and rumours commenced about Hugh Colborne committing wickedness against Katherine, Rosamund, or a scullery maid at the residence who was with child out of wedlock. Geoffrey Hancock broke with Hugh, damaging the business. Her father no longer stayed at the residence. Mrs. Colborne remained there but only as a wraith of a woman. Rosamund was not spared reproach either. For many, what she said at the trial and her silence afterwards smacked of calculation by a daughter facing a difficult future that she had brought upon herself. In such circles, Rosamund was not just a scheming bitch, but a lying, vindictive one.

James remembered the tongue lashing that Rosamund had given him during the *Sinclair* trial. During their increasingly terse tea times, he wanted to encourage her to have the courage, like Susannah, not to remain silent. Each time, he did not find that courage with her. Something had happened in her family or at the residence, but James did not know what. Something had to happen for her future not to be grim, but she had not shared her plans, if any, for what was ahead.

He understood that asking for her hand would be honourable because marriage offered her a way to avoid hardships on the horizon. But he had not asked. It was not honour that he wanted. Jemmy Oakeston had seen it. He had been, for too long, enamoured with what was "bright and shiny" about Rosamund. The real Rosamund—a woman of spirit, secrets, and scars—eluded him. He so often did not grasp what she was thinking and feeling. He did not understand her hopes and fears. He did not know what he meant to her.

His failure to draw her out, grow closer to her, and become her confidant upset him. The anger begat misbehaviour. He became aggressive with Bones, too often applying the riding crop in pent-up ire rather than necessity. In a midnight fit, he shattered the creaky chair in his room, smashed the wood and rattan into ever smaller pieces, and burned the debris. One late night at the court, toiling alone in eye-straining candlelight on some tedious matter, he upended the table in the clerk's office, scattering papers, pens, and ink every which way. Each spasm, each new temptation, was a pathetic setback in his efforts to exhibit a more virtuous and manly confidence in his life's endeavours.

In calmer moments, often in the hours before dawn when sleep was a stranger, he wondered whether Rosamund wanted to be drawn out by him. He could believe that she might grow weary of him. However, she insisted on continuing to see him for tea on Saturdays. Perhaps interaction in the present circumstances also frustrated her. He could have forced the issue over cups of Ceylon, but the thought of not seeing her anymore unsettled him. So he remained stranded and somewhat desperate. Could an unexpected visit elicit an unguarded reaction from Rosamund and clues about her true feelings?

He guided Bones off the way normally taken. He wanted to approach the residence on small paths—more like infrequently used trails—wending through unkempt meadow dotted with scattered, tangled stands of trees. This area extended to the walled garden of the residence. He and Rosamund sometimes walked these paths during his visits.

Once, as they strolled the paths after he had fully recovered from his fever, Rosamund had suddenly stopped and said, "I want to show you something."

She had left the path and struck out through thick grass. It took him some moments to follow because such a detour was unprecedented, and his confusion made his legs leaden. She outpaced him and disappeared near some old, gnarled trees. He slowed down because he could not see where she went. Then her hand protruded from the copse and waved to him. He squeezed through a nearly invisible gap amidst the trees and undergrowth and walked up behind her. He waited for her to move or speak, but she remained silent and still.

He looked around to see an irregular oval of tightly knit grasses, vines, shrubs, and trees supporting an interwoven canopy of branches shielding the space beneath. After scanning the enclosure, he focused on where Rosamund had her eyes fixed. At first, he did not see it. As his sight adjusted to the mottle of light and shade, the remains of an ancient building emerged. Not much, perhaps all that survived of a once grand structure.

"Here," she took his hand, something she had never done, and led him opposite where the remnants of two walls formed a corner. Extending along and out from the walls was a mosaic floor laid by craftsmen ages past. The tiles were beautiful. They formed geometric patterns, but nothing that suggested Islamic influences. The colours—blues, reds, yellows—were, even dappled by the canopy, still stunning centuries after creation.

Gazing at the ruin, he realised that Rosamund must tend to it. No vines clung to the walls; no weeds grew among the tiles; no dirt dulled the mosaic's colours. Perhaps she and Maggie had discovered and cared for it; a rite Rosamund now continued alone.

"I don't know why," she said barely above a whisper, letting go of his hand and moving wayward strands of her hair back in place. "But I imagine the bed chamber of a Roman villa, where a man and a woman lay together in love."

Her confession surprised him. He had never heard her say anything romantic. Just as he wondered whether he should kiss her, she turned, walked to the gap in the copse, and left—without saying another word. After struggling to understand what had just happened, he followed. Once outside, he saw her striding toward the residence. She never looked back. She had not mentioned it again. His memory of the mosaic was a haunting reminder that he really knew nothing about her.

As he turned Bones onto a smaller path about half-way to the residence, he noticed a brown horse munching grass near a poplar tree. The reins hung down, dragging on the ground as the horse stepped into fresh grass. It was saddled and appeared, in the sharp light of the new morning, to have dark, wet legs and haunches from grazing on dew-covered vegetation. He saw nobody around, so he rode on. He dismounted on reaching the front entrance and walked Bones to the stables at the side of the residence. The stable hands were accustomed to him, and, despite the early hour, they made no fuss when he handed over the reins. He told them about the horse, but their sullen reaction suggested that stray horses sometimes appeared, or that they simply did not care. He went back to the front entrance and rang the bell. Her response should be telling, he reassured himself.

However, awkwardness reigned as the servants reported that Rosamund could not be found. Their reaction appeared genuine and not feigned to soften any refusal of Rosamund to see him. No one else could greet him, the servants said, because Mrs. Colborne was visiting friends in Adrianople. He took his leave, telling the servants they need not inform Rosamund that he had called. He returned to the stables and collected Bones himself. It was a wasted effort, but at least he had seized the idea and done it. He slowed Bones to a lazy walk, let the horse nibble grass, and decided to ride by Rosamund's secret ruin.

After wrong turns and confusion, James found his bearings and directed Bones down a more familiar path. He had not gone far when he reined Bones to a stop. He saw Rosamund emerge from the copse and start walking toward the residence. She was wearing a light-coloured robe or frock and carrying something draped over her arms. The morning haze made it hard to tell what. Her dark hair cascaded down her back past her waist and swayed as she walked. He had never seen her hair this way. She had probably been tending to her secret ruin in the morning cool, explaining why the servants had not found her.

On Bones, he could reach her before she entered the garden. He could take her hand, lead her into the secret ruin, kiss her, know her desires. When doubts come to conquer. He hesitated; Emma died. He tensed, leaned forward in the saddle, and raised his riding crop.

Chapter 22
Jerusalem

Edmund looked at his pocket watch again. It was unlike either of them to be late; for both James and Mehmed to have missed the meeting was even more curious. He still wanted Mehmed involved with the court, and the way his trial had ended made Edmund confident that keeping Mehmed as a clerk would create no problems. Edmund continued to believe that the hybrid code of criminal procedure could be a model for reforms that the Ottomans—and other oriental societies—would need to undertake in cooperation with Europeans over the rest of the century. But he suspected that Mehmed might have other ideas.

Before the trial, Mehmed seemed ready to break with the court over the *Enoch Wright* incident. Having lost his accommodations while in gaol awaiting trial, Mehmed had asked Edmund to increase his sentence from one day to two weeks so that he could work on a project as a guest of the "Hotel Hornby." Mehmed refused to do court-related work, joking that his sentence did not include hard labour. Mehmed had completed his sentence yesterday, and missing the meeting was perhaps another sign that he was pursuing a new path.

Edmund also wanted to tell James and Mehmed the good news concerning his efforts to reform the judicial functions of the British consular service in the Ottoman empire. Despatches from the Foreign Office in the latest diplomatic pouch handed victory to the Supreme Consular Court. One despatch enclosed an expensively printed response from Lord Russell, the Foreign Secretary, rejecting the complaints from the English Committee of Constantinople and supporting the reforms being "carried out under the able superintendence of E Hornby."

The Foreign Secretary reinforced a central tenet of Edmund's strategy—the positive effect British reforms could have on the Ottoman government. In Edmund's favourite part, Lord Russell described the reforms as "calculated not only to insure justice being done in the several British Consular Courts but also to serve as an example and as an encouragement for the improvement of the Turkish Tribunals, the defects in which gave rise to the extraterritorial jurisdiction conferred by successive Sultans on Christian Sovereigns."

In the same diplomatic pouch was a despatch in which the Foreign Office instructed Edmund to extend the approach developed at Constantinople throughout the consulates in Ottoman domains. He had already started down this path by sending Donald Logie to Smyrna, and with the Foreign Office's new instructions, he would have Henry Wroth go to Alexandria. In a private note enclosed with this despatch, Edmund Hammond, Permanent Under-Secretary of State for Foreign Affairs, shared that the Foreign Secretary was exploring the expansion of Edmund's reforms to British consulates in the Far East.

The Foreign Office had routed the British factions aligned against the court—an outcome beyond anything Edmund had expected. It expanded the horizons for his contributions to the British empire and the cause of justice among nations—horizons that James and Mehmed could explore alongside him. He would have to tell them another time as one more glance at his timepiece told him that the day's other business could wait no longer.

Emelia Hornby was also astonished, but not as thrilled, at the turn of events. She dutifully planned a celebration—dining and dancing at the *Hôtel d'Angleterre*. They kept the celebration private, a chance for them to be together after dark days at the court and at home. After dancing, they took tipsy turns toasting people who made it possible—Lord Stratford, the Sultan, Fuad Pasha, Wroth, Logie, Bingham, Lord Russell. When Edmund raised his glass to toast the Queen, Emelia playfully protested, "I will not toast her. I mean, really, in all this, where is your knighthood?"

Shortly after the celebration, Edmund was in his study one evening sipping Scotch. Emelia peeked in and noticed his demeanour. Knowing how gloom descended when Edmund had too much solitude, Emelia joined him and encouraged him to talk. He reminded Emelia of her concerns about how hard he worked, how often he was away, and how much his responsibilities burdened her. But his duties in Her Majesty's Service had just multiplied in ways that he could not fathom. He stared into his Scotch before wondering whether he could work harder or sacrifice more. Emelia understood that Edmund did not need wifely huzzahs. She had to help him clarify his fears.

"You have always calibrated your efforts to the task at hand, no matter how demanding. What really worries you?" she probed.

He swirled his drink in the tumbler. "I don't want this to be like Jerusalem."

The response was peculiar. She hoped that his fears involved the price their relationship would pay for implementing what the Foreign Office had in mind. Although she had said nothing to Edmund yet, she was done with the East. She would not stay here much longer, or go to the Far East, for her husband's legacy or Her Majesty's glory.

"Edmund, what do you mean?"

"Remember, right before Bingham arrived, I took the steamer to Jaffa and then was in the saddle the rest of the day and night riding to Jerusalem. Though well dead without sleep, we scrambled up the Mount of Olives at dawn, and there it was. What a sight. I should take you."

"Yes, you've promised before, but now isn't the time to make you feel guilty." The attempt at levity nearly betrayed her discontent.

He did not notice. "The Golden Gate, the Temple Mount, the mosques and minarets, the Church of the Holy Sepulchre, all resplendent in the rising sun. It was as if this place promised what the future should be. Ordered, plural, just, spiritual, beautiful. My, it was glorious."

He went quiet, and Emelia did not wish to disrupt the pensive silence.

"Then we descended into the city. And Jerusalem became what history always becomes. Degraded, dilapidated, dirty, despotic, disconcerting." He stopped speaking and took a drink.

"You are cheery when you don't sleep." Her next attempt at humour drew no reaction.

"We believe that we know what law and justice should be," Edmund resumed. "But when we descend from the mount of our making into the city belonging to others, what do we become?"

"Law givers, peace makers," Emelia offered.

Edmund made that little noise he used when dismissing her thoughts. "Romans, Arabs, Crusaders, Turks—all believed the same entering Jerusalem. But the Jews hated the Romans. The

Crusaders hated the Arabs. The Mahomedans hated the Christians. Now we come. With our law. Our courts. Our justice. Our civilisation. We defend what the Ottomans despise. We celebrate what they curse. Will it be the same in the Far East? When does it become necessary, or just, to take another approach, to have a different vision?"

"Would you like more?" Emelia pointed at the decanter, but Edmund shook his head and swallowed the last dram before continuing.

"I recoiled at the star and crescent flag flying above Jerusalem. My distemper edged close to the mentality of the Crusaders, who attempted to destroy a religion and a civilisation that they made no effort to understand. As you know, I have nothing against Mahomedanism. It's not incompatible with morality or good government. But I was perturbed by that unfurled flag, as if Mahomedans had built a mosque in Weybridge.

"This agitation was likely my response to being forced, at Jerusalem, to engage in the dismal rituals we endure at Constantinople—protesting treaty violations, the capricious exercise of government power, the conditions in gaols, etcetera. What I see descending into the political affairs of men convinces me that these rituals are necessary. But whether at Constantinople or Jerusalem, my words are received as arrogance born of prejudice made potent only by the possession of superior power.

"In my discontent, I proposed that the European powers should buy Jerusalem, or obtain a concession over it, as France did with the Suez Canal. The Turks are weak enough, I argued, to be tempted by a large sum, and the Europeans are strong enough to pay."

"Did you persuade them?" Scepticism was clear in Emelia's voice.

"No, except for the Frenchman dining with us, who said that my idea simply reflected how the world works—the strong do what they can, while the weak suffer what they must. A sentiment, he claimed, from ancient Greece."

"Are you afraid that what you do here and, perhaps, in the Far East, reflects this sentiment?"

"No. The sword of justice has two edges. The weak never suffer what they must for long. They eventually forge violence and law into weapons, and their defiance becomes power that changes a people's destiny."

"You're afraid of this power?" Emelia tried again.

Edmund's countenance darkened. "I fear the Jerusalem we are making."

Chapter 23
Bon Mots

Mehmed wanted to tell the judge that he was not coming back. He anticipated the conversation being easier. He explained his reasoning. His association with the court had brought him nothing but trouble. He had been subjected to government surveillance. He had been vilified in the English colony as a religious fanatic. He had been hunted by the police for sedition. He had faced criminal trial for defending the honour of British subjects. The *Enoch Wright* incident was the final straw. He could no longer work for the court.

Judge Hornby listened, nodding at times as if sympathetic. But the judge took the explanation badly. He told Mehmed about the Foreign Office's decision to expand his reform strategy throughout Ottoman dominions and perhaps in the Far East. These developments, the judge claimed, gave Mehmed the opportunity to participate in a noble effort that could guide law around the globe. The moment was one in which Mehmed could help countries achieve common purpose in pursuit of a shared, universal justice.

Mehmed listened, nodding at times as if Judge Hornby had said something interesting. However, he refused to come back. The judge asked whether he would continue to work with James on the code without being a clerk. The request produced a bitter exchange.

"The code," Mehmed's voice dripping with disdain, "is a mirage. You and Fuad Pasha thought you glimpsed something shimmering on the horizon, an oasis that you were desperate to believe was there. But your camels have just marched around in circles."

Judge Hornby took offence. "The code is real; it is started; it can be finished."

Mehmed shook his head. "The code has never been a priority. You, Wroth, Logie, Bingham, the dragoman, or the constable always had something more important or urgent for me to do. Meanwhile, you contort the capitulations to make them mean whatever you have the power to demand. And you want to expand this approach across the Ottoman empire and even farther east. The code, remember, was supposed to make unequal, unjust treaties relics of a prejudiced past."

"I thought you agreed that the code was the only way to move our empires to a better place in terms of law and justice. I thought you understood—it is either the capitulations or the code." Judge Hornby stabbed a finger into the desk for emphasis.

"No. There is another way," was Mehmed's last word.

Upon leaving the judge, Mehmed ran into Henry Wroth. Unsentimental as always, Henry shook his hand, "Best of luck." Mehmed wanted to say goodbye to James and collect the item that he was keeping safe, but James was out with the dragoman. As he left, Mehmed wondered whether he would ever set foot inside the court again once he started down the path of confrontation.

Mehmed had spent his time in gaol drafting a manifesto for law and justice reform in the Ottoman empire. He undertook this effort to prepare himself for his next position. Hasan had arranged for him to join the Ministry of Justice once he had completed his gaol sentence. Mehmed also needed to write the manifesto for himself, to get his ideas organised in a way that could inform his future. He was not writing a code, such as the one Judge Hornby and Fuad Pasha had conceived. It was a conceptual argument for reform not subservient to European ideas or pressure. He intended the manifesto to convince religious and political leaders to reform from within, on Islamic and Ottoman terms.

It was not a screed against Europeans, although he wasted much foolscap venting about the capitulations before feeding those pages to the gaol fire. As Hasan had predicted, he did learn from Hornby, including that Ottoman legal practices and judicial institutions were often wanting. Mehmed had been with the dragoman to Turkish prisons and was ashamed of what he saw. He had accompanied Hornby to Turkish legal proceedings, and he was often embarrassed by the behaviour of Turkish officials responsible for judicial tribunals. He had eluded the Ottoman police to avoid being put to death for sedition, hardly a reassuring episode concerning law, justice, and power.

However, he wanted reforms anchored in *sharia* or Ottoman law rather than European law. He risked cloaking European ideas in native garb because Ottoman law already incorporated much from Europe. He needed help, and he drew on Hasan's knowledge and wisdom. Without mentioning Mehmed, Hasan contacted *muftis*, *kadis*, and *imams* for advice on issues Mehmed encountered in writing his manifesto. One of the most difficult involved how to navigate between following extant jurisprudence, the path conservatives favoured, and challenging the centuries-old accumulation of legal precedent, the approach reformers preferred.

Mehmed wished to recover how the Koran enabled the people of Islam to retain their identity and prosper in modernity. This desire to reform from within did not, however, make the manifesto free of risk. Laws, he believed, served the greater goal of justice, but each rule had to be, in its own way and context, just. Legal reform could not avoid confrontation with prevailing laws and concepts of justice.

The manifesto's purpose challenged the religious and political order in the Ottoman empire. Many Ottoman leaders and subjects believed the Koran and the Sultan's authority to be immutable. Anything emanating from them—especially law—was, by definition, just. However, immutability encouraged principled inflexibility in the application of *sharia* and unprincipled expedience in the exercise of political power.

The empire had never confronted the nature, scale, and pace of the transformations now unnerving its peoples. Such roiling change pulled *sharia* in incompatible directions. Some acknowledged *sharia*'s limitations, which relegated it to becoming doctrinaire within a shrinking sphere of application. This perspective reinforced the view that *sharia* was too antiquated for the modern age and should be phased out as a path to justice. Others argued that *sharia* governed change as it did all things, producing the need to extirpate whatever new was incompatible with it. This view nourished attitudes about *sharia* that were dogmatic and violent.

For Mehmed, things were not better with the Sultan's authority. As *caliph*, the Sultan was a source of justice. However, new Ottoman laws bearing his imprimatur borrowed heavily, if not exclusively, from Europeans. These laws made the Sultan appear a weak and passive supplicant to foreign, infidel ways. Legal reform had become little more than a desperate tactic to buy time for something more rooted in the nation to germinate. Political exigency has, however, ever been a poor source of justice.

Mehmed searched, but neither seeds nor husbandry seemed forthcoming from the empire's leaders. This failure wasted the time that tactical retreats generated. Europeans, seeing *sharia* as archaic and inadequate and the Sultan as weak and pliable, usurped legal reform and exploited the situation to their advantage. The Ottomans confronted the incessant expansion of the capitulations and the irrepressible conviction that European law provided the only path to justice.

In his manifesto, *sharia* was not fatally brittle in the face of change, and Ottoman legislation should be based on ideas from within rather than from without. These arguments challenged prevailing views about *sharia* and the Sultan's authority as immutable sources of justice—views that persisted despite the incoherent mess that law in the Ottoman empire had become.

Most dangerously, the manifesto critiqued how sultans had exercised their authority. The draft highlighted disquiet among religious leaders about the willingness of sultans to import foreign law and notions of justice. The text faulted sultans for adopting laws that parroted European legislation. It criticised how sultans handled relations with the European powers.

In its final sections, the manifesto argued that continuation of present trends would lead, at some point, to the end of the Sultan's power and Islam's role in law and justice for the Ottoman peoples. Such arguments were not novel, but they were usually expressed by nationalists or radicals seeking to end what they believed were anaemic political institutions and antiquated legal rules. It would be easy for paranoid political officials and fearful religious leaders to read his manifesto as a radical call for extremism.

By the time he left the gaol, Mehmed had a complete draft. It was too raw, long, complicated, hastily written, and—potentially—incendiary. It needed revision. No one else had read it, not even Hasan. He had only one copy, which he always kept with him.

He was excited and nervous about the draft. He wanted to discuss it with others. One thing he admired about the English court was how the barristers talked, argued, debated, and joked about everything, including the British monarchy. He intended to share a revised draft with the barristers, but English judges and lawyers were not his audience. How could he share his ideas with Turks without incurring the wrath of the palace, the Porte, or religious leaders?

Asking Hasan to circulate the manifesto within the law school or the Ministry of Justice was not a good idea, at least not until he was confident that it would cause no trouble for anyone who read it. Instead, he imagined sitting in a coffee house, explaining his arguments to fellow Turks, and hearing their reactions. It was an idle thought. The manifesto was too lengthy and complex to digest over a few cups of coffee. At most, he could share bits of it over days of coffee and conversation, and with time, help people understand its purpose. This thought gave him an idea.

Training in *sharia* involved studying rulings on legal questions, or *fatwas*. One of his favourites was associated with the great jurist Abu Hanifa and concerned circumstantial evidence and criminal offences. Typically, a *fatwa* begins with a question: "What happens if Amr finds a wine jar in Zeyd's possession?" Then comes the answer: "Abu Hanifa—may God have mercy on him—went on a Pilgrimage, and, in Medina, he saw people surrounding a man. They said, 'He has a wine-skin, and we should punish him.' Abu Hanifa responded, 'He has the instrument of fornication with him, too. So, stone him.' And they left the man alone and dispersed."

Mehmed decided to take arguments, issues, and questions from the manifesto and formulate them on slips of paper in the style of *fatwas*. He would leave the slips, surreptitiously, around coffee houses in Constantinople. The strategy was to make complex ideas accessible, start conversations, and prepare the ground for the manifesto's eventual appearance.

Translating the manifesto into pithy text on paper strips proved difficult. For some arguments, the question-answer format did not work. Or, if he managed to develop a question and an answer, the size of the slips made it impossible to communicate clearly or with nuance. Instead, he sometimes found it easiest to pose a question, but leave the answer blank to prompt the reader to ponder the question and possible answers. He decided to distribute his first batch of slips without mentioning the experiment to anyone.

He chose a coffee house that he did not frequent but that had a reputation for lively conversation among patrons. He divided his slips into small envelopes with *Bon Mots* written on each. He arrived early and placed the envelopes around the coffee house where customers would find them. He avoided being noticed, left unobserved, and decided to wait in a nearby market square until returning later to eavesdrop. However, he was de-

layed. Foreign diplomats and their security escorts entered the
square to take water for their horses. One *cavass* glanced in his
direction, stared for a moment, and dismounted. The *cavass*
walked toward Mehmed, who pretended not to notice. As the
cavass got closer, Mehmed heard humming. Mehmed stepped
out to greet Halil.

Halil flashed a conspiratorial grin. "Ah, now I find you. We
searched for you after the Sultan's ball. Well, some of us searched
harder than others."

"I wish that I could say I'm sorry," Mehmed replied.

Halil's face lost its cheerfulness. "You need to be careful. You
embarrassed the police. The ministry has brought in people from
the military. They work in teams. They train new agents using
you, given how good you are at evading surveillance. You're being watched and followed. Someone is, I bet, observing us now."

"Won't you get in trouble?" Mehmed forced himself not to
look around.

Halil ran his fingers over his moustache. "No. You're not suspected of committing crimes now. But you've made the police
angry and the palace suspicious, and they want to keep an eye on
you. If you cause problems, you won't escape again. Don't get into any more trouble."

The *cavass* returned to his horse. Mehmed cast his eyes
around. Leaning against the wall at the opposite corner of the
square was a man who must have appeared while he was with
Halil. Mehmed knew not to stare, so he glanced away. After a few
minutes, he looked again. The man was still there, but he locked
eyes with Mehmed, bowed his head with respect, backed away,
and disappeared.

Mehmed suspected that he was being watched, even after he was cleared of involvement with the seditious pamphlet and had agreed to join the Ministry of Justice. For the moment, he was in no danger from cat-and-mouse games. But, if they followed him here, they knew he had been at the coffee house—and they would track him back there. Why that mattered was not clear as he dithered about whether to return to the coffee house.

Mehmed finally began to make his way back. As he turned the last corner leading to the coffee house, he saw commotion in front of it, with police, mounted and on foot, attempting to control a seething crowd. Mehmed became tense, but more alert. The crowd offered ways to be inconspicuous. Easing into the crowd, he asked someone what was happening.

"I don't know," the man replied. "The police dragged a man out of the coffee house. Someone said there was blasphemy."

Something was terribly wrong, but Mehmed could not fathom how his slips could have produced accusations of blasphemy that had people rioting. But he knew that he had to leave because, as Halil had warned, he needed to stay out of trouble.

"*Inshallah*," he muttered to himself about what he must do, hoping that Allah was willing.

"What do you mean? Allah doesn't will blasphemy!" the man next to him shouted, causing Mehmed to move around the edge of the crowd.

The man followed and continued to yell at Mehmed, calling him a blasphemer. Someone grabbed the strap on Mehmed's satchel, causing him to lurch backwards. He spun out of the strap, leaving the satchel in someone's hands. He dove into the crowd and, spying a riderless horse at the crowd's edge, she toward it. He mounted the horse, kicked it hard, and raced away from the coffee house.

He urged on the horse, knowing that the commotion, the crowd, and the escape would give him a few hours. But they knew he had visited the coffee house earlier and had returned. They would compare the slips of paper with the contents of his satchel. They would come for him. He did not have much time to plan his next steps. But first, and despite the risk, there was one thing he had to do.

Chapter 24
Body and Soul

Henry Wattling hated taverns. The smell, the services, and the clientele were painful reminders of his days of debauchery and violence. Silas Benson, who had invited him to meet, probably wanted to send a warning before Henry departed for Africa. A warning was well advised. Of late, his attitude lacked Christian sensibility, which worried Silas and Maude Benson. The Bensons had helped put his life back together and nurtured his new calling. As sin leavened guilt, he went to them to repent. He told Mr. and Mrs. Benson that he had again sought out, and been rejected by, Rosamund.

Silas and Maude had harshly reprimanded him. Mr. Benson fulminated like the fire-and-brimstone preacher that he was. Normally gentle, Mrs. Benson cuffed his head repeatedly for lusting after a woman contemptuous of God's commandments. In tears, he had conceded that he must ask God to forgive him, no matter how many sins he had committed, and to forgive Rosamund, no matter how many commandments she had broken. But repentance did not involve a full confession, which he feared would have pushed the Bensons beyond even their capacity for forgiveness.

At the brothel, he had paid the prostitute to dress like Rosamund, wear her hair like Rosamund, and smell like Rosamund. He paid to watch her let down her hair, undress, and service a brute he knew from his miscreant days. He paid the lout to whip the naked, unsuspecting woman with the black leather and silver metal belt she had taken off. He intended the sordid, violent episode to achieve what prayer had not—exorcising Rosamund from his life.

Benson was late, and the tavern keeper gave Henry annoyed looks for not purchasing food or drink. Henry opened his Bible. He had barely found the desired passage when a hand reached down and closed the good book. Henry raised his head to see Hugh Colborne. Before Henry could say a word, Hugh sat opposite him at the table.

"I nearly didn't recognise you, Henry. That beard makes you look like the ruffian that you once were, and it's going to be uncomfortable in Africa," Hugh remarked.

"Mr. Colborne, I'm expecting Silas Benson." Henry felt uneasy with Hugh Colborne.

"Benson isn't coming. I sent the invitation."

Henry flashed confusion. "You? Why would you pretend to be Mr. Benson?"

"Because I feared that you wouldn't accept my invitation after what happened between you and my daughter. I encouraged you to see her. You did—thank you, son—but she mistreated you again. I apologise, Henry, and I beg your forgiveness."

Henry was not receptive to contrition expressed through deception.

"My daughter," Hugh continued, "it's worse than I thought. She treated you badly, again, but this time, you experienced manipulation of my daughter by someone who has led her down the path of sin and put her body and soul in jeopardy."

"I want nothing more to do with your daughter." Henry could sense perspiration forming on his forehead.

"I do not wish for you to have more contact with the woman you wanted. It can only lead to more temptation, more urges, more sins." Hugh picked at Henry's scabs.

Henry leaned back, retreating from Hugh and the feelings welling up. But he could not avoid the truth of it—the temptations, the urges, the sins, the wounds.

"No matter how much she has humiliated me," Hugh shifted forward, "I am her father, responsible for my wayward child. So, can I, a desperate father, beg you, a soldier of Christ, to save her body and soul? Henry, she's a weak, confused, and sensuous woman vulnerable to manipulation by men interested in possessing her, violating her."

Still leaning back, Henry crossed his arms as a shield. "Your daughter doesn't strike me as weak, confused, or vulnerable."

"That's what I thought, but I was blind. Now I see that she has been misled by men she trusted. When she rejected your love the first time, Geoffrey Hancock poisoned her against you. When she refused you again, James Bingham did the same. Both acted out of jealousy."

"Hancock and Bingham, jealous of me?" Henry was not persuaded.

"Think about it," Hugh was ready. "Hancock believed himself a friend to sad, lonely, beautiful Rosamund, and, with his wife dead from the cancer, he wanted her. But you, as her husband, would have thwarted his desires, so he turned her against you."

Henry blamed himself for failing with Rosamund. He had never considered that she might have been manipulated.

"As for Bingham," Hugh continued, "you had the courage to ask Rosamund to marry you—something the coward can't do.

He fears that you'll steal her away because you have the fortitude he lacks. Bingham convinced her to lash out at you."

Henry knew this was balderdash. His visit to Rosamund after reading his father's note was spontaneous. Bingham could not have known about the note or the visit. Henry's discomfort with Colborne deepened.

Henry hesitated but went ahead. "At that trial, what she said—was that Bingham as well?"

"No," Hugh had prepared for this. "Hancock again. Slander me, take over the business, and then prey on vulnerable Rosamund who will need a husband or suffer a dismal future."

Henry disbelieved this convoluted and disingenuous explanation of Rosamund's behaviour, but reluctantly asked, "How does any of this help me to save her?"

"Bingham isn't going to marry her. He wants to exploit her unfortunate situation to have immoral relations with her."

Hugh paused dramatically before delivering the decisive blow. "He wants to dress Rosamund like a whore, fornicate with her, and then punish her for the deed."

Henry swallowed hard, nearly choking in the effort. How did Colborne know? What did the merchant want for that sin to remain secret? Was all that Hancock and Bingham nonsense a contrived prelude to blackmail? Henry uncrossed his arms, unclenched his hands, and put them flat on the table to calm himself.

He raised his face to meet Hugh's. "What do you want?"

Hearing the strain in Henry's voice, Hugh laid his hands on top of Henry's. "Teach Bingham a brutal, bloody lesson he'll never forget."

Henry felt sweat running down his neck as the *quid pro quo* became clear—an act of violence to ensure that another act of violence stayed secret.

"I'll arrange the rendezvous, and let you know when and where," Hugh continued.

"What if he doesn't come?" Henry feared what Colborne might do if Bingham foiled the plan.

"I'll include sufficient enticements to make sure he does." Hugh had the answers.

Trapped, Henry said nothing.

"But you must do it quickly because you are leaving for Africa soon," Hugh roughly seized Henry's hands to ensure the message was clear. "Unless there are developments that end your life as a missionary and put you in gaol for a long time."

Hugh then stood, went to order a drink, and engaged in boisterous conversation with the tavern keeper. As Henry collected his things to leave, Hugh turned with his ale, pointed at Henry, and loudly addressed the tavern. "Let me buy a round for everyone and toast Henry Wattling and the one final service he shall render me before he leaves to honour God in Africa."

Amidst the cheers for the free round, Henry weakly smiled, put on his hat, and left the tavern. Once outside, he breathed deeply to calm himself. He wiped his brow with a handkerchief. He walked slowly to where he had tethered his horse. Colborne's informants had done well, and now the merchant threatened to destroy him if he did not attack Bingham.

But what had Bingham done to deserve violence? Was Colborne seeking revenge against the barrister? Against Rosamund perhaps, for whom marriage to Bingham was her escape from a frightful fate? Revenge for what she said at that trial. For slandering her father. For manipulating society. For violating the truth. For destroying people. For her cruelty. Like daughter, like father.

Henry mounted his horse greatly agitated. He would not beat Bingham senseless. But given Colborne's threat, he should leave Constantinople sooner than planned. He needed to be done forever with this forsaken city.

Hugh Colborne accepted the gratitude of patrons quaffing the free round and then stood alone at the bar sipping ale. He didn't give a tinker's damn what Henry Wattling did next.

Chapter 25

Sovereignty

The messenger was worried. "I'm only paid by the sender if I give the letter to him personally."

"You can wait until he returns," Henry Wroth said. "Or again, just leave it. We handle correspondence here all the time. Mr. Bingham will get it today just as if you handed it to him."

The messenger did not move, so Henry asked, "Who's the sender?"

The messenger hesitated before tentatively responding, "Colborne."

"Ah," Henry said, knowing Rosamund's penchant for sending correspondence to James at the court. "Then you can be assured that, if you leave it with me, that letter will be the first thing Mr. Bingham reads once he's back."

The messenger still hesitated. Henry rolled his eyes and fished some coins from his pocket and dropped them one by one into the boy's hand until his palm was sufficiently greased to leave the letter. Henry put it on top of the documents stacked on the table in the clerk's room.

James was with Judge Hornby in the Ministry of Justice at the Sublime Porte. The Minister of Justice, Ahmed Pasha, had asked to discuss the *Enoch Wright* case. Edmund brought James, who knew the legal issues. Both barristers suspected that the meeting would involve more unpleasantness with the Ottoman government. Ahmed Pasha set the tone by making them wait for hours on a bench in a hallway outside his office. Judge Hornby had dozed off, his head propped against the wall and his mouth agape.

James had never been inside the Ministry of Justice. He watched the people bustling in and out of the minister's office. He then loosened his legs by walking around. He thought that he glimpsed the *mufti* whom Mehmed knew at the end of an adjacent corridor. Perhaps Mehmed had started his position at the ministry, and the *mufti* was visiting him. Meandering back to the bench, he wondered whether Mehmed had forgotten about that gift from Rosamund. He wondered whether he had done the right thing that morning when he saw Rosamund leave her secret ruin. James eased back on the bench, leaned his head against the wall, and closed his eyes.

The judge and law clerk were embarrassed when the Minister of Justice woke them up. As he led them to his office, Ahmed Pasha apologised for the delay, blaming it on urgent matters piled on the usual crush of demands.

"I asked you here today," Ahmed Pasha began, "to inform you that we are proceeding, in civil law, against the English owners of the *Enoch Wright,* who are responsible for operating a tugboat on the Bosphorus in violation of Ottoman port and coastal water regulations."

"Your Excellency," interrupted Judge Hornby.

"We aren't here," the minister interrupted the judge's interruption, "to debate our course of action. I am simply informing you that we are starting legal proceedings against the owners of the *Enoch Wright.*"

"Will you," the judge interrupted again, "grant me the courtesy of informing you that your course of action is illegal?"

"You and your staff have made the British government's position clear. I do not need to hear it again," Ahmed Pasha replied.

"Your Excellency, you are turning a legal matter into a diplomatic dispute. It won't end with you and me," Judge Hornby protested.

"The British government invariably turns legal issues into diplomatic disputes, so it's our turn," the minister replied. "Our actions should communicate that we will, from now on, aggressively challenge claims of jurisdiction made under the capitulations. We have placated and prevaricated long enough. Now we are going to defend and assert our sovereignty."

Judge Hornby and James were then unceremoniously ushered out of Ahmed Pasha's office. As soon as they were well away from the office, the judge moved James by the arm into a stairwell.

James spoke first, "They're taking legal action against the owners of the *Enoch Wright*? Not the captain and crew?"

"Clever," Edmund responded. "They're asserting sovereignty but not through criminal law. It forces a fight over the treaty, a fight they want over this incident. Let's head back to the court, but after that, I'll brief the embassy, and you'll find Mehmed. Tell him about the political risks that the Ministry of Justice will run in taking this course of action. If you can't locate him, find the *mufti*, and persuade him to talk some sense into Ahmed Pasha."

—

Hasan stroked his beard as he sat waiting. It was a soothing habit, even when things seemed to be falling apart. Sometimes there was nothing to do but wait for the world to come around. He closed his eyes, his fingers making slow revolutions around his whiskers.

Eventually, the door opened. He kept his eyes shut as people shuffled into the room. He heard the chair opposite scrap across the floor as someone sat. Papers thudded onto the table. No one spoke. When the room went quiet, he opened his eyes.

"Teacher," said the man across the table, "we need your help."

Hasan did not recognise the man, who was in European clothes. He glanced at the three people standing behind the man, only one of whom wore a police uniform. Hasan nodded that he understood. The man placed an envelope on the table with *Bon Mots* written upon it.

"Please, can you take the slips of paper out of this envelope?" asked the man.

"Please," responded Hasan, "can you tell me who you are?"

"My apologies. I am Bakir Nazim, the new Deputy Minister of Police. I am investigating an incident that occurred yesterday."

"I was teaching yesterday and witnessed no incident."

"We haven't asked you here as a witness. We want your help with evidence found at the scene," Nazim said.

"An envelope?"

"Containing slips of paper. Please, take the slips out of the envelope, read them, and tell us what you make of them," the deputy minister requested.

"These slips are obviously of some concern to you. Can you enlighten me as to what troubles you about them?" Hasan did not want to appear too eager to help.

Nazim would not play along. "We can talk about that after we hear your thoughts."

Hasan opened the envelope, retrieved the slips, and began to read. A trace smile peeked through his beard. When he finished, he straightened the slips and returned them to the envelope.

"What do you think? What's the purpose of these slips?" Nazim enquired.

"I think a student tried to be a teacher, and now you're asking a teacher to explain a student. It would be easier to ask the student." Hasan pushed the envelope to Nazim.

The deputy minister of police was not amused. "I'm asking about the purpose of the slips. I'm not asking who wrote them."

"You're asking me to tell you what this person intended without informing me who did it. It would be easier to help if you told me who wrote the slips." Hasan thought he could string things out a bit more.

The deputy minister scratched his temple in frustration. "Teacher—"

Hasan held up his hand for Nazim to stop. "Most, but not all, of the slips are written in the style of *fatwas* used in teaching *sharia*. There's a question, then an answer. Studying *fatwas* helps students to understand the law and the reasoning behind it. It looks as if someone was attempting to teach something to the reader, or at least make the reader think, and discuss over coffee."

"I didn't say anything about a coffee house," Nazim asserted.

Hasan feigned surprise. "Neither did I. I merely said coffee, which can be taken at home, a mosque or, yes, a coffee house."

"Don't play games, Kazim Hasan."

The *mufti* ignored the bluster. "One slip describes how extensively *kadis* are trained in *sharia*. It then asks whether, in government tribunals, it is acceptable for those presiding to have no legal training. Its answer is, 'Yes, legal training is not required to apply law and administer justice.'"

"That sounds like the attacks that Europeans make on our justice system, our government, and the Sultan," the deputy minister argued.

Hasan shook his head. "No, you'd make a poor law student. Let me teach you. Deputy Minister Nazim, what's the first thing on the slip?"

"I don't know."

"Please open the envelope and find the slip in question," Hasan requested.

Nazim whisked the envelope to one of the men behind him, who fumbled through it to find the slip. He handed it to the deputy minister, who slapped it on the table. The *mufti* understood the gesture, so he read the first sentence of the slip out loud.

"So, deputy minister, what law is the first line emphasising?" Hasan asked.

The deputy minister's exasperation almost boiled over, "*Sharia*."

"Correct. Now, the slip asks whether it is appropriate for those presiding over government tribunals, which do not apply *sharia*, to have little or no legal training. What is your answer, based on what the slip tells you about *sharia*?"

Nazim did not reply.

"Don't be shy, you can answer. If we extensively train experts to apply *sharia*, should we not also extensively train experts to apply the Sultan's legislation? Your answer?" Hasan persisted.

When the deputy minister still did not respond, the *mufti* tried again. "Let me rephrase the question. Do you agree with the answer on the slip—that, in the pursuit of justice, it is acceptable not to train experts to apply Ottoman law?"

Hasan waited a moment or two but did not expect Nazim to speak, so he proceeded with the lesson. "Where does this slip mention European views, European laws, or European anything? You claim that the slip contains European criticism of how we exercise our sovereignty. Tell me, where is that criticism on the slip?"

Nazim still did not respond.

"Isn't it asking the reader to think about whether we should change based on our own traditions?" Hasan continued. "Rather than reflecting on it, you saw what you wanted to see, what confirms your fears, what tempts your prejudices, what suits your interests, what scares your sovereign. The incident yesterday arose from the same self-serving reactions."

"These slips incited a riot," the deputy minister said. "Religious leaders have condemned them for mocking *fatwas* and *sharia*. Other slips—so-called *mots de la guerre*—have appeared around the city threatening Europeans for slandering Islam. And you're telling me that these slips are teaching people to learn from Islam?"

"Not all are about learning from Islam," Hasan replied. "Some reflect common sense. Others are, well, confusing. But yes, the optimism about man's willingness to stop and think proved a miscalculation. I suspect those rioting, issuing words of war, crying blasphemy, interrogating people, and conflating sovereignty with justice have not read the *bon mots*. Sadly, slips of paper proved a poor choice to communicate something important—we can change on our terms and not on those dictated by others."

"So you know who wrote them." Nazim removed a hand-written manuscript from a folder and pushed it toward Hasan.

"Do you want me to teach you what this means?" The *mufti* risked Nazim's wrath.

"No. This document is treasonous. It attacks the Sultan and his exercise of religious and political authority," Nazim said.

"You are a poor student," Hasan responded.

"We don't know whether it has been shared among those who are hostile to the Sultan—shared in ways that try to avoid the fate of traitors who propagate sedition. We don't know whether it has been shared, for example, with you," the deputy minister replied.

"It hasn't been shared with me, nor has it been shared with anyone," the *mufti* asserted.

"There's only one way you could know that," Nazim shot back.

"And that's the only reason I'm here," retorted Hasan. "So ask me what you really want to know."

———

James stayed atop Bones as Judge Hornby stabled his horse and went inside the court building. He then rode off with Halil to find Mehmed. James thought the task futile. He was never going to persuade Mehmed to do the court's bidding even if he managed to find the Turk. Mehmed could be at the Sublime Porte, on the European side of the strait where he once lived, or anywhere in-between. As they rode off, James noticed that Halil was not his dynamic, avuncular self. He did not take the initiative in the search or hum and sing, something James always enjoyed when Halil provided his escort.

"No songs today?" James asked.

"My apologies, but I am tired and thirsty after this long day. It's Ramadan," Halil said.

James dismissed Halil to let him break his fast, telling the *cavass* that he would head home and thus no longer needed an escort. Instead, James rode alone around the Pera district looking for Mehmed in various places, coffee houses and the like.

As afternoon progressed into evening with no sign of Mehmed, James switched, as the judge had ordered, to the equally hopeless search for Hasan. Fatigue was coming over Bones. He found a water trough for his horse to drink while deciding where to look for Hasan. Only one place came to mind—the Ottoman law school. Perhaps the *mufti* lived near it. Mehmed had mentioned that the school was across the Bosphorus in a neighbourhood close to St. Sophia. James had been to St. Sophia only once for a miserable standing-about in a frigid drizzle while the Sultan did something or other at the ancient basilica.

Retracing the route that the court staff had taken that day, he rode down to the water to take a *caique* across the strait. Evening was evolving into night as he secured Bones for his return. The bare-chested *caiquejee* moved with alacrity to power the small vessel toward old Stamboul. He was a magnificent Turk, with gleaming muscles honed from rowing across the water and a green turban glinting with the light coming alive in front of James. Lights, thousands of them, illuminated mosques across the old city. Each mosque visible from the Bosphorus had lamps and lanterns strung between minarets, walls, and domes. Some lanterns were shaped like flowers, birds, and ships and appeared to float through the air. This fantastical sight brightened as the old city came closer with each stroke of the *caiquejee*. Nothing James had seen in England at Christmastide rivalled this display of religious thanksgiving.

After securing the *caique* on the other side, the *caiquejee* helped James disembark and thrust a pomegranate into his hands. "*Iftar*, bono Johnny, *iftar*!" exclaimed the *caiquejee* in encouraging James to partake in the evening meal that ended the day's Ramadan fasting.

James began to make his way in what he thought was the direction of St. Sophia, but the great edifice, so clear in crossing the strait, became impossible to see on foot amidst the tangle of buildings in the old city. People filled the streets in response to the call for prayers reverberating among and above the buildings. James joined one surging flow, guessing it was headed toward St. Sophia. He was wrong and ended up before a different mosque—he did not know which. The mosque received the worshippers, leaving James alone before it. The building had a simple, abstract grandeur, made more striking by the lamps and lanterns illuminating its walls, galleries, cupolas, and minarets. He stood still soaking in its magnificence.

The passing of a dog reminded James that he had a mission, but he had no idea where he was or where he needed to go. He scanned the square, picked the biggest street leading off it, and ambled down it without expecting the effort to lead him to Hasan. The street, and others he aimlessly took, were empty and quiet. He stopped at an open café, ordered coffee, cut and pulled the pomegranate apart, and slowly ate it. A group of old men, some in turbans and some in fezzes, sat nearby drawing on narghiles. The most ancient of the group nodded his turbaned head at James.

Well after James had finished his leisurely repast, the streets filled with people leaving the mosques. He left piasters for his coffee and merged with the flow, letting it take him wherever it went. The wave eventually deposited him by a garden. A puppet stage stood in the middle of it, and a few coins in the hand of someone standing before a gate gave James entrance. He leaned against a tree and watched Turks, adults and children, gathering in front of the stage. The scene reminded him of when he had watched Punch and Judy as a boy with his father. The audience, he recalled, was laughing and clapping as the puppets pummelled each other. His father clipped his ear and demanded to know why he was not enjoying the show. He had replied, "It's like late at night, with Mum, when you come home from the pub."

The crowd roared as the curtain on the stage opened to reveal shadow puppets illuminated from behind. The puppets moved exquisitely through the skill of a master puppeteer. The translucent puppets—made of coloured paper or vellum—were jointed, allowing arms, hands, legs, feet, and heads to move. The children began yelling *"karagoz"* as one puppet took centre stage. James had no idea what tales were being told. The *karagoz* appeared to be a rival of another, more sophisticated puppet. The crowd, adults and children alike, seemed familiar with the characters and what was taking place. Everyone was having a good time.

James paid closer attention when a puppet with a Union Jack dress, golden crown, and sceptre appeared. Some conversation or argument unfolded between the *karagoz* and Queen Victoria, and the crowd fell quiet, suggesting that this scene was not anticipated. Her Majesty raised the sceptre as if to knight the *karagoz*, but the sceptre's next motion took the head off the puppet. Silence descended over the garden. The shadow of a hand appeared and attempted to put the head back on. It swivelled and fell again. The curtain abruptly closed, and murmurs rumbled through the garden. James became uncomfortable as people, including children, began staring at him, as if he was complicit in the decapitation. James watched the crowd disperse, but not without final glances thrown at him as people departed.

The *caique* ride back was choppy, as the rising wind drove swells across the water. James turned to watch the illuminated mosques of old Stamboul retreat as the strokes of the *caiquejee* bit the water. James found Bones where he had left him, and he steered his horse toward the Hornby residence. There was no point stopping by the court. Whatever had accumulated could wait until tomorrow. No stable hands were around when he arrived. He settled Bones into a stall and went into the residence. He did not see anyone.

In his room, the long day's events flooded through his mind, but he was too exhausted to process it all. He laid down, intending to rest only for a moment before jotting down some notes for Judge Hornby on his search for Mehmed and the *mufti*. Instead, he fell asleep.

—

He slipped the watch back into his waistcoat pocket. The appointed hour had long passed, but the mark never showed. They would still demand compensation. He readied the payment.

"That's right, guv. You pay though me boys didn't get to play, just like last time."

"Easy money, then."

"A bit more makes it sure we don't tell no one 'bout these jobs."

A bit more appeared, duly anticipated. The cost of doing business.

Chapter 26
A Turk, A Mahomedan

As was his habit, James rose before dawn. Having fallen deeply asleep, James felt, for once, refreshed in waking. After changing clothes and having some bread and fruit, he left before anyone in the residence was stirring. Although stable hands were around somewhere, he saddled Bones and, in the fresh morning, enjoyed a pleasant ride to the court.

On the clerk's table, James found the usual stack of documents. After sorting the top bits and pieces on pending cases and other court business, he found something unexpected—a familiar light blue envelope addressed to him. He opened it to discover that it was from Rosamund, but it was not in her hand. The letter informed James that she was with a friend who had given birth. Probably Maggie, James thought, visiting from Malta. Rosamund apologised for dictating the letter while helping with mother and child. Given her present commitments, she had two favours to ask. First, she wanted him to meet Henry Wattling and deliver her apologies for her behaviour and her best wishes for his new life in Africa. The letter came with a wax-sealed note that she desired James to hand directly to Henry. The letter concluded by saying that, for the second favour, she wanted to see James on Saturday for tea and hear him ask "a very welcome question."

James set the missive down. He looked again at when and where he was supposed to have met Wattling—last night at a tavern near the Galata docks. Hadn't Wattling departed for Africa? Hadn't Rosamund reconciled with Henry? However odd it all was, he would have delivered her message and the note had he received it in a timely way. And she wanted to hear a "very welcome question"? Was she realising that he was the only way out of her predicament?

He picked up the sealed note intended for Wattling's eyes only. He turned it around in his fingers. What did she want to say secretly to Henry? It was none of his business, but he could not make sense of any of it—the dictated letter, the arranged meeting, the private note. He broke the seal and unfolded the note. Blank. Not a word. He gaped at the empty paper, as if hexed.

After the spell subsided, he retrieved an ashtray, found matches, and set the letter and note aflame, dropping them into the ashtray as the burn took hold. He disposed of the ashes, wiped the ashtray, and opened windows to clear lingering smoke. He could feign ignorance, telling Rosamund that he never received a letter. The ruse would not prevent him from asking the question. As distraction from the discomfort of more deception concerning Rosamund, James began slogging through the stack of legal documents.

Judge Hornby arrived at the court thereafter, with Henry Wroth on his heels. James met them outside the judge's office and informed Edmund that he had not found Mehmed or Hasan. Henry interjected that, last night, tavern chatter suggested that the Mussulman fanatic was in trouble again, something about a riot at a coffee house. James mentioned that he might have seen Hasan yesterday at the Ministry of Justice, but this information did not clarify whether Mehmed was in trouble.

Edmund turned to go into his office but paused to clasp his hand on James's shoulder. "Son, ask Rosamund to marry you. Stop prevaricating, for her sake at least."

Henry signalled for James to come into his office. Henry closed the door and told James that, yesterday, Frederick Guarracino had taken statements from a woman and a man who alleged that Henry Wattling had whipped the woman with a leather and metal belt. Henry asked whether James had heard anything about Wattling or his whereabouts. James shook his head, deciding not to mention the burned letter and note. Henry wanted James to know that, based on the statements, the court had issued a warrant for Wattling's arrest.

Uneasy about the morning's developments, James began to return to the clerk's room. He encountered a man in the hallway whom he did not recognise. The man needed to talk urgently with Judge Hornby. James ushered him into Hornby's office, and the man closed the door in James's face. Henry happened to witness the scene and leaned against his office doorway. Then Edmund's voice blasted beyond his office, "Beaten?"

Spooked, James and Henry looked at each other, and Henry moved to stand by James.

"Beaten?" they heard Edmund say again, this time with more anguish than astonishment.

Henry knocked and opened the door. Edmund gestured for Henry and James to come in. The man glanced at the two barristers, then turned to the judge. "Yes. Alive, but badly beaten."

The judge sat down as if his knees gave out, elbows landing on the desk and head falling into his hands. Edmund lifted his head and, barely above a whisper, asked again, "Beaten?"

"I've never seen such a thing," the man choked up. "May God have mercy."

"Sir?" Henry managed to say.

"Rosamund Colborne was attacked last night." Edmund's head stayed in his hands.

The sentence concussed the room.

"Attacked?" Henry repeated in disbelief.

James then realised that everyone was looking at him.

"James, my God," Henry said with affection, something that James had never heard from him before.

"Your Honour," started the man who broke the news.

"Sorry, Henry, James, this is Morris Fletcher. He works at the Colborne residence," Edmund interrupted, but no one shook hands.

"Your Honour," continued Morris. "We have the perpetrator. Found him last night near the residence. Hands and clothes covered with blood."

This information was electric.

"We locked him up but couldn't find the constable last night. You need to send Williams to arrest him and put him in your gaol. Dr. Hoyland's at the residence," Morris explained, his voice catching again. "I'm sorry, I've never seen such a dreadful thing."

"Who is he? The perpetrator," asked Edmund, who was back on his feet.

"A Turk, a Mahomedan."

This information was disconcerting.

"What's his name?" Henry jumped in.

"Hasn't given his name or answered questions," replied Morris.

"Has he said anything?" Henry probed.

"He made one request," responded Morris.

"What was it?" Edmund demanded.

"That Your Honour be informed," Morris said. "That's why I'm here."

"The attacker knows Judge Hornby?" Henry was confused.

"Don't know," Morris replied. "He asked that the Supreme English Judge be informed. Speaks English."

"A Turk who speaks English asked that the Supreme English Judge be informed that Rosamund Colborne has been attacked?" Henry attempted to summarise.

"Your Honour," said Morris, "I should get back. Katherine is in shock, and we're trying to find Hugh to let him know."

Fletcher did not wait for a response before leaving. The office fell silent.

"It can't be," mumbled Henry, who crumpled into a chair and threw his head back as if to curse the heavens.

"No." James grasped Henry's meaning.

"Mehmed." Edmund completed the terrible conclusion.

Chapter 27
Compromise

James sat on the edge of the bed, holding his aching head in his hands. He had not slept. The tragedy had tossed, turned, and tormented him throughout the night. Rosamund had been savagely beaten. Mehmed was in the consular court's gaol. News of the attack—and the inevitable rumours—had roared like wildfire across the British community in Constantinople. From within the residence's dining room, he could hear another embassy attaché blasting Judge Hornby with more of Ambassador Bulwer's anger.

He had already asked for Bones to be saddled and prepared to ride, but James did not know where to go. Should he comfort Rosamund at her residence? Console Mehmed in the gaol? Contain the damage at the court? Perhaps he would let Bones shamble wherever the horse wished to go—just to escape the nightmare of it all.

James dragged himself to the stables, where, to his surprise, Halil was on his mount, waiting.

"The judge is probably not going to the court today," James said to the *cavass*.

"I am here for you," Halil replied, his face tense.

James led Bones from his stall and mounted. "I can ride to the court without a security escort, just like every other day." At least he had decided his destination.

Halil nervously shook his head. "I go with you this morning." Possibly sensing its rider's uneasy mood, Halil's horse snorted and side-stepped nervously.

James could see that Halil was worried but determined to see James to the court safely. "Is there something I should know? That the judge and the court's staff should know?"

Halil calmed his horse by stroking its neck. "No. I just have no good feeling about this morning." A feeling, he did not add, fermented by furtive whispers among his colleagues last night.

James did not have the energy to argue with Halil, so he shrugged and guided Bones forward. Instead of riding alongside, Halil spurred his horse ahead of Bones. Once clear of the residence, the *cavass* signalled for James to follow him in a direction different from the one normally taken to the court. James halted Bones, intending to insist that Halil tell him what was going on. Before Halil could wheel around, Ottoman police emerged, as if from nowhere, and surrounded James.

Halil powered his horse through the cordon, and James had difficulty keeping a spooked Bones from bolting. Although Halil was riding tall in his saddle, James realised that the *cavass* did not know what to do, which unsettled him given Halil's usual confidence.

One man stepped forward. "Mr. James Bingham, I am Bakir Nazim, Deputy Minister of Police. I am arresting you for the assault on Miss Rosamund Colborne."

"Nazim," Halil placed his horse between the deputy minister and Bones. "You will not arrest someone under my protection. This is my oath as a soldier, and my honour as a man."

"Deputy Minister," James began, "any criminal case involving two British subjects falls under the jurisdiction of the British consular court. You have no legal authority to arrest me for that crime."

"Then I will arrest Halil, as a criminal," Nazim stated with relish.

"I have jurisdiction to arrest him," Nazim spoke to James, pointing at Halil. "He is an Ottoman subject who is, at this very moment, opposing the exercise of the Sultan's authority. That crime does not end well for the guilty—especially at the *Bagnio*."

Halil turned in his saddle to look at James, his eyes filled with confusion and fear.

"Or," Nazim began to walk towards Bones, "we can ride to the English court, and you can turn Osman Mehmed over to me. If I do not have jurisdiction over you, then you do not have the authority to arrest him for this crime—but I do."

James perceived menace in Nazim's desire to arrest Mehmed not related to the attack on Rosamund, but he did not understand the reason for it. James looked at Halil, who shook his head against agreeing to Nazim's proposition.

James saw that Halil was in an impossible situation and sensed that Mehmed was in some sort of danger with the Sublime Porte. It was time for him to be decisive.

"Deputy Minister," James shifted Bones to speak directly to Nazim. "Halil is protecting me under the authority of the Sultan, so his actions in doing so cannot be criminal. But he protects at my discretion. I hereby release Halil from his duties today, and he shall leave here unimpeded. Then you may arrest me."

Halil brought his horse alongside Bones. "No, Mr. Bingham," he said in a low voice, "do not capitulate."

James glanced at Nazim, who nodded his agreement to the compromise. James grasped Halil's arm. "Please go. But, my friend, come and sing me songs at the *Bagnio*."

Halil did not move or speak, but tears formed in his eyes. James placed a hand on Halil's shoulder and shepherded him and his horse through the cordon.

—

Edmund paced his office in a desperate effort to contain his emotions. Now, more than ever, his responsibilities as a representative of Her Majesty's Government and an advocate for the rule of law required dispassion. But could he act without bias? Within a day of the news of the attack on Rosamund, the Ottoman police had detained not only James Bingham but also Hugh Colborne on suspicion of committing criminal assault against her. It was, Edmund believed, retaliation for his detention of Mehmed as a suspect for the same crime. Justice was imperative for the victim and the suspects, but the British and Ottoman governments were in a standoff.

The situation stirred up gale-force political winds. A seething Ambassador Bulwer had personally tongue-lashed Edmund about the British community's fury over the attack on an Englishwoman by a Turk, who had previously assaulted the woman's father and threatened Christians with violence. The ambassador frothed about the Ottoman government's "barbaric kidnapping" of British subjects. Turks were outraged that the British claimed jurisdiction over the crime and were convinced that the consular court would not treat Mehmed fairly. The detention of Bingham and Colborne signalled that the Sublime

Porte opposed British jurisdiction, and Rifat Pasha made it clear to Ambassador Bulwer that he wanted Mehmed in Ottoman custody for the crime of sedition.

Edmund feared the crisis could undermine London's backing for the court and the expansion of consular judicial reform through Ottoman dominions. The blame would fall on him if the case became a disaster for Her Majesty's Government. This crisis could damage everything that he had built and destroy the Foreign Office's interest in taking his strategy to the Far East.

He also felt deep guilt. His clerks were both suspects in the same heinous crime. James in a Turkish gaol brought back horrid images branded into his memory by visits to Ottoman prisons. And that poor girl, whom Edmund had hoped James would marry, was struggling to recover. No matter how much he detested Hugh Colborne, the man deserved the presumption of innocence and a fair trial—neither, he believed, a Turkish tribunal would accord him.

Edmund had already taken initial steps in responding to the crisis. He telegraphed Donald Logie and asked him to return to Constantinople to provide support with James in Ottoman detention. Donald came immediately and set to work on the jurisdictional questions. The judge assigned Henry Wroth the criminal law issues. He sent Frederick Guarracino to visit Bingham and Colborne to ensure their treatment was acceptable. His wife kept him informed about Rosamund.

Preliminary discussions confirmed Edmund's sense of the critical issues. What happened to Rosamund was a criminal offence under English law and the Ottoman Imperial Criminal Code. The most contentious issue was whether the consular court should treat Bingham and Colborne as suspects. Edmund argued that they should not without evidence akin to what the court had against Mehmed. Donald and Henry pushed back, noting that collecting evidence required interrogating Bingham and Colborne, which was, in essence, treating them like suspects. Donald added that not doing so would expose the court to charges of granting Englishmen favourable treatment—exactly the prejudice Turks complained about concerning Mehmed's arrest.

With his experience in criminal law, Henry raised questions that chipped away at Edmund's stubbornness. Hugh Colborne, Henry noted, might have had a motive for attacking his daughter, especially after her testimony at Mehmed's trial. Such a credible motive meant that, no matter what court had jurisdiction, Colborne should be interrogated. Where was he on the night Rosamund was attacked? Can he corroborate his whereabouts at the time of the assault? Edmund more readily accepted Henry's analysis concerning Colborne than he did for James.

"Do you believe," Edmund angrily asked, "James capable of such evil?"

"No, I don't believe that James beat Rosamund," Henry answered. "But Edmund, what we believe isn't the measure of what justice demands. We must ask the difficult questions. We cannot have justice without answers. Where was James on the night of the attack?"

Judge Hornby shrugged. He knew what he had tasked James to do but not where James had been that night.

"So, we don't know where James Bingham was on the night of the crime," Henry was in full barrister mode. "Have you searched his room for evidence related to the crime? For blood on his clothes? For evidence that could exonerate him?"

Edmund shook his head, realising that he would have to order Constable Williams to search James's room.

"How interesting," Henry started pacing. "And Mr. Bingham lives in your house. Have you talked to anyone about the suspect's whereabouts on the night of the attack or the status of his relationship with Miss Colborne?"

"Are you suggesting James had a motive to smash up Rosamund?" Edmund protested. "He wants to marry the girl."

"Really?" Henry intoned, acting as counsel for the Crown. "Has the defendant asked the victim to marry him?"

"No," replied Edmund.

"If the accused wants to marry her, why hasn't he asked, after so many months, so many cups of tea, and so many chances, including the obvious opportunity that the young woman's desperate fate has created?" Henry pressed.

Edmund had no response.

"Could it be," Henry continued, "that the alleged perpetrator has not asked because he feared that she would reject and humiliate him—as she did Henry Wattling? That she had, in fact, been manipulating him all along?"

"I see your point," Edmund conceded.

"No, let me finish," Henry wanted to complete the case. "Are members of the jury to believe that passions enflamed by unrequited love cannot be a motive for criminal behaviour?"

Henry paused dramatically. "Have you asked the victim who attacked her?"

Henry knew, as did Edmund and Donald, that no one had questioned Rosamund. Her injuries rendered her unable to endure the preliminary examination normally undertaken in a criminal case.

The harder questions involved jurisdiction and criminal procedure, and how these issues forced the desire for justice to cope with the demands of politics. The court could not claim treaty jurisdiction over Mehmed because he was no longer a clerk at the court. The capitulations did not accord the court jurisdiction over crimes because the victim was British. The Ottoman claim of jurisdiction over Mehmed concerning the crime was correct.

But, as Henry explained, Mehmed would be prosecuted under the Ottoman temporary code of criminal procedure adopted earlier in the year. Edmund had excoriated this code in a despatch to the Foreign Office for failing to ensure appropriate pre-trial treatment and lacking procedures for a fair trial for suspects. The barristers believed that admitting the Ottomans had jurisdiction meant abandoning Mehmed to injustice. Remember, Henry noted, the police and the palace had wanted Mehmed detained before the attack on Rosamund. The Ottomans would prosecute Mehmed for sedition, which compounded British concerns about an unjust trial.

The British government had ironclad jurisdiction, Donald argued, over Bingham and Colborne. The victim and suspects were all British—the classical basis for British extraterritorial jurisdiction in Ottoman domains. Bingham and Colborne were in Ottoman custody in violation of the treaty. Exchanging Mehmed for Bingham and Colborne satisfied no one on the British side. Even Ambassador Bulwer—always prowling for ways out of diplomatic imbroglios—understood the British community would erupt if the Turk who almost every British subject believed was guilty of beating an Englishwoman near to death was handed over to the Ottomans.

While pacing his office, the judge knew the solution must be legally sound and politically acceptable. Ideally, he should recuse himself from presiding over Mehmed's trial. But, even if one were available, a different British judge might rule that the court did not have jurisdiction, turn Mehmed over to the Ottomans without securing the release of Bingham and Colborne, and cause the court irreparable political damage.

He contemplated various alternatives, but he gravitated toward a compromise—a joint criminal trial of all the suspects. The Ottomans could conduct preliminary investigations with Bingham and Colborne, supervised by the court's dragoman. The court could do the same with Mehmed, with Ottoman officials present. Should Miss Colborne recover sufficiently to undergo preliminary examination, the court would conduct it. The information from pre-trial efforts would be submitted to an *ad hoc* tribunal presided over by British and Ottoman jurists who would decide the case as equals.

He had not worked out the details. But with the Ottomans threatening to start proceedings against Bingham and Colborne, he needed to present his proposal to Rifat Pasha and Ahmed Pasha. After inking his pen, a painful irony paused his hand. His proposal for achieving justice would be stronger if James and Mehmed—two of the suspects—had completed the Turkish-English code of criminal procedure that he and Fuad Pasha had envisioned long ago.

—

Constable Williams opened Mehmed's cell for Hasan to enter. He slammed the cell door shut and stood outside, with arms crossed in disapproval of Judge Hornby's decision to let Hasan speak with the attacker of Rosamund Colborne. Hasan ignored the constable, cut off Mehmed's expressions of respect and gratitude, and bluntly spoke his mind. Mehmed went cold.

"Teacher," he finally spoke. "How can we? We don't know who attacked her."

"Someone attacked her, and it wasn't you," Hasan replied forcefully. "Don't you believe he had a motive?"

Mehmed did not answer.

"He was tortured because of what happened after you—his rival at the law school and a clerk at the hated English court—defended an Englishwoman. He attacks her, gets revenge on you, and strikes a blow against the English. Even better, you have her blood on your hands, and the English and Ottoman governments come after you."

"No," Mehmed reacted, "he didn't break to avoid or end the torment. He didn't betray me. Why would he attack an innocent woman?"

"Mehmed," Hasan lifted his student's chin so that their eyes met. "Go back to before we met. Remember your shock when your sister was violated and then killed herself. Remember your shame when your mother slit the guilty throats. Remember your guilt when you did not fight the Russians. Remember your bitterness when you were starving on the streets, when you had to steal to survive, and when your father forced you to clean away the dregs of others. All of these stoked a rage that nearly destroyed you. And you don't think that Ali—a man tortured and deemed uncivilised—could unleash his fury on the English?"

Mehmed was nearly in tears. "No, he didn't give me up. How can you ask me to accuse him to save myself? That would be illegal, unjust, dishonourable."

Hasan did not hesitate. "Illegal? You don't know who attacked her. Unjust? All that needs to be done is to raise the possibility that Ali had a motive and might have done it—and then let the law take its course. Mehmed, you are innocent. You must be part of the search for truth and justice. Please compromise. Don't confuse honour with what is legal and what is just."

Mehmed gripped the *mufti*'s hands. "Promise me that you won't mention Ali's name in connection with this crime to anyone."

Hasan hesitated, but the conviction in Mehmed's request made him consent.

Hasan nodded and said as he stood to leave, "I hope Ali is wrong."

Mehmed's eyes flashed confusion, and Hasan did not want to part with doubt prevailing.

"I hope Ali is wrong that you are the biggest fool of all."

Chapter 28

A Mystery

"Miss Colborne," Judge Hornby began. "We are pleased that you are well enough to come before this court, and we hope that our proceedings do not hinder your recovery."

Rosamund, seated in a chair in front of the witness box, gave an appreciative nod for the judge's sentiments. Although a valiant effort had been made, the attempt to conceal the lingering damage to her face was not successful.

"Miss Colborne," Judge Hornby continued. "Your recovery did not progress sufficiently for you to participate in a preliminary examination, as typically required in criminal matters before this court. Counsel for the Crown and the defence agreed that the best course was to permit you to answer questions at trial. The Crown and the defence also agreed to forgo opening statements to reduce your time as a witness. You accepted this approach. Do you still wish to proceed?"

"Ask me your questions," Rosamund answered.

Edmund looked across the overcrowded courtroom, glanced at the jury, and again addressed the witness. "Miss Colborne, this trial only involves one accused person, Osman Mehmed. The Ottoman government refused to release James Bingham and Hugh Colborne to this court for this case. Under English law, suspects in criminal trials cannot be prosecuted *in absentia*. Mr. Bingham and Mr. Colborne are British subjects protected by the law. Do you understand?"

"Ask me your questions," Rosamund stated.

"One last preliminary," Judge Hornby continued. "The Ottoman government has provided us with statements taken from Mr. Bingham and Mr. Colborne for proceedings against them under Ottoman law. These statements were given in the presence of representatives of Her Majesty's Government. Today, the Crown and the defence might reference information from Mr. Bingham and Mr. Colborne provided by the Ottoman government. Representatives of the Ottoman government are present today to record your testimony, and they might use your testimony in their prosecution of Mr. Bingham and Mr. Colborne. Do you understand?"

"Ask me your questions."

Edmund nodded in Sebastian Knight's direction, and Knight stood to question Rosamund on behalf of the Crown. Usually for Edmund, the start of the Crown's case before a jury marked the moment when the process of discovering the truth merged law with justice. Today, however, the moment was not restorative. The British and Ottoman governments had failed to establish a shared tribunal to assess the innocence or guilt of three men accused of the same crime. The Sublime Porte rejected his proposal. It began proceedings against Bingham and Colborne, which forced Edmund's hand in starting the trial for Mehmed. The Ottoman government was taking an uncompromising stand, just as the Minister of Justice had promised. In a case full of oddities, it was an act of defiant sovereignty that Mehmed—the only suspect not being prosecuted under Ottoman law—would have applauded.

However, the Ottoman refusal to compromise perplexed Edmund. The Sublime Porte's approach flagrantly violated the capitulations. Although Edmund disagreed with them, Ahmed Pasha's arguments in the *Enoch Wright* case at least engaged with the law. However, refusing to accept the court's jurisdiction under treaty law for a criminal matter involving only British subjects—Rosamund, James, and Hugh—was legally radical, diplomatically offensive, and politically incendiary. Of course, the Ottoman government accused him of violating the treaty in putting Mehmed on trial, but in the balance of power between the two empires, the Ottomans had far more to lose in a tit-for-tat treaty fight.

It was some, if not much, comfort that the Ministry of Police had confined James and Hugh under appropriate conditions. Edmund had visited them to confirm what Frederick Guarracino reported about the standard of treatment. Things appeared to be in order, although the two men were bearing confinement differently. Hugh had maintained, as much as possible, his grooming and attire. James had not, letting his whiskers grow into a scruffy carpet and his clothes darken with grime. Edmund thought that Hugh had probably bribed the fleas to bite only James.

"Miss Colborne," Knight began. "Osman Mehmed has been accused of committing the crime of assault resulting in serious bodily harm. You have had the chance to review the charge and discuss it with the Crown and Judge Hornby. So, let me ask, did Mehmed attack you as laid out in the charge against him?"

Rosamund did not hesitate. "I do not know who attacked me."

In the dock, Mehmed fought the urge to look at Rosamund—the first time he had seen her since the attack. He concentrated instead on faces in the crowd. He locked eyes with Hasan, who executed a nearly imperceptible nod. Farther along he spotted Wroth and Logie sitting together and whispering. At the back of the courtroom, he saw Ali, who was staring straight at him without any expression.

"What do you remember about that evening?" enquired Knight.

"I went for a walk, about dusk, in the area behind our house. There are paths back there, and cool air in the evenings. Quiet walks there help me think, sort things out, make decisions."

"What decisions were you wrestling with that evening?" Knight followed up.

"Your Honour," Maurice Butt stood to protest. "What was on Miss Colborne's mind that evening bears no relevance to the question before this court."

Before Judge Hornby could speak, Rosamund answered, "I have decisions to make because I face changes in my life brought about by my own actions."

Virtually everyone in the courtroom knew the dilemma that Rosamund faced in being cut off from money and family.

"Did anyone know," Knight continued, "that you were taking a walk that evening?"

"I called to my mother that I was going for a walk, but I don't know if she heard me."

"Do you remember anything before the attack began? Did you see, hear, or sense anything?"

"The last thing I remember was the sound of the breeze rustling in the trees as night fell."

"What did you do after the attack started?"

"I tried to scream, from instinct, to survive, but I don't know if I made any noise. Then I pleaded for it to stop, begged to make it stop—and it did. But he started again."

"How do you know it was a man who attacked you?" Knight probed.

"I assume from the damage done that a man attacked me."

"Did you know Mehmed before you were attacked?" Knight asked.

"Yes."

"How did you know the accused before the attack?"

"I first became aware of Mehmed through James Bingham, who worked with Mehmed at this court. I didn't meet Mehmed until the Sultan's ball, when Mr. Bingham, with whom I attended the ball, asked Mehmed to escort me for the rest of the evening because he had to leave with Judge Hornby on court business."

"Is it possible that the accused was jealous of your relationship with Mr. Bingham?" The question caught Rosamund by surprise.

"No. I do not believe that Mehmed was jealous of Mr. Bingham," she answered, keeping her eyes fixed on Knight.

"Miss Colborne, the accused defended your honour at the Sultan's ball by confronting your father. This chivalry forced him to go into hiding from the Ottoman police because he was accused of supporting seditious Turkish radicals and starting the Slap-an-Englishman crime spree. To spare you more distress in the witness box, he pled guilty to criminal assault of your father before this court and served a term of imprisonment. Through it all, you continued your relationship with Mr. Bingham. Isn't it possible that this hot-blooded young man, so willing to defend your honour and well-being, could have been jealous of your affection for Mr. Bingham?"

Crimson appeared amidst the black and blue on Rosamund's face. "I ... my relationship with Mr. Bingham is of no concern to this court."

"In fact, Miss Colborne, it is," Knight insisted. "So, you will have to answer my questions about how your relationship with Mr. Bingham might have affected the accused and provided a motive for attacking you."

Rosamund stayed quiet for some moments. "When I spoke with Mehmed before his trial for slapping my father, he told me that I did not need to apologise and that he alone was responsible for his actions. He did not blame me or Mr. Bingham. He did not blame my father. He never said anything, or acted in any way, that would lead me to believe he was jealous of Mr. Bingham."

"Thank you, Miss Colborne," Knight shifted to the next set of questions. "In his statement under preliminary examination, the accused admits being in that area near your residence before the attack and admits having your blood on his hands and clothes after the attack. Yet he claims that he did not attack you. So first let me ask, do you walk on those paths behind your residence frequently?" Knight asked.

"Yes."

"Did you ever walk with the accused on those paths before the night that you were attacked?"

Rosamund began to answer, but then closed her mouth.

"Miss Colborne?" prodded Knight.

"No," replied Rosamund.

"Did you ever encounter the accused on those paths as you walked them?" Knight continued.

"No."

"Did you arrange to meet the accused to walk on those paths before or on the night that you were attacked?" Knight followed on.

"No."

"Did anyone else arrange for you to meet the accused that night?"

"No."

"In all the times you walked on those paths, how many times did you see the accused walking on them?"

"Never."

"Never," Knight repeated for emphasis. "How many times did you see anyone else walking on those paths?"

"I have walked those paths with Mr. Bingham, but other than Mr. Bingham, I have never seen anyone else on those paths."

"Never," Knight repeated once more. "Now, let me note that Miss Colborne's testimony accords with the statement provided by Mr. Bingham to the Ottoman police. Mr. Bingham also never recalls seeing anyone else on those paths or in that area behind the Colborne residence. He saw a horse once, but never people. Now, Miss Colborne, don't you find it curious that the accused just happens to be walking on those paths, which no one other than you and Mr. Bingham apparently seems to do, on the night that you were attacked?"

"That area is not private property. It is a common area where anyone, Christian and Mohammedan, can walk without being suspected of committing crimes," replied Rosamund.

"The accused was detained near your residence, with your blood on his hands and clothes, and he claims that he found you after the attack. You, as well as Mr. Bingham, have testified that you have never seen anyone else on these paths. Isn't it odd that, of all the places to walk at night, and of all the nights to take a walk on these paths, the accused just happens to stumble across you, miraculously, after you were savagely beaten?"

"Your Honour," Butt was on his feet. "We do not need, and justice does not deserve, such prejudicial innuendo."

"Mr. Knight," Judge Hornby said, "interrogate not insinuate."

"My apologies, Your Honour," Knight said with a small bow toward the judge. "Now, Miss Colborne, we need to understand how the facts that we have make sense. Why was the accused found near your residence with your blood all over him?"

"I am the victim, not the accused." Rosamund took umbrage at being asked such a question.

Knight ignored her reprimand and turned to the jury. "It is a mystery. The two people who have walked these paths many times never recall seeing anyone else. Then, on the night Miss Colborne is attacked, the accused says that he was walking these paths when he happens across her beaten body. According to him, he did not come into that area because he heard screaming or sounds of violence. He does not claim to be using the paths to reach another destination. He says that he was there because it is a safe and secluded place—something he claims is hard for him to find as a man wanted by the Ottoman government for sedition. But that safe and secluded place on that night?"

Rosamund was not sure the question was for her. She looked at Judge Hornby for guidance.

"Miss Colborne," Knight continued before the judge could respond. "Let's solve this mystery, shall we?"

Knight stepped toward Rosamund to address her directly. "On the night in question, the accused was in the area where you are attacked. So, we have the accused at the scene of the crime. We have evidence of the crime on his hands and clothes. Our mystery then boils down to motive. Why would the accused attack you?"

Rosamund interrupted, "I have no reason to believe that Mehmed would attack me."

"Miss Colborne," Knight replied in a tone suggesting the interruption was not appreciated, "in law, we must look beyond what you believe. Now, many see these facts and assign guilt because the accused is Moslem. And this has angered the Turks, and this anger is directed toward this court, these proceedings, and perhaps you. I hope, Miss Colborne, that you would agree with me, and with this court, that the accused cannot be found guilty simply because he is Moslem."

Rosamund nodded, but tentatively, unsure where Knight was heading.

"Miss Colborne, are you aware that the accused objects to the exercise of British jurisdiction in the Ottoman empire?"

"Yes," Rosamund answered, expecting Knight to probe how she was aware of Mehmed's objections. But he did not.

"Are you aware that the accused despises the capitulations agreed by treaty between the British and Ottoman empires—the very treaty provisions that are the foundation for this court?"

"Yes."

"The capitulations that gave this court jurisdiction over the accused when your father brought a claim of criminal assault against him?"

"Yes."

"The capitulations that permitted this court to imprison him for criminal assault?"

"Yes."

"The capitulations that the accused believes this court violates in putting him on trial now?"

"Yes."

Knight pivoted to face the jury. "The accused comes that night, as he has described, to that area behind Miss Colborne's home to quieten his tortured mind. He encounters her by accident—it is an improbable coincidence. But he sees her earlier than he claims. He becomes angry. She symbolises everything he hates—British power, privilege, and prejudice that the treaty capitulations force upon the Ottoman people. She is the daughter of a British merchant who used a British court to convict him of a crime under English law. She is the romantic partner of a British barrister who imposes the capitulations through this British court. This daughter, this merchant, this barrister, this court, and this law are civilised because they are British, but he is uncivilised because he is not. Enraged, he attacks her, not in any premeditated way, but in a crime of passion—a crime of political passion."

A hush fell over the courtroom, and Knight exploited the quiet. "After this spasm of violence, his effort to find help and his distress when found with her blood on his body arise from guilt about what he had done. Guilt made more painful by the innocence of his victim. Guilt made more searing by his religious faith. Guilt that, in the cold fear that evil leaves behind, turned into lies. A cowardly transformation common in men who commit crimes of passion, whether Christian or Moslem, civilised or uncivilised."

A voice from the crowd broke the silence, "Hear, hear, mystery solved."

Applause rolled like thunder around the courtroom.

Judge Hornby tried to bring the court to order, and it took much bellowing to achieve. Knight was already seated at the prosecution table when Maurice Butt rose for the defence and waited for the noise to abate completely.

"You walked on these paths with Mr. Bingham. So Mr. Bingham knew the paths and that you walked on them, correct?" Butt began.

"Yes." Rosamund's irritation with more questions about paths was palpable.

"Mr. Bingham had knowledge of where the crime took place and the habits of the victim of the crime. He cannot identify anyone who can verify his whereabouts on the night that you were attacked."

Butt paused, and members of the jury looked in unison at Rosamund.

"Now," said Butt, holding up an index finger. "We need a motive. Do you, Miss Colborne, have any reason to believe that Mr. Bingham might have attacked you?"

Rosamund glanced at Judge Hornby. "Mr. Bingham is not on trial here."

"You are correct, Miss Colborne," Butt continued. "But the Crown bears the burden of establishing that Mehmed is guilty of the alleged crime. It is a great misfortune that this court cannot examine the suspects together. But my duty, as defence counsel, is to identify possible explanations for the crime that the Crown did not explore. Do you understand?"

Rosamund nodded and shifted uncomfortably in her chair.

"So, is it possible that Mr. Bingham was upset that his efforts to court you were unsuccessful, and that he was angry enough to attack you in a place that you frequented and where there would be no witnesses?"

"I have never seen Mr. Bingham angry," Rosamund replied.

"Mr. Bingham walked with you on these paths in courting you for marriage. Is that your understanding of Mr. Bingham's intent?"

Rosamund appeared either perplexed or vexed by the question. She looked at Judge Hornby, as if to ask whether she had to answer. The judge nodded.

"You should ask Mr. Bingham that question."

"Miss Colborne," Butt came back firmly. "Answer the question."

"Yes," Rosamund answered crossly. "He was courting me for marriage."

"But there has been no marriage after many months of seeing Mr. Bingham and being with him at the Sultan's ball and other events in society. Despite all this effort, Mr. Bingham has not won your hand—a source, no doubt, of frustration and embarrassment given that everyone knew the purpose of the endeavour. A humiliation that resembles what some previous suitors endured in seeking your love."

"Do you have a question, Mr. Butt?" Rosamund snapped, unhappy with the suggestion that her behaviour was the problem.

"Oh, Miss Colborne, I most certainly do," Butt firmly replied and paused for effect before continuing. "At the confrontation between Mehmed and your father at the Sultan's ball, did you tell your father—and everyone watching—that you had been manipulating James Bingham?"

Knight smacked the prosecution table with his hands in standing up. "Your Honour, Miss Colborne is not on trial today. This line of questioning is offensive and unjust."

"Let me finish, Your Honour," Butt quickly countered. "The mystery that Mr. Knight conjured for the jury is more complicated than his speculations permitted."

Edmund looked at Rosamund, who was beginning to appear drained and vulnerable. However, he knew what Butt was attempting to do, and it was not unjust. He nodded at Butt to proceed, and Knight sat with disgust at the decision.

"Miss Colborne, did you declare at the Sultan's ball that you had, all along, been manipulating Mr. Bingham?"

Rosamund said nothing, but her eyes and posture provided all the answer Butt needed.

"Isn't it possible—nay, probable—that Mr. Bingham learned of your very public declaration that the courtship was not an affair of the heart but was, in fact, a cruel charade?"

Butt did not wait for an answer. "We have a man with a plausible motive to hurt you—in a true crime of passion. He knows that you walk on those paths. No one can confirm his whereabouts on the night of the attack. And you cannot identify Mehmed as your attacker."

Butt slowly put his hands on his hips, a gesture that heightened anticipation of his next words. "However, perhaps the perpetrator is not James Bingham. Perhaps the culprit is not Osman Mehmed. Perhaps," Butt paused again to enhance the drama, "the perpetrator is your father."

Murmurs began, but they quickly subsided as the desire to listen overwhelmed the temptation to whisper.

"In his statement to the Ottoman police," Butt resumed, "Mr. Colborne could not provide any witnesses to corroborate his whereabouts on the night that you were attacked. We can safely presume that Mr. Colborne has familiarity with the area behind his residence and knew that his daughter walked there. So, is it true, Miss Colborne, that your father cut you off financially and is forcing you back to England alone and penniless?"

"Yes." Rosamund looked down into her lap.

"In your testimony at Mehmed's trial for common assault, based on a claim that your father brought to this court, did you testify that your father, at some earlier time, committed a criminal act against you, your mother, or someone else?"

"Your Honour," Knight was quickly on his feet again. "Miss Colborne did not complete her testimony. She made only a vague statement that was never clarified at trial but that launched a thousand sordid speculations in society. We should not subject her to such prurient questions. And Mr. Colborne is also not on trial today."

"Your Honour," Butt said before Judge Hornby could respond. "She can clarify why her father might have had a motive to harm her. This case offers so little on which to defend the accused. We have no witnesses of the crime. None of the suspects has an alibi. The victim cannot identify her attacker. I beg the court for leeway to mount a defence."

"Approach the bench," Hornby instructed Knight and Butt.

Rosamund slumped and appeared on the verge of slipping from her chair. She straightened her back to steady herself. She retrieved a handkerchief tucked between her wrist and sleeve and dabbed perspiration from her forehead, trying not to smudge the creams and powders applied to hide her injuries. She replaced the handkerchief and raised her hand to her face, closed her eyes, and ran the back of her fingers slowly down her battered right cheek.

She was at her bedroom window but had seen no stars that cloudy night. She was sad. She missed her mother's bedtime visit, but her mother was often caring for the soldiers when night came. She turned when he entered and took two steps toward him. She smelled smoke and whiskey but did not see his hand whip around. It exploded against her cheek. He grabbed her hair, yanked her from the floor, and slammed her face down on the bed. His knee went into her back, and he stuffed something into her mouth. He tore her nightgown, forced her legs apart, leaned over, and, in a foul whisper, said, "Here's a message for our Miss Nightingale. Tell her." When he had gone, she removed the gag. Breathing heavily, she touched the pain, brought her hand up, blood on the fingers. She stifled a scream in the bed. Tears rolling, she touched again, felt blood, and buried another scream. Anger stirring, she reached with intent, gathered blood, and smeared it on her nightgown. She reached with purpose, raised her hand, and streaked it down her arm. She reached in defiance and striped blood across her face. Like her mother, covered in the blood of violence. With her mother, she would disobey, never speak of it, and suffer.

Rosamund lowered her hand into her lap and opened her eyes.

The gathering at the judge's bench ended. Knight sat down at the prosecution table, and Butt returned to the defence table and prepared himself to ask the next question.

"Miss Colborne, Judge Hornby asked me to rephrase my question," Butt explained. "After your testimony at Mehmed's trial, were your father's business and personal reputations damaged?"

"My father raped me when I was a girl."

The courtroom became incapable of sound. The only movement was Katherine Colborne slowly and silently rising from her seat. Rosamund met her mother's despairing eyes. Trembling, Katherine lowered herself back onto the bench, making no noise, tears streaming down her face.

Butt stepped toward Rosamund, the sound of his feet on the floorboards directing everyone's attention back to her. "Miss Colborne, the final question. Did your father attack you?"

Rosamund looked down into her lap again for many moments before lifting her eyes to the courtroom. "I do not know who attacked me."

"Miss Colborne," Judge Hornby struggled to speak and started over to find his voice. "Miss Colborne, thank you for your endurance today. We have faced many challenges in this case, but of this we are sure—that you, an innocent victim of a brutal crime, have been faithful to the cause of justice and have demonstrated the courage that only the virtuous possess."

Rosamund acknowledged the judge's words with a small nod, but unexpectedly, her time as a witness did not end.

Chapter 29
Conviction

From the back of the courtroom, a bearded, rough-looking man appeared and walked down the centre aisle toward the front. He carried himself as if he had the right to commandeer the proceedings. It was such an unusual sight that, initially, no one moved or spoke.

After moments of confusion, Judge Hornby recognised him. "Henry, what are you doing?"

Henry Wattling stopped directly before Rosamund. "I have a question for the witness."

Edmund did not hear what Henry said, but he stood to emphasise his authority. "Henry, there's a warrant out for your arrest. Are you here to surrender?"

Henry ignored the judge. "I have a question for the witness."

"Constable Williams, arrest this man," Edmund called out.

Before the constable took two steps, Henry had pulled an army revolver from under his coat and rested it on his shoulder, pointing up and away from Rosamund. Edmund signalled with his hand for the constable to hold.

"Now may I ask the witness a question?" Henry took his eyes off Rosamund to glare at Edmund. "A question that will reveal the truth, as well as the true nature of her character, things that your law and your court have failed to discover."

"Henry, put the gun away. We are here for justice, and you are a man of God." Edmund kept his voice stern but calm to hide his fear about the threat of violence.

"Then we should finally have justice in this court and before God, rather than more deceit," Henry replied, turning to face Rosamund again.

"Constable Williams," Edmund raised his voice, but he stopped speaking when Henry levelled the pistol inches from Rosamund's head.

The immediate danger of violence silenced the courtroom, until a rending sob interrupted the confrontation, "Henry, my boy, no!"

Mary Wattling had scrabbled to her feet and stumbled toward the end of her bench, creating a tangle of bodies in her wake. As she turned into the courtroom's centre aisle, she tripped and fell hard, her head slamming the floorboards with an awful sound.

"Henry, I beg you, put the gun down." Garrett Wattling stepped over his wife to approach his son.

"Not another step!" Henry pressed the barrel against Rosamund's forehead.

Everyone in the courtroom went still except Garrett, who knelt to place a hand on his prostrate wife. Mehmed then slowly stood up in the dock. Henry gave Mehmed a dismissive look, as if the Turk was no one and nothing in this moment. Returning his attention to Rosamund, he pulled the muzzle from her skin but kept it pointed at her head.

"Miss Colborne, I have a question," Henry spoke loudly to ensure everyone was listening.

Rosamund did not move. She could not understand why Henry was before her, rather than in Africa or on his way there, or why she must answer his question at gunpoint. Sensing her pulse quickening, she considered pretending to faint. But she wanted no more dissembling. She leaned forward, bringing her forehead closer to the revolver. "Ask me your question."

Henry hesitated, not expecting Rosamund to challenge him, and she seized the silence. "You failed as a soldier. As a merchant. As a Christian. But here you are, once more, this time as some species of lawyer threatening violence and pretending that your depredations have a higher purpose."

Henry straightened the arm holding the gun, but he did not speak.

"Ask me your question or get out."

This provocation loosened his tongue. "You are here, according to this judge, as an innocent victim demonstrating courage in the search for the truth. But, if you are not innocent, if you have not told the truth, then justice will be the victim. My question goes to the heart of the matter—whether you have been honest, faithful, and virtuous with your family, among our community, in this court, and before God."

"Ask me your question," Rosamund said less vehemently, unsure about what question could possibly be coming.

"In this court, you have been cruel, rather than courageous. You have accused your father twice of a heinous act when his innocence or guilt was not being weighed on the scales of justice. As other females have done in this court, you accused a man without evidence, none, to support your allegation. But you did so when he could not protect himself. When he had no Queen's Counsel to defend him. You blackened his name to defeat his attempts to temper your cruelty. You ruined your father to save yourself from the ruin that your madness has made of your life."

Henry's voice gained confidence. "And you slaked your thirst for hurting people beyond this court. You humiliated me, but then I was deaf, dumb, and blind. I never asked myself why you so publicly and relentlessly condemned my feelings, my character, and my morality. And, as everyone is aware, you have been most cruel to James Bingham. But you went to such lengths to humiliate him that you committed one sin too many."

Henry paused, lowering the revolver to hang by his side. Rosamund searched Henry's face but found nothing to help her understand what he was talking about.

"You can prove your virtue against all these accusations if you have, in fact, been courageous, faithful, and innocent in your words and deeds," Henry began again.

"Today, before this jury," Henry stretched out his arms as if upon the cross, "you testified that, on the fateful night, you pleaded for the attack to stop, that you begged to make it end."

Henry paused again, and almost reflexively, Rosamund nodded confirmation.

"What did you say—as an innocent, faithful, and virtuous woman—in that moment of absolute truth?"

Rosamund looked perplexed by the question, a reaction shared by judge and jury.

Henry returned the gun to point at her forehead. "Why did you beg to make your punishment stop? Why did you plead for mercy?"

Rosamund then understood. "You."

"Tell them!" Henry angrily commanded, causing more confusion throughout the courtroom.

"You did this," Rosamund's accusation added to the bewilderment.

"Tell them that you are with child!" Henry yelled.

Amidst gasps around the courtroom, Rosamund stood with difficulty. "You did this to me."

"Tell them—" Henry's voice collapsed as Rosamund stepped forward, pressing her forehead into the muzzle of the gun.

The defiance unnerved Henry, who stepped back, releasing the gun from her skin. She pressed her forehead against the revolver again.

"You cannot destroy me," Rosamund spoke without fear or anger. "You return again and again after I reject you. You cannot have peace because I can live and love without you. You want everything that I deny you—my body, my love, my forgiveness, my submission. Now you come, one last time, because I defy the violence that your civilisation calls justice."

The gun began to waver, as if Rosamund's words heaped irons upon it. Henry stepped back again. Rosamund let the space between the gun and her head evidence his retreat.

"You cannot have justice because you do not have what justice requires—conviction. Conviction born from sacrifice that diverts life into an unforgiving void. Conviction that overcomes pain and fear by refusing to capitulate. Conviction that staunches the blood and slows the tears. Conviction that witnesses against the wrongs, even when it is never clear, never certain whether, in the decisive moment, right will prevail over might."

Rosamund suddenly felt unsteady and on the verge of fainting. She laid her hand on Henry's chest to stop from falling. Her touch tore him open. He lowered the gun, and, tears welling, he helped her sit down. He tenderly kissed the top of her head.

Henry Wattling turned from her, took a few paces toward the astonished congregation, put the revolver under his chin, and pulled the trigger.

Chapter 30
That Morning When

The gunshot brought chaos—people screaming, scrambling, falling. Judge Hornby was still on his feet when Henry pulled the trigger, and he recoiled, crashing to the ground. As he got up amidst the confusion, he saw Williams manhandling Mehmed out of the courtroom and Rosamund laying on the floor in front of the witness box.

"She's down!" Edmund yelled and stumbled badly in trying to get to her.

Others were also rushing toward her. Dr. Charles Hoyland bulled through the panic and reached her first. On one knee, he wheeled his arms about to clear the crowd away. He whispered to Rosamund, touched her flushed face, and recalled treating her after the attack. He had not returned to the Colborne residence much after attending to her in those early, harrowing hours because, with her injuries, rest, time, and patience were the best physicians. Katherine Colborne had nursing skills, and she had kept him informed of Rosamund's condition. He sensed that she had just fainted and would recover if people would give her space.

As he bent over her, legs and knees jostled him. He caught his balance by putting his hand briefly on Rosamund. He pulled it away and did not move for a few moments. Charles placed his hand on Rosamund again, where he had before, but this time with a doctor's intent. He withdrew his hand, stood, and stared at her.

"Is she dead?" someone shouted. The question brought him back to the courtroom. He instructed men and women standing nearby to keep the crowd away from Rosamund. He motioned to Katherine, who shouldered through the scrum to join him in an empty part of the courtroom. There, after listening to the doctor, Katherine leaned a hand on the wall to steady herself, and Charles eased her into the nearest seat as she started to weep again.

Despite his instructions, people pressed too close to Rosamund, who still lay on the floor. Furious, Charles returned to shoo away the crowd, but in doing so, he triggered gasps.

"Stand back, everyone, for Christ's sake, get back. She is with child!"

Amidst the commotion that this declaration caused, Charles got Rosamund on her feet and moving toward an adjoining room where she could recover. He started to shut the door, but Edmund stopped it with his foot and squeezed in. Once the doctor appeared content with how Rosamund was resting on a cushioned bench, Edmund grabbed his elbow and directed him to the opposite side of the room.

"She's with child?" Edmund whispered.

"Yes," replied Charles.

"But she wasn't violated in the attack." Edmund leaned closer to Charles.

"She wasn't," Charles assured the judge.

"It happened after?" Edmund was thoroughly confused.

"No," Charles said.

"My God, that means Wattling ... I thought he was mad." Edmund could not contain his surprise, before his mind raced in one direction. "How far?"

"Probably three months," the doctor estimated before returning to the task at hand. "Now, Edmund, let me look after her and arrange to get her home. You, I imagine, have other matters that need your attention."

Edmund gripped the doctor's arm and let go. Once back in the courtroom, he noticed that it had been mostly cleared, with Guarracino shifting the last people out. Someone had placed blankets over the body of Henry Wattling. Edmund walked up behind Guarracino as he ushered disoriented stragglers through the courtroom door.

"Frederick, as soon as you can, collect Bingham and bring him here. The Ottoman police had representatives here. They'll know what happened, and they should release James," the judge instructed.

"What about Hugh Colborne?" Frederick asked.

"He can go to hell," Edmund growled.

"What should we do with the Turk?" Frederick enquired.

"What?" The question failed to register with Edmund.

"Mehmed. What do we do with him, after this?" Frederick pointed into the courtroom.

"Set him free. Mystery solved," Edmund replied as he took leave of the dragoman.

Edmund went to his office, where his wife was waiting. They shared a long embrace.

"For as long as there is a court at Constantinople, a trial never to be forgotten," Emelia said as she released her husband from her arms. He kissed her forehead.

"Wattling," he said shaking his head in disbelief, his voice barely a whisper.

"Expecting." She lifted his chin to smile into his eyes with a mother's happiness.

"Good God." His face darkened as he stepped back from his wife.

"Edmund, what is it?" Emelia would not surrender his hand.

"Mehmed. I told Frederick to let him go."

"He's innocent. He should be free."

"No, the Ottomans want him for sedition. I've just released him into their hands." His body tensed and turned toward the door, but he had no idea what to do.

"Go, see if he's still in the gaol," she released his hand.

Edmund rushed out and headed toward the gaol, but Mehmed was gone. Edmund tried to convince himself that Mehmed could evade the police, as he had done before. However, he was going to do everything he could. He ordered the deputy constable to mount up and look for Mehmed, who refused because Mr. Williams had instructed him to stay at the gaol until the constable had dealt with Wattling's body.

"Damn you, I'll do it myself." Edmund marched to the stables, where he was met by Henry Wroth, who counselled the judge not to ride out without a security escort.

"Where the hell is Halil?" Edmund demanded.

"Edmund, calm down. We told him that his services weren't needed during the trial. You should not go without an escort. You know this." Henry's hand firmly held the judge's shoulder to emphasise the need for restraint.

Edmund broke contact with Henry and turned away.

"He's gone, Edmund. You won't find him. If anyone can keep safe, it's Mehmed," Henry tried to reassure the judge. "Come back inside, Edmund, please."

After Edmund returned to his office, Donald Logie popped in to tell the judge that his wife had gone to the Colborne residence. Edmund remained sufficiently agitated that he could not decide whether to smoke or drink, so he did neither. He started pacing around his office.

"Where's Guarracino?" he muttered, growing impatient with the pointless pacing.

He returned to the courtroom to assess what still needed to be done. Wattling's body was gone, but shards, splatter, and stench from the bullet remained. He went to the judge's bench and sat down. Then came the emotions. He fought back, but they prevailed.

He took jurisdiction over the case when the court had none. He placed an innocent Mehmed in danger of being convicted. He put two innocent Englishmen in jeopardy. He never suspected Wattling. It took violence from a broken man to expose the truth in his court. The still-suffering victim of a brutal crime was with child out of wedlock by his junior law clerk. He crawled underneath the judge's bench and succumbed to a convulsing body.

Edmund did not know how much time had passed under the bench. He eventually emerged, made himself presentable, and returned to his office. To his surprise, Guarracino and Bingham were within, chatting. James had tamed his scruffy beard and shambolic hair with copious amounts of water and a brush.

"Where's Colborne?" Edmund asked, without welcoming James.

"They're keeping him until we hand Mehmed over," Frederick answered.

Edmund asked Frederick to leave so that he could talk with James. Edmund closed the door behind the dragoman.

James spoke first. "Sir, Henry Wattling—I thought he had departed for Africa."

"Clearly not," was Edmund's terse response.

"Sir, I must tell you something." James squared himself.

"I should think so," Edmund said with unintended anger.

James cocked his head at the judge's tone. "Sir, the morning we learned of the attack on Rosamund, I came to the court early, before anyone else."

"What are you talking about?" Edmund shot back.

"I came in early and discovered that a letter from Rosamund had been delivered for me the previous day, when we were at the Sublime Porte on the *Enoch Wright* case."

"A letter from Rosamund? On that day?" The judge was not expecting this from James.

"Her letter asked me to meet Wattling that night to send her good wishes and deliver a private note to him."

Edmund was astonished. "To meet Wattling? On the night she was attacked?"

"It sounds bizarre, but given what just happened, I needed to tell you," James said.

"Where's the letter?" The judge held out his hand.

"I burned it." James broke eye contact.

"You what?" Edmund was incredulous.

"I burned the letter and the sealed note, which the letter said contained something Rosamund wanted to communicate privately to Wattling."

"You burned the letter and the note? You aren't making sense." Edmund struggled to focus his bloodshot eyes on James.

"I opened the note. I shouldn't have, but the note was blank. Not a single word."

"So you burned it?" Edmund's confusion about the tale growing.

"No. I burned the letter and the note because, well ... because seeing that blank note—it was the moment that I accepted what I could not bring myself to admit before, and the burning brought finality." James appeared embarrassed, and Edmund gestured for James to continue.

"That I wasn't going to marry Rosamund. That I didn't love her," James confessed.

"Good Lord, son, are you serious?" Edmund blurted out.

James had not anticipated that response.

"Didn't Frederick tell you?" Edmund suspected that they were talking past each other.

"He told me Wattling revealed that he attacked Rosamund, then killed himself."

"Oh, James, I thought he told you."

"Told me what?" James furrowed his brow.

"Rosamund's expecting," Edmund responded.

James went still and silent.

"Rosamund's with child," Edmund said again.

"From the attack? Did Wattling?" James could not articulate his discombobulation.

"No, from before." Edmund grasped the young man's arm.

"Before?" James was unmoored.

"It happens, James. The question now is, what will you do?" Edmund tried a fatherly tone.

"What will I do?" James's eyes flashed incomprehension.

"Yes, you. Wattling said that Rosamund pleaded for the attack to stop because she was with child. I thought Wattling had gone mad, but apparently not."

James formulated no response. He felt stripped of his truth.

"Look at me, son. Answer me, are you the father?" Edmund pressed with more intensity.

"Sir," James wrinkled his forehead. "How far?"

"Perhaps three months." Edmund sensed that a confession was near.

James closed his eyes, desperate for an explanation. He scoured his mind for what could have happened ... that morning. When he paid an unexpected visit. When she was leaving her secret ruin. When her dark hair was down. When ...

"James?" Edmund's tone became very stern.

"Sir, will you excuse me?" James entreated.

Edmund put his hand on the young man's shoulder before James left the office. He watched James go down the hallway and into the clerk's room and shut the door.

From the back of a musty cabinet, James retrieved the cigar box tucked behind old court papers. He set the box on the table, lifted the lid, and retrieved what was inside. He unwrapped the brown paper that he had used to protect it. He removed the blue ribbon and unfolded the white cloth. He slowly sat down, putting his elbows on the table and his head in his hands. He stared at it. He lowered a hand and gently touched it. A smile formed as he felt his life finally open. He would go to her, take her hand, and give it to her. So that she could decide how to be full, alive, and free. He placed it in his suit pocket.

After watching James disappear into the clerk's office, Edmund turned to his desk, intending to sit and release stress. Instead, he looked out of the window and watched the sun illuminate clouds passing over the city. *She will be alright if the boy does the right thing,* he assured himself. Just as he turned from the window to sit down, footsteps returned from the hallway. James reached his office before Edmund was halfway to the door.

"Sir," James began. "Do you have a horse here, at the court?"

"Yes, Sultan's here," Edmund answered awkwardly.

"Hornby, with me." James headed for the stables, leaving the perplexed judge trailing behind.

Chapter 31
Another Boy, Another Girl

James and Edmund led Bones and Sultan from their stalls. Halil sauntered into the stable yard on his mount. "Greetings, Supreme English Judge and Junior English Clerk. I heard that you, judge, might need an escort. I saw your dragoman at the ministry."

"Halil, your timing couldn't be better. We're on a mission," Edmund replied.

"Where are we going?" Halil enquired.

"I don't know. The Junior English Clerk's in charge. We'll follow him."

James and Edmund mounted their horses, and James led the trio into the streets of Constantinople. It did not take long before James sensed that Bones, trotting with confidence, knew the destination. Bones scarcely needed guiding off the road into an unkempt area of meadow and trees. James led the troop to the front of the residence, where they dismounted. Halil took the reins and walked the horses to the stables. James pulled the bell on the door. It opened to reveal Dr. Hoyland.

"Ah, gentlemen, I was just leaving. Rosamund, she is feeling better. Judge, your wife is inside. And what have we here? Mr. James Bingham, your ... well, son, go to her," Charles remarked with a knowing smile and a pat on James's shoulder as he went on his way.

James marched ahead, leaving Edmund to catch up. James knew where to find her.

She was on the same small divan where she usually sat during his visits. Her eyes registered astonishment when he entered the room. Katherine Colborne gasped on seeing him, and Emelia Hornby smiled when her husband appeared seconds later.

Her voice broke the silence, "Mr. Bingham, it is not time for tea."

James laughed at the quip, walked up to Rosamund, and held out his hand. "I want to show you something."

She did not speak. She did not move.

"If you are able, take my hand—I want to show you something." James leaned closer.

She had not forgotten. She remembered showing him. But the look on his face—she could not immediately discern his intent. Sensing her confusion, James leaned closer still and gave her a small nod. Her mind cleared and her heart was full. Yes, he remained a good man.

She began to stand up, and her mother protested, imploring her daughter to rest. Rosamund ignored the plea, and, with help from James, was on her feet, her hand in his. As they walked into the garden, she squeezed his hand, and he replied, "Don't worry, I'll carry you."

James and Rosamund went through the garden, out the gate, and onto the paths they had walked together. They knew which ones to take, what turns to make. When they arrived where wilder grass and meadow grew, James cradled Rosamund and carried her toward her secret ruin. She rested her head against his shoulder.

Upon arriving at the copse, he set Rosamund on her feet. He looked into her eyes, reached into his pocket, and gave the gift to her. She put a hand over her mouth in surprise upon seeing again the small artifact of blues, reds, and yellows. He stepped through the nearly invisible gap and extended his hand to help her into that timeless space. Once inside, she laughed softly when she saw him, her eyes dancing with happiness. James stepped aside and bowed his head as she went to him. He smiled as the two lovers embraced under the mottled dome of light and shade. He turned and exited through the gap. Once outside, he strode toward the residence without looking back.

With evening advancing, Rosamund back in her home, and the gap nearly invisible again, James, Edmund, and Halil led their horses to the front of the residence, where they mounted.

"Halil," Edmund addressed the *cavass*. "Can I count on your discretion?"

Halil smiled as only he could. "I can say, in all honesty, that I didn't see a thing."

"You're an honourable man. I cannot thank you enough." Edmund's feelings were true.

Halil patted his horse's neck. "Thank you."

"But," Edmund shifted from thankful to cheerful. "You're good at something else."

Halil and James looked at each other in anticipation.

"You can sing, sir. So, for our journey home, a song, please," Edmund requested with an inviting grin.

"What would my English friends like to hear?" The *cavass* cleared his throat in preparation for his performance.

Edmund looked past the clouds hanging on the horizon and toward the setting sun. "The one that ends with another boy, another girl, and the happiness love promises."

Chapter 32
West and East

James sipped coffee as dawn broke over Constantinople. Recent events had left him exhausted and, after the peace he had felt bringing Rosamund and Mehmed together, anxious. He and Judge Hornby had been neglecting their duties. Donald Logie delayed his return to Smyrna, but he could not stay much longer. James knew that it was time to get back into things, especially with Henry scheduled to leave for Alexandria.

His nerves jangled from uncertainty about what would happen to Rosamund and Mehmed. One ordeal had ended, but another had begun. Sympathy for Rosamund as the innocent victim of a heinous crime evaporated as she experienced the opprobrium that society reserves for unwed, expecting women. Rosamund's refusal to identify the father made malicious whispers far easier, more delicious, and highly contagious. Forgotten amidst the salacious slander was her testimony. James became the target of disdain as well because many in the British community believed that he—the man everyone knew was courting Rosamund—was the father but was too cowardly to take responsibility. Everyone in the small circle who knew the truth understood that it was only a matter of time before one of them, without malice aforethought, would say too much in some private or social setting. Then prudish tongue-wagging would turn truly vicious.

Mehmed remained in hiding to avoid the Ottoman police because the palace and the Porte still considered him, and his ideas, a seditious threat. The consular court could no longer protect him. Although the secret ruin had served Mehmed well as a hiding place, believing it would remain secret would ensure his ruin. Nor would those who once defended him do so again, not with more serious allegations of sedition hanging over Mehmed and not if they learned that he had fathered a child out of wedlock with an Englishwoman.

James let Bones plod and meander on a circuitous route to increase the chances that Judge Hornby would be at the court first. The judge was trying to help Rosamund and Mehmed. In her situation, returning to England—with or without Mehmed—was an even more forbidding path for Rosamund. In his predicament, Mehmed should not remain in Ottoman lands. James desperately wanted to know what Edmund had done, or planned to do, for them. But the judge was not there when he arrived. Only Wroth and Logie were present. All three barristers avoided difficult conversations by keeping their heads buried in the unending legal work.

Judge Hornby did not appear at the court that day, or the next. Nor had James seen him at the residence. The judge's absence, combined with the strain of handling legal matters with torqued emotions, made the court building funereal. On the following day, with still no sign of Edmund, Henry Wroth could no longer help himself when morning tea was served.

"James," Henry began. "You really don't know where Edmund is? Things are piling up."

James shook his head. Henry looked out of the window. Donald swirled milk into his cup.

"James," Henry turned from the window. "You knew them best. And you had no idea?"

Henry's face suggested that the question was unfair, but James did not resent being asked. "I did not know."

This time James gazed out the window. Donald stopped stirring his tea.

"We never suspected Wattling," Henry changed the subject. "Until what she said about her father, I thought the jury would convict Mehmed. It had evidence and defensible grounds for doing so. What an injustice would have been done."

"What I don't understand," interjected Donald, "is why she didn't exonerate him. The father of her child?"

James blew on his tea to cool it. "She answered truthfully the most important question she was asked. She could not identify her attacker. She could not exclude Mehmed, her father, or me. If she had revealed her relationship with Mehmed, she might have made the Crown's case stronger. The prosecution could have spun a more credible motive for Mehmed to attack her—to kill her or cause a miscarriage. A true crime of passion. No alibi for the time of the attack, plausible motive, found near the scene of the crime with the victim's blood on his hands and clothes. Your Honour, we find the accused guilty."

"And testifying that she knew Mehmed did not attack her would have invited questions about why she excluded only Mehmed, questions that might have forced her to admit their relationship," Henry added.

"Yes," Donald said, "but, after what she said, it would have been so very easy for her to say that her father attacked her. The jury would not have convicted Mehmed had she done so."

"But he didn't attack her, at least not on that night. The bastard," James replied. "And Wattling's appearance would have revealed her as a liar if she had done so."

Henry leaned back in his chair, crossed his arms, and looked impressed. "She told the truth and protected Mehmed as best she could."

Donald raised a sceptical eyebrow. "But was she too economical with the truth? She implied that she only knew Mehmed superficially and, except for the Sultan's ball, had never spent time with him."

"No," Henry leaned forward, "I've thought about this. She answered the Crown's questions precisely, giving away no more information than the questions sought. Remember, Donald, when Knight asked her if she had ever walked on those paths with Mehmed? She hesitated but said no. The Crown never asked her whether she had relations with the accused. And she said she was out walking to make decisions that her own actions necessitated, such as being with child."

"Everyone assumed—well, at least I did," Donald shared, "that she was referring to the awful position her father had put her in. But she must have known that she could not hide her condition much longer, forcing difficult decisions. Should she manoeuvre James into marriage? Should she return to England alone and suffer the consequences? Should she run away with Mehmed?"

The barristers went quiet, aware that Donald's questions underscored Rosamund's uncertain fate.

"She would have made a fine lawyer," Henry finally observed.

"And a better judge," Donald added.

"But probably not a good diplomat," James added, causing all three barristers to smile.

"But you," Henry pointed a friendly finger at James. "How did you figure it out? Not only that Mehmed was the father but also where he was hiding. You did so miraculously because you had no idea about that before. Come on, enlighten us, or I'm going to give you all the bankruptcy cases until I leave for Alexandria."

"When I was journeying here on the *Sphinx*," James began.

"No, don't start in Genesis. Right here, in these offices, it just came to you, so start with Revelations," Henry prodded to Donald's amusement.

"When I was on the *Sphinx*," James continued, prompting eye rolls from Henry and Donald, "a husband and wife tried to teach me that I would never understand what I am living unless I opened my eyes, my mind, and my soul. After failing too often, and being accused of fathering a child, I finally did so."

"And?" Henry insisted.

"Imagine the bed chamber of a Roman villa, where a man and a woman lay together in love," Bingham replied. He scooped up his teacup and saucer, nabbed a biscuit, and headed to the clerk's room before his perplexed colleagues could make any sense of his answer.

That evening, after Henry and Donald had left, James remained at the court to sort out backlogged legal documents. He laughed at the pile of bankruptcy cases newly placed on the table. As he organised the papers, someone came into the court building. The sound of the door that closed shortly thereafter was unmistakable.

James knocked on the door and opened it before Judge Hornby could respond. Edmund was gazing out of the window of his office, staring over the rooftops stretching down to the confluence of the Golden Horn and the Bosphorus. He did not acknowledge James's entrance.

"Edmund?" asked James firmly.

Edmund turned, and James was taken aback by the exhaustion on the judge's face.

"They're gone, James," Edmund said with sadness.

"Gone?" James did not understand.

"We secured passage for them to America."

"America?" James's voice was full of disbelief and loss.

Edmund did not elaborate. James, he believed, would in time understand.

"James, is everything straightened out here?" Edmund asked.

"Is everything straightened out?" The question's harshness did not escape Edmund's notice.

"We go on, James. The law goes on."

James had to ask, "Did we do them justice?"

Edmund left the question suspended between them. "I've been summoned to the Foreign Office in London."

"Edmund, we are badly behind. Donald's going back to Smyrna. Henry's departing for Alexandria. You're leaving for London. I cannot manage everything here by myself."

"Don't worry, James. You are coming to London with me. New flesh and blood will arrive here before we leave. There'll be a court at Constantinople after we're gone," Edmund said.

After we're gone? Edmund's sudden detachment from what he had sacrificed so much to create baffled James. Was Edmund returning to England? Was he as well? James wondered whether his time in the East was at an abrupt, incomplete end. Despite everything he had lived at Constantinople, James did not yet have the measure of himself as a man, or of his civilisation, on the scales of justice.

"Why do you want me to come to London?" James pressed.

Edmund did not answer and stared out of the window again. James sensed that the judge's eyes were transfixed by something very distant, past the Asiatic side of the city and beyond the hills of Anatolia.

"Because, James," Edmund finally replied. "We are going to build a court in China."

***

Author's Note

As historical fiction, *A Court at Constantinople* weaves imagination into people, places, and problems recorded in archives, journals, autobiographies, and academic research. The novel sprang from my interest in the "standard of civilisation" in international law during the nineteenth and early twentieth centuries. The standard categorised countries as "civilised" or "uncivilised" based on European concepts of politics, law, and justice. Today, the standard of civilisation is a disconcerting chapter in the history of international law because it reflected and enabled political, religious, and racial prejudice. But once upon a time, it shaped how European and non-European governments and peoples interacted.

The standard of civilisation was applied through, among other things, treaties that European states had with the Ottoman empire and other non-European countries. Certain treaty provisions—called "capitulations"—gave European governments jurisdiction over certain legal disputes and activities within the territories of other nations. Many of these treaties were signed before the standard of civilisation became part of international law in the nineteenth century. The term "capitulations" originally described headings in the treaties and derived from the Latin *caput* for head, heading, or chapter. After the standard of civilisation became an international legal principle, treaty provisions granting "civilised" European states extraterritorial jurisdiction within "uncivilised" countries became associated with other meanings of capitulation—defeat and surrender.

How civilised states exercised extraterritorial jurisdiction also served as a model for reforms that uncivilised countries had to implement to become equal members of international society. For example, the Ottoman government—often called the "Sublime Porte" after the decorated gate that provided access to the government's buildings—pursued political and legal changes through its *tanzimat* (re-organisation) reforms. Technological changes in transportation (steamships, railroads), communications (telegraph), and military weaponry (mass-produced rifles, better artillery) heightened the pressure that uncivilised nations faced to change their political systems, laws, concepts of justice, and identities as peoples.

The implementation of the treaty capitulations caused political and legal problems that civilised and uncivilised diplomats, lawyers, merchants, and individuals had to confront, navigate, and resolve. My research explored how the standard of civilisation informed the day-to-day activities of lawyers working on issues that arose as political and economic relations intensified between different civilisations.

Lawyers such as Edmund Hornby, an English barrister who served as the chief judge of Her Britannic Majesty's Supreme Consular Court at Constantinople, before having a similar role in China and Japan. The introduction to Hornby's autobiography described him as a "great and industrious representative of his country" who served as "Consular Judge in three Empires which had by his time lagged far ... behind the progress of Occidental civilisation" [1]. The emergence and global application of the standard of civilisation in the nineteenth century shaped Hornby's activities during his time in Her Majesty's Service. After Hornby finished his diplomatic career, he participated in efforts to develop international law to bring nations closer to peace.

A Court at Constantinople draws on diplomatic correspondence between Hornby and other lawyers at the Supreme Consular Court and the Foreign Office in London. The novel uses cases, incidents, and controversies that Hornby and his colleagues addressed with their counterparts in the Ottoman government. As additional primary sources, I used, among other things, Hornby's autobiography, and the memoir that his wife, Emelia, published about her journey to and time in Constantinople during the Crimean war [2].

The experiences in the historical record tell very human stories about how law affects individual lives, why law and justice are often at odds, and what justice should mean in a diverse but rapidly shrinking world. I have taken liberties with these stories to craft them into the lives of my characters. In so doing, I tried to keep in mind that my imagination did not walk alone.

Notes:

1. D. L. Murray, "Introduction," to *Sir Edmund Hornby: An Autobiography* (1928 [posthumously published]), p. v.

2. Mrs. Edmund Hornby, *In and Around Stamboul* (1858).

About the Author

Anthony Earth is an international lawyer and foreign policy expert who has advised governments, international organisations, and companies all over the world. He has written extensively on legal and political issues and has recently delved into outer space law and policy.

Anthony is a first-generation American, born to British parents in the Texas panhandle and raised on the plains of Kansas. He studied political science and English literature at the University of Kansas, earned graduate degrees in international relations and law from the University of Oxford, and received his J.D. from Harvard Law School.

Read more at anthonyearth.com.

Printed in the USA
CPSIA information can be obtained
at www.ICGtesting.com
LVHW090914051123
763096LV00007B/195